WHEN THE RIVERS RISE

The Rivers Series
Book I

Shelley,
Merry Christmas!

Joey Jones

A Novel by 2022
JOEY JONES

ISBN: 978-1-948978-12-5 (MOBI)

ISBN: 978-1-948978-11-8 (EPUB)

ISBN: 978-1-948978-10-1 (PRINT)

For my nieces and nephews:
Andrew, Josh, Allee, Brooke, Zac, Lilly, and Harper.
Being your Uncle Joey is one of my proudest titles.

Also by Joey Jones

THE DATE NIGHT JAR

"A beautiful love story, capturing the poignancy of both new affection and the power of deep, lasting devotion. Readers of Nicholas Sparks, Debbie Macomber, and Nicholas Evans should add THE DATE NIGHT JAR to their reading list." –Jeff Gunhus, *USA TODAY* Bestselling Author

A FIELD OF FIREFLIES

"This is a tale of tragedy, romance, heartbreak and, ultimately, redemption. With lyrical writing and strong character development, Joey Jones effortlessly pulls readers in." –Kristy Woodson Harvey, *USA TODAY* Bestselling Author

LOSING LONDON

"I read the entire book in one day... I could not put it down! WOW!! LOSING LONDON was incredible; I laughed, I cried, and I'm still in shock." –Erica Latrice, TV Host, Be Inspired

A BRIDGE APART

"Filled with romance, suspense, heartbreak, and a tense plot line, Joey Jones' first novel is a must read. It is the kind of book you can lend to your mom and best friend." –Suzanne Lucey, Page 158 Books

Acknowledgments

It's nearly unfathomable to be able to hold up all five fingers on one of my hands when asked how many novels I've written. *When the Rivers Rise* is one of my proudest works. It's set in my hometown, and the book is about how hurricanes can shape people and places. There is an abundance of amazing people who helped make this book become a reality. First and foremost, I would like to thank God for giving me the ability to write and planting that passion within my soul. Branden, my oldest son, recently graduated high school, and I am excited to watch him become a young man. Parker, my little guy, is always by my side. I love hearing him call me Daddy and watching the smile grow on his face as he runs to my arms.

I would also like to thank my wonderful family. My parents, Joe and Patsy Jones, taught me about the essential aspects of life, and I hope I leave a legacy that makes them proud. My dad now lives in Heaven, and I miss him dearly. My mom, who is my breakfast partner and one of my best friends, is the most humble person I know. My brothers and sisters, DeAnn, Judy, Lee, Penny, and Richard, are some of my closest friends. In many ways, their support is my foundation.

My editors, Erin Haywood, Donna Matthews, and Krisann Blackwell, are incredibly talented at polishing my writing. My graphics designer, Meredith Walsh, has done a fantastic job with all of my novel covers and supporting pieces. Bob Peele (Sozo Fine Art Photography) is responsible for my author photo. Our photoshoots are always memorable. Polgarus Studio made the intricate process of formatting the interior of this novel a breeze. Once again, Deborah Dove has worked her magic creating the book blurb. Brian Edwards deserves a special thank you for answering my many police related questions.

Lastly, I would like to thank some people who have been influential throughout my life. Some for a season, but each for a reason. Thank you to Amber Gray, Andrew Haywood, BJ Horne, Billy Nobles, Cathy Errick, Diane Tyndall, Jan Raynor, Jeanette Towne, Josh Haywood, Josh Towne, Kenny Ford, Kim Jones, Mitch Fortescue, Nicholas Sparks, Ray White, Rebekah Jones, Richard Banks, Steve Cobb, Steven Harrell, and Steve Haywood. It is a privilege to call each of you my friend.

WHEN THE
RIVERS RISE

1

*E*ven though he only had a high school education, Niles North knew one thing for sure. If Hurricane Florence was going to barrel into New Bern, North Carolina, later this week, like some meteorologists on the weather channels were predicting, he was packing his bags and evacuating with his five-year-old son. The two of them would travel far enough away that they wouldn't feel a single raindrop from this monster of a storm. He shared this plan with Mickey Banks, his best friend since elementary school, as they took a break after mowing their first lawn on this muggy Monday morning. When working, Niles's chin-length hair was almost always pulled back. The shaved sides, cut short from one ear to the other, had been a lifesaver throughout the summer months in the sweltering Eastern North Carolina heat.

Risking his own life was something Niles had done in the past and would probably do again for the right reasons, but his son's life was more precious than anything he owned or anyone he'd ever known. There was absolutely no way he'd let Riley stay here and ride out this storm.

"Niles, you know that crazy ex-wife of yours isn't going to let you leave here with Riley," Mickey exclaimed after he gulped from a bottle of water while sitting on the tailgate of his rusty pickup truck. The vehicle was attached to a rickety trailer that had seen better days, but it hauled the landscaping equipment just fine.

Smelling like cut grass and with his clothes soaked in so much sweat it looked as if he'd been swimming in one of the nearby rivers, Niles shrugged his shoulders. The September sun felt like it was beaming down nearly as hard as it had during the hottest days of the year. Glancing at his bare ring finger, which he'd subconsciously begun to rub with his thumb, he realized once again that Mickey knew the details of his life nearly as well as he did. In fact, his best friend knew the ups and downs like he knew how to dissect a lawnmower engine.

"Well, my son is not staying here in New Bern; it's too big of a risk. They're saying this thing could hit land as a cat five."

A category five hurricane meant 157 mile per hour winds or higher—enough force to level a house. Both Niles and Mickey had grown up near the coast, even been through their fair share of hurricanes, and survived. They had handfuls of memorable stories to tell, like the one about the time they walked to the river in the eye of the storm. Without warning, the winds picked up, and the sea began to spray their bodies like a rogue water sprinkler stuck on high. The pine trees towering above their heads started bending like rubber poles, and for the next seven minutes, both of them wondered if they'd ever see the fourteen candles that would be on their respective birthday cakes that year. Mickey's parents' house was nearly a mile from the river, and as they'd sprinted for their lives, the trees threw limbs at them while rain that felt like darts pelted their maturing bodies.

"You best come up with a better plan then," Mickey suggested, tossing an empty bottle into the bed of the truck where it rolled around before coming to rest amongst a scattered array of other containers, cans, and random items that the two of them had flung back there over the past week or so.

Neither Niles nor Mickey barely remembered living anywhere

else unless the short time Niles spent at boot camp counted. That was a story he was and wasn't proud of, depending on which day he was telling it and who was asking. Their families had never fled a hurricane; however, a category five hadn't impacted New Bern during their lifetimes.

"If she won't let me take Riley somewhere safe, then maybe I can talk her into taking him to her aunt's house in Kentucky," Niles considered out loud as he ran his fingers through his dirty blond hair and pulled it back a little tighter in a rubber band.

Honestly, at this point, there was no way of knowing if the storm would hit the area. One thing Niles learned from this town during his twenty years and 300 and some odd days of life was that weather had a mind of its own, especially when it came to a hurricane brewing in the Atlantic Ocean. One day the prediction would be for a direct hit along the coast of Florida, and the following day the path would change, and South Carolina would become the bullseye. Basically, no one, not even the experts, really knew where the storm would end up or whether it would increase to a catastrophic hurricane, decrease to a tropical storm, or flutter away altogether.

Mickey threw his hands up as the two of them hopped out of the truck's bed, needing to finish loading up so they could move on to the next job. Their phones had been continuously buzzing the past few days with everyone on God's green Earth asking to have their lawns cut as this storm approached, which was good because the two of them had been scrounging for business all summer.

"If you give her some cash, she might be able to fill her tank with enough gas to make it there," Mickey teased.

Niles stared up at his best friend, who was nearly a foot taller, and for the longest time had reminded him of a dark-haired carrot top. In addition to resembling that guy, Mickey thought he was a comedian, too.

"I'm not giving her more money; I already pay enough in child support."

"You mean drug support," Mickey sneered.

Niles jabbed his buddy in the ribcage, and the sudden gasp for air that exploded from Mickey's mouth explained that the blow caught him by surprise. "I've asked you not to call Eden a druggie."

"What do you want me to call her, your baby mamma?" Mickey badgered with a snicker as he caught his breath and straightened his lanky body.

Niles lunged at him again, but this time his friend was ready for a second strike. Mickey quickly stepped back and began to circle just like when the two of them were sparring in the backyard. They'd grown up taking karate classes together, and now they both studied mixed martial arts. Niles was faster and stronger, but Mickey was long and elusive.

"Just call her Eden or Riley's mom," Niles reminded his friend for what seemed like the thousandth time.

"Dude, don't be so uptight, she's your ex, not some chick you're dating."

An old lady in a nightgown stepped onto the porch about twenty yards from where Niles and Mickey were squabbling, wasting precious time as they waited for her to write a check. "Y'all boys did a good job," she complimented in a screechy southern voice that perfectly matched the first word of her sentence.

Niles and Mickey smiled and said, "Thank you," nearly in unison as the woman with a cane and curlers in her hair handed over payment for the work completed. The lawn between the house and where Mickey had backed in the truck and the trailer looked like a different yard from the one they'd set eyes on forty-five minutes ago. Weeds had taken over the sidewalk, and the bushes looked as if they were growing horns. Niles had driven the riding mower while Mickey buzzed around with the weed eater and the hedge trimmers. At the next yard on their list, they would switch tasks, and this song and dance would continue until the sun sank below the horizon.

Mickey slid into the truck and twisted the key as Niles climbed in from the opposite side. The engine turned but didn't crank right away. It took a couple more twists, and a few pumps on the worn gas pedal before the muffler spat a cloud of black smoke into the air and pushed the truck onto the black pavement.

Mickey usually drove because the title was in his name, but he and Niles always split the gas when they used the truck for work. It was only a handful of months ago when the two of them had sat on the deck surrounding their treehouse home and decided they were fed up with the cruddy pay and long hours they'd been putting in while working for the longest standing landscape company in town. Between the two of them, they scrounged up enough cash to start their own lawn service business. Sure, they lacked one of those zero-turn mowers and enclosed trailers they were spoiled by having at their previous place of employment, but at the end of the day, they knew the equipment wasn't as important as the hard work. Heck, together, they had single-handedly built a 500 square foot treehouse equipped with heating and air conditioning, indoor plumbing, and a fully-functioning kitchen. The initial idea for the place where Niles, Mickey, and Riley now called home had come about when Niles, not long after the finalization of the divorce, was surfing the Internet for an economical way to build a small house. When he came across a website named Tiny House Listings, he instantly found himself fascinated by the options that were out there. Some of the tiny homes he came across were on wheels and could be moved anywhere in the country on a moment's notice. He had no need for one of those since his son was here. Other houses were built on a slab in the middle of nowhere, and he'd even discovered houses made from old cargo containers that had been settled into downtown districts in metropolitan areas. Those were nifty but not really what he needed either.

When Niles came across a photo of a livable treehouse, he knew exactly what he wanted. It hadn't taken much convincing to get Mickey, who had lived with his parents up to that point, to jump on board. Of course, Eden hadn't missed an opportunity to make fun of him living like a grown-up boy, but he and Mickey had been able to use the knowledge gained from working in construction to create a home that met building code requirements. Sure, it had taken about five visits from the inspector before obtaining approval, but in the end, the stuffy man who always showed up in a suit and tie stamped the document just like he had for every home built by a licensed contractor.

"If there's ever a hurricane," the inspector warned as he pointed his expensive ink pen at their house in the trees, "I suggest vacating this property."

Even though Niles hadn't given the man's suggestion much thought at the time, it made sense because the home was attached to a cluster of hardwoods that danced in the wind like every other tree in the forest. Fortunately, Niles and Mickey had learned about specialty springs to attach to the trees and the main parts of the structure that would help secure the home when the wind blew, but he doubted they would all withstand sustained triple-digit winds. Not that the everyday home was capable of that feat either, especially ones near the river like theirs. Technically, they now lived in a small community called Bridgeton, which was just across the Neuse River from the town where they'd grown up, but most of their time was still spent in New Bern, whether hanging out with friends or working.

Niles and Mickey cut one more lawn before stopping for breakfast at The Country Biscuit. They'd be eating later than usual since their customer had asked for help with hurricane preparation: moving loose outdoor items into the garage, boarding up the windows, and carrying bulk packages of bottled water into her house. These services weren't listed on the homemade business cards they'd been passing out all over town. Even so, both of them thought it made sense to take advantage of the opportunity to earn a little extra cash, especially if they were going to be out of town for a few days to dodge the hurricane.

"If Eden doesn't let you take Riley with us, we should still head west to the mountains for a few days; we can party and meet some babes," Mickey suggested as he parked the truck parallel to a vacant building across the lot from the restaurant. The two of them had ended up here for breakfast almost every day since branching out on their own.

"Us?" Niles questioned, furrowing his brow while thinking about how nice it was that the two of them could make their own work schedule. "I didn't know you were going with me."

Mickey lifted his voice along with his brow. "You'd leave your best man here alone to face this massive hurricane?"

Niles shook his head. He and Mickey did nearly everything together, and as Mickey had just pointed out, he had been the man standing next to him at the wedding when his future seemed so clear. The dude had also been there for him ever since, especially once he and Eden separated, which had been as muddy as the marsh between their treehouse and the Neuse River. Divorce was the hardest thing Niles had ever experienced, and he often lay in his bed at night thinking about how no human being should have to go through such torment, especially when a child was involved. That was by far the hardest part.

"We *might* take you with us," Niles finally said, laughing. "But we're not taking your truck."

"You better take me," Mickey exclaimed. "The truck is optional."

Niles pulled open the glass door that led into the restaurant, and the atmosphere was bustling. The place was always busy because they served the best tasting biscuit in town, but Hurricane

Florence had everyone out and about for a variety of reasons. Some of the locals wanted to talk with other residents about the storm, share stories, thoughts, and give opinions on where they thought the hurricane was headed. Others wanted to be out of the house as much as possible in case they ended up trapped at home without electricity once the uninvited storm arrived. Almost everyone who lived in Eastern North Carolina had experienced power outages, as short as part of a day up to two weeks due to past hurricanes.

Just inside the door was an area where locals posted business cards, and Niles felt proud when he saw his and Mickey's displayed among the others.

"Hey, guys," one of the waitresses called out as she scurried from behind the thigh-high front counter with two beverages in her hands, heading to one of the tables in the dining area. "You know the drill, sit wherever you'd like," she offered swiftly.

Niles and Mickey usually sat in one of the corner booths in the second room, separated from the main area by a glass wall nestled atop a knee-high bricked frame. Today, the booths were all taken, so they plopped down at the only open table in the front room where the television was broadcasting the local news station. The words BREAKING NEWS were flashing across the bottom of the screen, and the chatter in the restaurant lowered to a hum as the recognizable meteorologist spoke. Wearing a black suit jacket, he was standing in front of a map highlighting the coast of North Carolina and pointing directly at the names of three cities: Wilmington, New Bern, and Morehead City. As he showed the future radar, the red circular hurricane symbol that had always reminded Niles of a saw blade was spinning, heading right for their hometown.

"When the rivers rise," the weatherman warned in a somber tone, "you don't want to be in any of these areas."

2

Eden Franks slept in this morning without intention. Last night had been rough, and sleeping hadn't been comfortable ever since the accident. There was a time in her life when she'd woken up every morning by seven o'clock, eaten a healthy breakfast, and looked forward to the day ahead. Today, when Riley Cameron woke her by jumping onto the bed, she hadn't meant to shout at him. As the words, "What are you doing?" flew out of her mouth as sharply as the tacks holding the photos of the two of them on her walls, he instantly began to sob. The sound of the crying stabbed her aching head, but what hurt the most is when he'd run out of the room in his footed pajamas, chanting, "I want my daddy! I want my daddy!"

Hearing her son say that during *her* time with him was like an arrow piercing her heart. Riley had spoken those words for as long as he could string together a sentence, but he'd also been known to say, "I want my mommy." Now, since she and Niles were no longer together, she had no way of knowing when Riley wanted her when he was with his dad. The moment his little feet scurried into the hallway, she knew he didn't care to have anything to do with her. He'd run into his room and hadn't come out since. Eden didn't feel like a bad mom, she just wasn't as patient as she would like to be sometimes, but she was working on that. In fact, the new nerve medication was supposed to help keep her calm.

Medicine. When opened, her bathroom cabinet resembled a small pharmacy. Every day as she stared into the mirror, she held a handful of pills to take for the ailments that plagued her youthful body. As she studied herself today, she noticed that her naturally curly brown hair, which spiraled about midway down her back, was a matted mess. She didn't feel up to fixing it even though it looked horrible, and she hadn't felt like going into work either, which is why she'd texted her boss first thing this morning. Thankfully, he'd agreed to let her work from home again. Over the years, she'd learned how to sweet talk him even though he was the lawyer.

When at doctor's visits, Eden often felt like she was the one who needed a law degree to understand what they were talking about and why she needed so many different ones. In addition to her primary physician, she saw an orthopedist, neurologist, and a spinal specialist whom she was pretty sure was a neurosurgeon. Each doctor seemed to ask similar questions. "Where is your pain?" was their favorite.

"The pain is in my back," she always answered first because that was the area that hurt around the clock, but the minutes in her life often seemed to move as slowly as the hour hand in everyone else's. "And my neck, and my head, and my legs," she would eventually add. This point in the conversation is where she would start to tear up. "The pain is everywhere. All the time. It just doesn't go away."

This life wasn't how she envisioned living. Sure, some times were better than others, but most were nearly unbearable—until she dropped another pill into her mouth. *Thank God for medicine*, she often thought, but she also wondered if she would be taking pain pills, muscle relaxers, and so forth for the rest of her life.

"Honey, only take what the doctors prescribe," her mother often warned.

Eden knew that Grandyma—the name given to her mother by the grandchildren—meant well, but her mom didn't have a spine that felt like an inflamed stick.

Eventually, Eden was able to talk Riley out of his room for a bowl of Frosted Flakes. The kid loved cereal. He could eat it for breakfast, lunch, and dinner. Every day, probably. She sat next to him at the kitchen bar as they watched the television in the corner of the living room. He seemed to be over her snapping at him earlier, but now he was upset about not being able to watch cartoons. When she'd pressed the power button on the remote, the channel she'd fallen asleep watching on the couch reminded her that a hurricane was headed in their direction. Last night, she hadn't been concerned about it, but she'd also been in another world. This morning, things felt a little more serious. The weatherman was talking about the river rising and a chance that the storm could produce life-threatening winds. When she heard that part, she nearly said a dirty word. She'd been trying her best not to spit them out in front of Riley because she knew he was at that age where he was going to repeat everything his parents said. The last thing she needed was Niles breathing down her injured neck about their son saying a four-letter word. She hadn't always used foul language as much as she had lately, but stress seemed to bring out the worst in her. It wasn't like Niles had never said a cuss word, but ever since Riley was born, the man—who'd been a teenager like her at the time of their son's birth—had cleaned up his mouth and his lifestyle. His sidekick Mickey Banks, on the other hand, hadn't changed all that much. He was still a womanizer and didn't have a filter on his mouth. This brought her to the idea that if Niles ever said anything about their son repeating a filthy word, she could blame it on Mickey.

"Mommy, I want to watch cartoons."

"Riley! Chill out," Eden yammered. "When I was your age, cartoons only aired on Saturday mornings. You kids these days have no idea how lucky you are to be able to watch cartoons all day long, play on your tablets, and have all those video games."

"I'm not watching them now," Riley combatted.

"What you need to watch is your mouth," she barked, holding her pointer finger near his lips for emphasis.

Riley let his head hang down. "Yes, ma'am." He slurped in another spoonful of cereal before speaking again. "When do I get to go back to Daddy's?"

Really? "I'm not sure," she answered as calmly as possible even though her temperature was boiling. "It depends on what this storm does," she uttered with her eyes glued to the weatherman.

"Daddy doesn't let me play video games," Riley announced.

Eden rolled her eyes without letting her son see the gesture. "I know," she murmured. "And he rarely lets you watch TV or play on your tablet either." *The guy who'd once licked beer off...* nevermind, she didn't want to remember that night or anything else about her ex-husband. "I'm sorry, honey," she consoled.

Riley shook his head left to right, his cheeks filled with soggy flakes of cereal and more milk than one mouth should hold. "It's okay, Daddy and I do fun things."

"Things that are more fun than video games and cartoons?"

"Yes."

"Like what?"

"Zip lining," he revealed with a big grin on his little face.

This time Eden didn't cover her rolling eyes. "That's dangerous, Riley Cameron."

Eden and Niles had disagreed about calling their son Riley Cameron, but that was another story, and ever since the two of them split up, she had decided that she could call him anything she wanted. Sometimes she even called him Cameron without the Riley in front. Nudging her mind back to the comment her son had made, she still couldn't believe that Niles thought it would be a good idea to build a treehouse with a zip line that traveled from the kiddie play area in the sky to a landing spot fifty yards away in the woods.

"No, it's not," Riley argued. "Daddy makes me wear a helmet, and my vest is clicked in, so I can't fall even if I let go."

"Do you let go?" she checked.

"Sometimes," he admitted.

"Don't let go," she reminded him, wanting to forget about the idea of her son soaring through the woods like a flying squirrel. "What else do you do with your daddy?" She liked to ask Riley these questions because then she didn't have to interrogate Niles for information about what their son was up to when she wasn't around to supervise. It wasn't like her ex-husband would tell her anyway.

"We jump on the net and roll around or just lay there at night and look at the stars."

Oh yeah, she'd forgotten about the sizable hammock-like net that doubled as a fail-safe beneath the ropes course that surrounded the treehouse. The challenges the training area presented didn't seem feasible for a five-year-old, but Niles promised that everything was secure and ensured a professional inspector had checked it. Maybe she needed to call that man's office and make sure her ex wasn't pulling her chain.

"That sounds like fun, Riley," she forced herself to say.

"The best fun we had lately was building the ark," Riley recalled with sparkles in his eyes.

Niles was always building something. He and Mickey had made the kid a miniature boat that resembled the one from the popular Bible story. She never could remember if it was Moses or Noah who built the ark. She had to give it to Niles and Mickey, though, the two of them could build almost anything. The little ship was tall enough for adults to stand inside, and it actually floated. At first, she expected it to sink due to all the heavy lumber from which it was constructed, but it scooted across the water as smoothly as a fiberglass canoe. A small deck circled the vessel allowing room for a person on either side to paddle. At first, Riley had begged her to let him put his stuffed animals in the ark, but she hadn't allowed it. She was afraid they'd all be ruined by water or be left outdoors to suffer the elements. Eventually, Niles had bought Riley lots of new stuffed animals to place in little cubbyholes created on the inside of the boat. She'd heard all about that specific trip to the toy aisle from the little boy sitting beside her at the moment who was holding his favorite stuffed animal, a monkey named Banana. This one never left home, and, thankfully, Riley had a second Banana at his daddy's house that was exactly like this one. Both of them had been a *welcome to this world* gift brought to the hospital by Grandyma.

Thankfully, Eden had been able to examine the ark firsthand when Niles and Riley rowed it over to her parents' house for her dad to check out. Both Niles and Mickey had worked for her father's construction company when they were in high school. It was kind of weird, but her dad and Niles still got along very well. Her mother kept in contact with him, too. "He's my grandson's dad," she would declare. "Why would I not maintain a healthy relationship with him?" Anyways, Eden's dad approved of the ark, so in the end, she was fine with it, too. Actually, it was still at her parents' house now after being left there following the last weekend Riley spent with his grandparents.

Eden's parents lived on the opposite side of the Neuse River from Niles, which was about a mile wide from their house to the far shore. When Eden and Niles were younger, he always promised that one day he would build her a big house on the land that his parents had given him, but that was old news. Now, he had built a tree fort on the five acres, and that land would probably flood when this hurricane came through. The elevation on her parents' side of the river was a bit higher, and their home had never flooded. After buying it, her dad had a company from Raleigh come in and lift the entire house and then brought in countless truckloads of sand to make sure it was raised high enough that it would never flood. "If the river comes into this house, everyone in downtown is in trouble," her dad guaranteed every time a storm threatened the area.

Eden rinsed her bowl in the kitchen sink and made Riley do the same. "Have you brushed your teeth this morning?" she asked.

"No."

"No, what?"

He shook his head. "No, ma'am."

"Now that you've eaten, you need to do that."

"Do I have to?" he whined.

"Haven't you had to every other morning for the past five years of your life?"

His answer came in the form of a shrug of his shoulders.

"Yes, you have," she reminded him. Why did kids hate brushing their teeth? Explaining to them that their teeth would rot if they didn't never seemed to make an impact.

When Riley headed to the bathroom, Eden retrieved her phone from the bedroom and dialed the most popular number.

"Mom, are you and Dad planning to leave if the hurricane is going to hit here?" she inquired. She didn't feel the need to exchange pleasantries since she'd already sent a *good morning* text earlier to let her mom know that she wouldn't need to watch Riley today.

"Darling, it depends on what the storm does over the next few days," she replied, which was how most people seemed to answer that question. Of course, there was a group of people in the area that would evacuate at the mention of a hurricane, and then there was a cluster of people who wouldn't leave if the forecasters told them the storm was going to wipe New Bern off the map. These folks felt the need to protect their home and community and go down with it if it came to that.

"Where will you go if you leave?" Eden queried.

"Probably to my sister's house."

"You're going to drive all the way to Kentucky?"

"Well, your dad will," her mom revealed with a chuckle.

Eden laughed. Her mother had never cared for driving. "Is it okay if Riley and I go along with you?"

"Of course, baby," she said before pausing for a moment. "Have you and Niles discussed that?" she asked.

"Discussed what?"

"You taking Riley with you."

"Why would I not take Riley with me?"

"Eden, Riley is his child, too. Don't you think he should have a say in it?"

"We're talking about Riley Cameron's safety, Mom. Why would I ask Niles if he wants our son to stay here with him while I evacuate to Aunt Becky's? I'd be worried sick about the little guy the whole time."

"Sweetheart, I'm not saying that Niles would want him to stay here, but maybe he would want to take Riley on a vacation since he doesn't get to see him as much as you do. That might be good for you, too; it would give you a chance to relax and spend some time with us and Aunt Becky."

Eden didn't care for her mother's idea, and she didn't feel the need to hide her feelings. "I have primary custody of Riley, so he should go with me."

"I understand your thinking, but maybe just run it by Niles so that it doesn't become an issue."

"Sure, Mom."

3

Reese Kirby was born, raised, and as an adult, still living in Chattanooga, Tennessee. In elementary school, when a teacher would ask what each kid wanted to be when they grew up, her answer without hesitation was always, "A police officer." Reese was the only girl in any of her classes who ever showed interest in wearing a badge. Many of the boys echoed her answer, and some students teased her for wanting to be a cop. They'd say things like, "Girls can't be policemen." Her daddy taught her the best answer to that statement: "Of course girls can't be policemen, but they can be policewomen." Upon offering that thought to the class, laughter would erupt, but rarely would any of the kids make a snide comment. Ever since she pounded little Tommy Waters on the playground for claiming she had cooties, no one messed with her.

Reese's father had been a highly decorated police officer, and he taught her early in life how to protect herself. He hadn't been happy about her bloodying up Tommy's nose, though. "Police officers are allowed to defend themselves, but we can't attack somebody just because they call us a name," he explained. "If that were the case, I'd be getting into fights every day," he revealed. "A police officer's job is to keep the peace, and the only time we revert to physical contact with another person is when there is no other option."

Vividly remembering that afternoon from more than fifteen years ago when her dad picked her up from school early for fighting, Reese buckled the belt that held her firearm, handcuffs, and badge. Then she slipped on a black suit jacket that covered her entire upper torso. The belt she wore these days as an investigator wasn't as hefty as the one she'd strapped on when part of the patrol unit. In addition to the items she now carried daily, that belt held a baton, pepper spray, and a variety of other self-protection items. Back then, the badge on her dark blue shirt read *Officer Kirby* just like her dad's had. In fact, his badge was proudly displayed in a shadow box on her nightstand. A small trunk tucked away in the bedroom closet protected an array of personal items that once belonged to the man who had always been her hero.

When Reese made it to the station on Ringgold Road, she headed to the conference room for the usual morning brief. Contrary to societal assumptions, there wasn't a box of doughnuts sitting in the center of the elongated table, which was surrounded by padded chairs. There were, however, bagels, and she grabbed one since she hadn't taken the time to eat breakfast this morning. She rarely did. Prior to leaving the house, she tucked her shoulder-length hair into a ponytail and scurried out the front door. She wasn't a girly girl by any means, but even so, she liked her hair. Many of the other female officers cut theirs short enough to be mistaken for men, and she didn't want to fall into that boat. Being slightly vertically challenged eliminated most of that confusion for Reese since most men were much taller than five feet. Technically, she was as well but only by two inches. The average American woman was five feet and four inches, which Reese knew based on research for a case that recently closed.

The conference room door made a recognizable sound when Captain Lawson walked in and pushed it shut. Instantly, Reese and the other three detectives surrounding the table turned out of respect and faced the man who, as usual, began to speak right away. "We have a special assignment, and I need a volunteer," the captain announced beneath his thick mustache. No one raised a hand, but instead, each of the faces began to look at one another as if in hopes that someone else would step up. "No takers?" he finally asked, studying his team as he spoke.

"Captain, it kind of sounds like a trick question," Dominguez, who was sitting two chairs down from Kirby, pointed out with a snicker. His black hair was shiny, curly, and matted to his head as always.

Almost all officers called each other by their last names, and the group here at the East Ridge Police Department did the same even though it was a relatively small agency. Reese, who was known to those in the chairs around her as Kirby, had considered taking a position with the Chattanooga Police Department where her dad had served but ultimately decided to accept one where she wouldn't feel like a small fish in a big pond. Plus, she didn't always want to be known as Kirby's daughter since he was somewhat of a legend in her hometown department.

East Ridge was nestled on the outskirts of Chattanooga and still in Hamilton County, where she lived. In hindsight, she felt like she'd made the right call. Everyone here was close, and the captain was relatively easy going, although stern. He allowed the team to spend time joking around when the situation didn't require seriousness. When officers were in the field, their persona almost always had to be all business. Inside the doors of this building, however, they were often able to let the walls down.

Johnson, the veteran in the department with a full head of gray hair to show for it, chimed in. "Last time you asked a question like that, Brown ended up walking out of Krispy Kreme with four boxes of doughnuts."

Remembering the moment, everyone in the room chuckled,

and Brown—who was the newest member of the investigations unit, and currently laughing with his cohorts—threw his bagel at Johnson. Sending the new officer out for doughnuts was a long-standing traditional prank at this station. As the crew regained their composure, Reese recalled her inaugural trip to the doughnut shop, especially when she walked out and watched all of the other detectives pull into the parking lot with their lights swiveling.

When Captain Lawson spoke again, the room silenced out of respect for the man who led the unit through thick and thin. "This is far more important than doughnuts," he explained. "Hurricane Florence is closing in on the East Coast, and I'd like to send one of you who is trained in special operations to help with whatever is needed; I wish I could send a whole team, but we're already shorthanded."

"Johnson can't swim," Dominguez reminded everyone. "And Kirby's so little, the wind might blow her over."

If Reese hadn't taken the last bite of the bagel that had been occupying her hand throughout this conversation, she would have slung it in Dominguez's direction. When she'd been promoted to detective, she rode along with him to learn the ropes. He was actually her favorite in the group.

Reese punched back. "Dominguez, you're the one who ate all those doughnuts that Brown picked up for us, so we know you wouldn't blow over."

Heavy laughter instantly filled the conference room, then Reese spoke again. "I'm the only one who doesn't have kids, so I'll volunteer for the assignment if no one else is keen on the idea."

4

"Y'all want sweet teas?" the waitress asked a few minutes after the guys sat down. Wearing a pair of black leggings and a heather gray t-shirt with a logo that matched the sign out front, she rested her hands on the edge of the table that Niles and Mickey occupied. Her fingernails were painted midnight blue, but they'd grown out a bit since she'd lathered them with polish, and they'd also taken a beating from restaurant work.

"Sure thing, darling," Mickey answered with a grin. He knew her name was Jenny, but he liked calling her names like honey, baby, and the one he'd chosen this time around.

Niles was pretty sure that the waitress and Mickey had spent time together outside of this restaurant. His best friend had always been quite the ladies' man, but as she walked away, Niles was thinking about the logo on her shirt rather than the woman beneath it.

"Her shirt made me think of something," Niles mentioned to Mickey.

"Like how you'd like to see her in a bikini?"

Niles shook his head. "I'm sure she'd look great in a bikini, but—"

Mickey cut him off like a dead branch. "She does, bro," he

assured his friend. "I've seen her in—"

Niles returned the favor, cutting off Mickey this time. "I wasn't referring to her body, I was talking about the logo on her shirt."

"Oh, there's a logo on her shirt?"

Niles smirked. "It's a rough outline of a red-rimmed plate with a fork on one side and a knife on the other."

"And your point?" Mickey asked with his elbows resting on the table as a confused look settled in on his face.

"We need a logo."

"Of a plate?" he questioned with one eye squinted.

"No, dummy. We need a logo for our business."

"We have one."

"We have our names in bold letters on our business cards; that's not a logo."

"Yeah, I guess you're right," Mickey agreed before pointing to the television where the weatherman was going on and on about the cone of uncertainty. "We could use the hurricane logo, it kind of looks like a lawnmower blade."

Niles chuckled again. Mickey had a way of making people laugh, and he didn't seem to care whether they were laughing with him or at him. He just spat out whatever came to mind and let the marbles fall where they may. "I think that logo is trademarked," Niles announced. "But it's a great idea, maybe a starting point."

"We need a name, too," Mickey suggested. "Hurricanes have storm chasers, maybe we could be the Lawn Chasers."

Niles furrowed his brow. "That's the dumbest thing you've said since . . . the bikini comment."

"Hey, I just made the bikini comment."

"Exactly."

"Well, the dumbest thing you've done lately is noticed the logo on Jenny's shirt rather than appreciating the beauty right in front of your eyes."

The two of them bantered back and forth about women's

bodies, logos, and making stupid comments until their breakfast ended up in front of their faces. Niles scarfed down scrambled eggs, grits, sausage, and hash browns while Mickey devoured a jumbo-sized bacon, egg, and cheese biscuit. The restaurant literally served a jumbo biscuit that was nearly double the size of a regular one, and Mickey ordered it almost every time they came to The Country Biscuit.

When they got up to pay, every seat was still taken, and there were a few people near the register waiting for a table. The crowd in this place was always diverse. It was one of those rare restaurants where on any given day, you were dining with lawyers, construction workers, nurses, boaters, and even homeless people. The establishment had an unwritten rule where if a person needed food and was willing to lend a hand by picking up trash in the parking lot, sweeping, or some other helpful chore, they fed them.

"How was everything, gentlemen?" the owner asked as she rang them up at the front counter.

"Delicious as always," Mickey answered, his hair swaying as he spoke.

"That was my first time having the sausage," Niles shared. "It was amazing."

"I get it from a local guy down at the farmers market," the owner announced cheerfully. "I'm all about locals supporting locals."

Mickey felt the urge to chime in again. "Well, if you need lawn maintenance, we're your *local* guys," he explained with a wink.

Niles was about to point out that the place didn't have a lawn. It was all blacktop and concrete, but he decided not to make his business partner look like an idiot—at least not until they walked into the parking lot.

Outside, beneath the rising sun, Mickey punched him in the shoulder. "It doesn't matter," he rebutted. "I bet she has a lawn at her house."

The next driveway they pulled into led to a gigantic home in one of the wealthiest neighborhoods in New Bern. A man with a wooden cane was walking up and down the long drive for exercise.

"I sure am tickled to see you, boys," he greeted as they hopped out of the truck. "The shorter this grass is when the hurricane comes through, the less chance of snakes slithering through here and surprising me during my morning walks."

Debris scattered about by hurricanes had a way of bringing creatures out of the woodwork, especially in areas with standing water or tall grass. The locals were well aware of this and knew to have their lawns cut prior to impending storms.

"Snake Savers," Mickey uttered in Niles's direction, using an Australian accent.

Niles didn't bother responding to Mickey but instead turned his attention to the homeowner. Based on a conversation they'd been having in the truck about a business name, he knew Mickey was throwing out another silly suggestion. "I bet that's how the best business names come about," Mickey concluded.

"Do you want us to cut your grass lower than normal?" Niles asked.

Not everyone realized it, but cutting grass too low could actually be destructive to a lawn depending on variables such as heat, water, and lack of exposure to other nutrients.

The man pondered the suggestion for a moment. "Sure thing, if you think it will help deter critters and such."

"It's probably a good idea," Mickey interjected. "There's no telling how much rain we'll get and how long it will be before the yard dries out again."

A few moments later, Mickey dropped the mower blade a level lower than usual as Niles began to edge the driveway. The two of them moved like clockwork as the sun climbed an imaginary ladder in the cloudless blue sky. The elderly man retreated to a rocking chair on the porch as soon as they began to unload, and with a grin on his face and a glass of ice water occupying one of his shaky hands, he watched them work. The earbuds the boys wore had music blasting loud enough to drown out the sounds of their machinery, reminding the man of the old days working in one of the local factories when he was around their age. His hearing would be much sharper today if ear protection had been required back then, but either no one in management realized the need, or more likely, didn't care enough to figure out how much damage was being caused to people's ears. Eventually, the company supplied the workers with bulky earmuffs, and he could remember being embarrassed to wear them when the women from the office would come around. This caused him to wonder if the two young guys mowing his lawn would wear earmuffs if they weren't able to listen to music. He only knew that was what they were doing because he'd asked them the first time they'd shown up back in the spring.

When the guys finished mowing, the older gentleman shook their hands just like every other time, told them the story about working in the factory and wearing earmuffs, and ultimately handed over a check written in what looked like chicken scratch.

"Thanks," Mickey said. "I bet you were quite the ladies' man."

The man snickered, and Niles wondered if he was recalling days past as he spoke, maybe seeing the face of a woman at the factory whom he had eyes for back then. Niles himself thought about women from time to time, even wondered if he'd eventually start dating. The weird thing was he never really dated. Eden had been his high school sweetheart, and he went to every school dance with her. He kissed a couple of other girls in middle school, but it was more like practicing than enjoying the game. The only woman he'd ever made love to was the one everyone knew he would end up marrying.

"This body has seen better days," the man admitted, grinning through his dentures.

As Niles's mind wandered, he let Mickey do the talking—a task for which he was always well prepared. After the divorce, Mickey told Niles that he was a lucky man because he had received a get out of jail free card. Said he needed to have sex with as many women as possible to catch up on all the missed opportunities he could have had in college if he hadn't married so early in life, which was a weird way to put it because neither he nor Mickey ever really considered filling out a college application.

"You're in good shape, Mr. Nelson," Mickey pointed out. "Still walking up and down this driveway with a cane. Not many men your age can or would do that." Pondering that thought, Mickey paused. "I bet you were chiseled in your day."

Niles nearly snorted—not because he couldn't imagine the old guy with a ripped chest and six-pack abs like the ones beneath his own sweaty shirt but because Mickey seemed so excited about this man's romantic encounters. On another note, Niles was always impressed by how Mickey seemed to remember everyone's name, even people he'd only met a time or two.

"Give us single guys some pointers," Mickey requested before the guy could entertain the previous thought Mickey had shoveled out.

Mr. Nelson squinted his eyes. "One day, you're going to meet a woman who will cause you to realize that every other woman on this earth exists for someone else. You'll figure out that she's the only one you'll ever need."

Pretty deep, Niles thought as his thumb traced the bottom part of his ring finger. *Eden*. That's how he'd always felt about Eden. But then—

"I don't know about all that," Mickey chuckled. "If I meet her, I hope I meet a lot of other women first. I'm in no hurry to settle down, if you know what I mean, Mr. Nelson," he announced, smacking the guy's bony arm with the back of his hand as if a mosquito had landed on it.

"I remember those days, young fellow."

"Niles here, he tied the knot before he realized there were other shoes out there to wear, but now that he's divorced, I'm trying to talk him into trying on some other pairs."

Once again, Niles nearly snorted. Mickey had a way with words, but as the ones his friend had just spoken traveled around in his mind, he wasn't sure whether to laugh or cry. Mickey also had a tendency to say things around people that most others didn't even think. He had no filter, which was both a good and a bad trait, depending on the situation.

"Women aren't like shoes, my friend; they're like a heart—you only need one," the man said.

"Some men need a heart transplant," Mickey uttered without skipping a beat.

This time, Niles did snort, but the frail man didn't react one way or the other. His face was as straight as a pencil. "If you lose your heart like I did a long time ago, you're right, you might need a new one. But, you only need one at a time," he said.

Niles wasn't sure if the gentleman was talking about his actual heart or comparing a woman to a heart again. There was a word for that, which he should have remembered from English class, but he had to admit that he had no clue. There were so many terms: irony, symbolism, analogy, metaphor . . . maybe it was one of those. He would ask Mickey later in the truck, but Mickey's grades in school had been worse than his. Eden would know, he thought, without meaning to think about her.

5

Eden was frustrated at how the conversation with her mother had ended. She always felt like her mom was playing devil's advocate on behalf of Niles. At least it had seemed that way ever since the accident that changed all of their lives. "It wasn't anyone's fault," were words that her parents seemed to mention over and over. But, accidents *were* usually someone's fault. Eden blamed Niles because, even though she couldn't remember the accident itself, he'd told her what happened just before it. Other than that, the next thing she recalled from that horrific day was looking up as she lay on the ground. A group of people hovered over her, some kneeling and others standing. At some point, there were flashing lights in her peripheral vision, but she couldn't remember if they were blue or red or some other color. They were bright and seemed to make her head hurt, she knew that.

As Eden thought about what she could remember from the accident scene, wishing she could watch it play out on video rather than hearing Niles's interpretation, her phone dinged, notifying her that she had a text message—from Niles nonetheless.

What is it called when a person compares one thing to another? the message on her screen read.

Eden threw her empty hand into the air as her cheeks rose,

causing both eyes to squint into question marks. Why was Niles asking this random question? She couldn't help but wonder if he wanted something and was trying to approach it from some weird angle.

Her thumbs began to dance on the screen as she conjured a reply: *Are you talking about an analogy?*

A moment later, a response from Niles popped up: *Like comparing a person to a storm?*

Eden huffed. *This is a timely analogy*, she whispered beneath her breath. Was her ex calling her a hurricane? All of a sudden, her mind shifted back to the earlier conversation with her mother. Instantly, she found herself wondering if her mom had called Niles and mentioned her plans to evacuate with Riley if the storm was going to be bad.

Yes, that's an analogy, she typed, deciding not to jump to conclusions as she wondered where Riley had gotten off to after brushing his teeth. As for herself, she'd settled onto the couch with her work laptop but had become glued to the television showing devastation from past hurricanes. Sailboats were toppling over, waves were splashing against buildings, and palm trees were nearly bending to the ground. The sounds of the gusting winds were blowing through the speakers, and in a way, she felt like she was there firsthand.

Ding. *Thanks!*

Eden cocked her head sideways. *That's it?* she queried.

Another ding. *Yes, thank you!*

She decided not to respond. Niles often texted her random things and would be all nice as if he had some ulterior motive. "Maybe he's just being kind," were words she could hear her mother saying. "Just because the two of you are divorced doesn't mean you have to despise one another," she also liked to point out.

Eden wandered toward Riley's bedroom, and the sounds of

little-human-made fire engine noises began flooding her ears as she inched closer. She could hear him audibly telling one of the characters in his head that he was going to rescue a cat from a tall tree. As she stepped into his room, she found her son sprawled out on the floor, running his cars and trucks through the carpet, making temporary lines with the plastic wheels.

"Honey, are you having fun?"

Oblivious to the fact that his mom had entered the room, Riley's eyes darted at the sound of her voice. "Yes, Mom," he answered as he went back to moving the firetrucks about.

"What do you want to do today?"

"Play," he said simply.

At least this time he didn't say, *Go to Daddy's*, she thought to herself.

"Mommy needs to go to the grocery store sometime today to stock up on some items in case the storm comes this way."

If the hurricane ended up being a category one or dropped to tropical storm status, she wasn't going to leave town. If it was a two, she might leave. Anything higher, she was pretty sure they would skedaddle with her parents.

"Like chocolate milk?" Riley asked, his focus still on rolling the vehicles.

"Sure, we can get some chocolate milk, but we also need batteries for the flashlights, bottles of water, bread, canned goods, and other necessities like that."

Anytime a hurricane threatened the area, the first shelves to become empty at the local grocery stores were the ones that held the bread and the water. Soon, there would also be lines of vehicles backed up at the gas station pumps if there weren't already. If she waited too long, there might even end up being a fuel shortage. People around here panicked when it came to hurricanes, and that wasn't necessarily a bad thing. The rule of thumb was to have one gallon of water per person per day for at least a few days, but over the years, she'd witnessed many people walking out of the market with a whole cart full. The hoarders were the ones who made it difficult for everyone to have what they needed.

"Mom, we probably need more cereal, too," Riley added, sounding all adultlike.

"The way you eat cereal, we might need to fill our cart full of it," she laughed, again thinking about those crazies who assumed they were the only ones who needed supplies.

His eyes lit up like the lights on the police car he was now using to chase the bad guys. "Are you serious?" he asked.

"I'm just being silly, son, but we'll make sure to get a couple of boxes."

Even if the power went out and the milk spoiled, she knew Riley would eat dry cereal. As she stood over him, gazing at her child as mothers often do, wondering where the time had gone and why he couldn't be a baby again, she could see Niles. She used to love how her little boy reminded her of his daddy—his expressions, his eyes, most of the features on his face.

Riley continued playing in his room for about an hour as Eden scoured through the cabinets and refrigerator, making a grocery list to include anything they might possibly need while trying to steer clear of items that would spoil if the power went out. Within thirty minutes, the two of them were in their shoes and out the door. Prior to leaving, Eden traded in her baggy shirt for a tighter one and replaced the lounge pants that had been covering her legs with blue jeans. She didn't spend as much time on her hair as she would if she'd been going into the office, but she made it look presentable.

At age five, Riley Cameron had graduated to a booster seat. One thing Eden made sure never to forget, no matter how big of a hurry she was in or even if she had the worst headache of her life, was to make certain he was properly buckled. When he'd been in a five-point harness car seat, she'd driven to the fire station at least once a month to take advantage of their free safety checks.

Once safe and sound, they made their way to the grocery store where the parking lot was already busier than a typical mid-morning on a weekday. There were always moms—whose kids were in school—shopping during the day, which reminded Eden that this time next year, Riley would be in kindergarten. She couldn't believe how quickly he'd grown up. It seemed like just yesterday, she hadn't even wanted to bring him to the grocery store because he was an infant, and she and Niles were worried that babies would pick up germs there. She knew she had been an overprotective parent during those early years, but she'd learned that most first-time parents were that way. On the flip side, there were some things that she was more cautious about now that she wished she had been more attuned to when her son was younger.

Riley still liked to climb into the back of the grocery cart, which always reminded Eden of when her little toddler used to climb into his crib at the age when most kids were climbing out. It was the cutest thing. When the boy was tired, he was ready to go to bed no matter what was going on at home, and he'd head that way on his own after saying, "I want to go to bed now." If she and Niles followed him, he went to the crib; if they didn't follow, he would work his way over the railing and lay down amongst his stuffed animals while holding Banana the tightest. Of course, the two of them always ended up going in and telling him goodnight, usually after peeking around the doorframe and giggling while he performed his monkey impersonation.

In the grocery cart, Riley pretended all sorts of things. Some days, he was a racecar driver steering around endcaps while others he was shooting at bad guys hiding behind jars of spaghetti. As they navigated the busy aisles today, Eden noticed that he wasn't asking for as much junk food as normal, and she figured it was because the store was inundated with shoppers. Like her, her little boy had been people watching and barely talking. When he had spoken, the first thing he'd asked was, "Why are all these people here?"

As Eden plucked items from the shelves, she crossed paths with a handful of people she knew, as usual in a small town. Some of them she would have rather avoided altogether, but the tight quarters on every aisle made that feat more difficult than usual. In fact, the grocery store could have used a few extra employees to direct traffic inside and probably outside, too. The cart at her fingertips was being bumped so often that she felt like a driver on a bumper cars ride, which was irritating because people were in way too big of a hurry. *The storm isn't coming today*, she thought about screaming out a handful of times. The only positive thing about the crowd was that most customers seemed to be in an abnormally chipper mood; for some reason, hurricanes always seemed to swirl excitement into the air. The best comparison for an event like this—and hurricanes in Eastern North Carolina were definitely an event—was Christmas shopping. Even though everything seemed chaotic, people, for the most part, were merry. Of course, there were always a few runts, too.

As expected, when she made it to the bread shelf, it was as bare as a newborn baby's bottom. She'd have to try back tomorrow morning much earlier because she knew the bread man delivered a truckload every day not long after the rooster crowed. Thankfully, the shelf that held the water was merely scarce, and she was able to snatch three gallon-sized jugs and a twenty-four pack of bottled water. Reaching for the jugs reminded her of those fish ponds where people toss in tiny pebbles of food towards dozens of gaping fish mouths and watch them fight like scavengers. At least ten arms were stretching into the same area. She was thankful that Riley hadn't seen the evil eye she'd shot the woman who nearly pushed her into the man rubbing shoulders with her on the other side. Eden had breathed out a cuss word but knew Riley couldn't have heard it over the commotion. The woman had, though; Eden knew that because the lady's eyes grew to the size of her hoop earrings and then she darted away. Eden snickered, thinking of how people were too easily offended these days. It wasn't like she was going to try to fight the woman or anything. She just wanted that lady to be a bit more respectful of other people's bubbles.

Once Eden and Riley made it through the madhouse and to the cash register area, the line she chose was as long as the one she'd waited in to upgrade her phone when the new model released. Today, each line of people with their carts was about the same length. Ironically, most of the customers standing in the lanes were occupied with their phones just like at the cellphone store. However, more conversations were going on than Eden expected, and she figured this most likely had something to do with the hurricane looming off the coast. The person in front of and behind her had each made comments to her about the storm. The middle-aged woman added, "I should have gotten some medicine, too," as she eyed the cough syrup in Eden's basket. Then the man, about her age, chimed in, "I should have gotten beer." Eden had grabbed a case with the same count as the bottled water. If she decided not to evacuate, she'd need the alcohol to help calm her nerves. Although the anxiety medicine was supposed to manage that, she knew her nervous system would be working overtime if left home alone with Riley while it was storming.

"Just don't mix that cough syrup and that alcohol," the woman suggested as though her comment wasn't common knowledge.

"I wouldn't think of it," Eden lied, knowing she'd done so quite a few times since the accident, but it had never caused her any serious problems. It was probably an old wives' tale, she assumed. Of course, she wasn't stupid enough not to realize that there was a limit to consuming alcohol with medication.

The man behind her—after a few glances in his direction, she began to notice was kind of cute in a scraggly way—offered his two cents again. "Just drink enough beer that you won't need the cough syrup," he suggested with a grin.

Eden snickered. The woman ahead of them rolled her eyes and turned her attention to the clerk, who was busy scanning groceries. The rough and sexy guy laughed, too, and Eden felt like the two of them were sharing a moment.

"I like your thinking," Eden offered.

"Maybe I should go to your hurricane party," he mentioned, smiling before letting his grin turn into a chuckle.

Eden looked him up and down as if scanning him like a barcode not even trying to hide her interest. "Maybe you should," she answered with a wink after noticing he didn't have a ring choking his finger.

She didn't normally pick up guys in the grocery store, especially while her five-year-old son was in the cart. Thankfully, Riley was buried in groceries and playing with the toy airplane she'd let him grab from one of the endcaps. Appeasing him with toys was easier than dealing with his tantrums when she wasn't feeling good.

Once Eden checked out, the cute guy asked if he could help her unload her groceries. "Sure," she answered, deciding that she didn't mind waiting since he only had about a dozen items in his cart. Otherwise, she wasn't certain she would have stuck around for him. It wasn't like he was Johnny Depp, although there was a resemblance.

"Can I borrow your pen?" Eden overheard him ask the cashier before walking out with her, their two carts rolling side by side.

Riley had glanced up at the guy a few times, but he hadn't said anything. He just kept flying his plane.

"What's your name?" Eden asked.

"Kirk," he revealed proudly.

"It's nice to meet you, Kirk," she replied, then shared her name. Since she didn't know him, she didn't think it would be wise to tell him Riley Cameron's name, and thankfully, he didn't ask. After strapping her little fellow into his seat, she joined Kirk at the rear of the SUV, where he was slowly loading bags. *Smooth*, she thought, letting a grin grow on her face. A few minutes later, after allowing an enlightening conversation to interrupt the task at hand, she and Kirk loaded the last bags, and he shut the hatch. Then, he handed her his receipt.

Eden furrowed her brow. "What's this for?"

"The important numbers are on the back," he relayed with a mischievous smile.

"Oh, are they?" she responded with a smirk, turning over the register paper to find his phone number, written sloppily.

"I'm serious about that Hurricane Florence party," Kirk confirmed. "I'll even bring more beer," he promised. "And a pizza or wings—whatever you like."

"We'll see," were the last words that Eden spoke before Kirk floated across the parking lot. She watched him walk away in tight jeans with holes in them and noticed that he wore them quite well. Once they'd exited the store, he'd dropped a pair of sunglasses from the top of his head to cover his blue eyes, and as they'd talked outside, she had kind of missed staring at them. She had no idea whether she and Riley would stay to face the hurricane, but if they did, Eden knew she wouldn't mind having Kirk's company.

6

eese spent a good part of the day roaming the city in her vehicle, an unmarked Dodge Charger with darkly tinted windows. East Ridge was one of those towns, like many others, where there were good areas and not-so-good areas. Of course, almost everyone knew the difference, especially law enforcement. In specific neighborhoods it was all but required to be with a partner before approaching a subject. Those were the areas where Reese took the most verbal abuse. Still, she let the crude names roll off her shoulders like a stream of water pouring from Ruby Falls, the tallest and deepest underground waterfall in the United States. Anyone who'd been anywhere near Chattanooga had a visual memory of the iconic red-painted barn roofs along the roadways that read: *See Ruby Falls*. As a kid, she had loved hopping in the elevator at the top of Lookout Mountain and then dropping twenty-six stories before walking through the caverns that led to the massive waterfall beneath the mountain. As an adult, she still enjoyed visiting the falls, but she spent much more time these days at the top of the mountain. The views there were breathtaking, to say the least. Recently, while on a date, she'd wandered around the castle area, which overlooked the Tennessee Valley and River. The best way she could describe looking down on the vast space beyond the mountain was to compare it to the view from an airplane. The tops of trees resembled dots painted on a canvas, large open fields appeared to be the size of tiny lawns, and tall buildings looked like miniature toys. She and her date had marveled about the sight as if neither of them had ever witnessed it before, but both were from the area and had been at the top of Lookout Mountain dozens of times. Unfortunately, the opportunity that particular evening hadn't turned into a relationship. On a positive note, if it had, she might be more hesitant about heading to the Carolinas this week. Being able to pack her bags and go anywhere she pleased without thinking about anyone else was one of the privileges of being single. There were downsides, too, like coming home to a dark house late at night and having no one there to welcome her into his arms. Ultimately, she always remembered that her relationship status, whether single or dating someone, was all about perspective. Within the past few months, she'd been able to take short trips on a whim during her days off. She'd visited Dublin and Bell Buckle, small cities in Georgia and Tennessee, respectively. Growing up in a relatively big city had given her an appreciation for quaint towns. She loved the feel of a place where almost everyone seemed to know everyone else, and people greeted strangers kindly when passing them on the street.

Thinking of the areas she'd visited lately, Reese wondered where in the Carolinas she would end up later this week. In the meeting this morning, the discussion had been about Wilmington, New Bern, and Myrtle Beach. She'd heard of all these places except for the middle one. After a quick search on her phone, she found out that New Bern was the smallest of the three cities, which made sense when it came to her not recognizing the name. However, she did know the name Pepsi-Cola, which she discovered had been founded in a downtown drugstore in this historic town. Apparently, there was a quaint museum store there now where customers could still get a fountain Pepsi for a couple of coins. She'd love to check that out, but even if she ended up there, she wasn't sure if there would be time for anything other than work. After she signed up for the adventure, the captain pulled her aside and shared stories about hurricane teams he worked with in the past. It sounded like crews pretty much worked around the clock with just enough sleep to wake up and start all over again the next day. This was fine with her because the reason she was going was the same reason she'd become a police officer—to help people.

One of the perks of taking the assignment was driving the department's Hummer, which generally rested in the city garage until needed for a case that involved mountainous terrain or muddy backroads. Dominguez was admittedly jealous of her as soon as he found out that she'd be cruising along the highway in his favorite vehicle as well as towing along the search and rescue boat. The whole special operations division had been through extensive water training and even prepared for flood situations. The Chattanooga area had experienced its fair share of flooding over the years, just not from hurricanes. Apparently, police departments from all over North and South Carolina were reaching out to stations that had specialized equipment for treacherous waters. It sounded like officials had decided that the potential for rivers rising well beyond their banks along the coast was even more of a concern than wind-related issues.

7

The dirty blond color of Niles's hair was always a little dirtier at the end of the workday. Today, he and Mickey felt like they had earned their money and then some. Now, even though they'd made it home, there was no purpose in taking showers. Work needed to be done in and around the treehouse to prepare for the storm. The first task they chose to tackle involved branches that would be in their best interest to trim back or cut down entirely to ensure that they wouldn't fall on the roof or damage the integrity of the structure.

Strapped into a harness, Mickey worked the chainsaw while dangling in mid-air as Niles maneuvered the ropes from ground-level. Each branch was tied off securely so that once sliced in half, it wouldn't freefall like the pinecones Mickey had been randomly tossing like grenades in his best friend's direction. The only reason Niles hadn't chunked something back at his buddy was because of the chainsaw. Instead, as he guided limbs to the ground, he decided he'd pay Mickey back later. This process took over an hour as the sun was firing shadow darts through the towering trees that surrounded the area. Rather than taking time to eat dinner, the guys decided on candy bars for snacks, not wanting to waste any daylight. This was something they'd become accustomed to from working in both the construction and landscaping industries. Sunup to sundown were the hours posted on the proverbial doors of those businesses.

"Have you talked to Eden today about taking Riley with us if we leave town to escape Flo?" Mickey asked after throttling down the chainsaw.

Mickey, along with many others, had nicknamed the hurricane Flo. People were saying that they hoped Flo would flow north and stay out in the ocean.

"Not yet," Niles answered as he squatted slightly to drag a good-size pine tree limb out of the area he'd been keeping clear in order to assist Mickey from the ground. His hands were sticky from the tree sap because he remembered too late that he should have worn gloves.

"You better not wait too long," he advised, shouting downward. "Eden is probably trying to decide whether or not to leave just like we are."

"I know, I'm just not sure how to bring up the subject."

"You should probably call her rather than text," Mickey suggested.

Niles's head swayed up and down in agreement. "I'd prefer to know if we're leaving before I discuss taking Riley. Because if we're not going anywhere, it's just a wasted conversation," he mentioned, breathing heavily as he dropped the limb.

"True. Maybe just call Eden and see what her plans are for the storm."

Niles had thought about going that route. "The only thing is, if she says, 'Riley and I are leaving town' then I've missed my opportunity to be the first to mention taking him out of town for safety reasons."

"Good point," Mickey agreed, working his way up the tree toward another branch that he and Niles had identified as risky. They'd targeted individual limbs simply because they were large enough to cause significant damage and others due to instability or weakness caused by a previous storm. "You want me to call her?" he asked with a snicker.

"Yeah, that will go over well," Niles answered sarcastically.

"C'mon, bro, you know how good I am at sweet-talking women."

"Ones that don't know you," Niles responded, chuckling.

"Really? I'm one of the good guys," Mickey proclaimed.

"I didn't say you weren't a good guy, but Eden isn't going to take you seriously if you call her asking if we can take Riley."

"I was just kidding about that anyway."

"I know," Niles confirmed.

"But what I'm saying is that you really think I can't sweet-talk girls who know me?"

"What's the longest relationship you've ever had?"

"Like a couple of months, maybe."

"Exactly. You jump from one girl to another just like you've been jumping around on those limbs beneath your feet."

"I get bored in relationships," Mickey admitted.

"Why?"

"Cause I don't like to sit around and hold hands and watch chick flicks."

"You like to sit around and play video games. What's the difference?"

"For real, bro? You're serious right now? You're on the verge of losing your man-card, Niles."

"Okay, that's not a good analogy," he said proudly, pretty sure he'd used the word analogy appropriately thanks to Eden's clarification.

"It's a horrible one. When's the last time you've seen a girl put her head on my shoulder while I'm playing a video game?"

Niles shook his head. "Probably never."

"That's right. Never. Women don't play fair. They want us to cuddle up with them and watch romantic movies that we don't give two cents about, but do you see any of them watching us play video games? Nope," he blurted out emphatically, answering his own question.

"So, you just need to find a woman who plays video games."

"They're as rare as . . ." he trailed off, searching his surroundings to find a comparison. ". . . as a dogwood tree," he finally spouted, pointing at one twenty-five yards in the distance.

Niles glanced at a tree he'd passed by a hundred times. One that Riley liked to climb, in fact. "You know there are several dogwood trees within eyesight, right?" Riley had climbed them all, over and over since he was two and a half years old.

"Whatever, you get my point. Look at how many pines and oaks are out here."

Niles let his eyes wander. "Point taken," he responded.

"I'll go one step further. A woman who likes playing video games is as rare as coming across a dog urinating on a dogwood tree."

Niles laughed out loud. "You're so dumb," he announced in the middle of the darkening woods, and for the first time this evening, he realized that the temperature had begun to drop.

Mickey cranked the chainsaw to drown out Niles's laughter and began to chisel away at the next limb. Tiny chunks of fresh-cut wood started spraying in every direction, landing on the ground near Niles's feet, where a bed of wood chips had already begun to form. When they finished with the branches on that tree, they moved to the next, and then to one more before it was too dark to safely operate a chainsaw, even with the spotlight they'd set up.

"Let's order a pizza," Mickey suggested as he unstrapped the gear, feeling as though he'd lost twenty pounds in a matter of moments.

"Gina's?" Niles asked.

Gina's was a local joint in Bridgeton and not far from the

house. Between the two of them, Niles and Mickey had probably eaten a hundred pizzas while they'd been living together. Usually, they drove the short distance up the road to pick up the pizza, but this evening they decided to call in delivery so that they could spend the time boarding up the windows. With their tool belts strapped on, they worked in unison like they'd done on dozens of construction sites over the years. Using their heads, they utilized the ropes system set up for the tree work, this time to lift pieces of plywood they'd picked up from Garris Evans Lumber Company on their way home. After hoisting a sheet onto the deck that surrounded the treehouse, one of them would hold it over a window while the other hammered a nail. The motion was like riding a bicycle, and it only took a few precise swings to reach the proper depth. Once the first window was boarded, the next one was done within a matter of minutes. By the time the pizza delivery guy's tires crunched the gravel on the long driveway, every piece of glass on the house was completely covered, and the smell of fresh wood was ever-present.

"We need some spray paint so we can write messages to Flo on these panels," Mickey suggested.

Spraying messages on boarded up windows was *a thing* when hurricanes threatened the coast. It was always interesting to see which notices would end up catching the eyes of the reporters in charge of the news cameras. Of course, none of those people would venture back here in the woods where they lived, but it would be fun anyway.

"Definitely," Niles agreed. "I have one we can write: Flo Away!"

Mickey laughed. "Good one," he offered. "Get the Flo out of here," he then reeled off, chuckling at his own idea before giving Niles a chance to process it.

"I like that."

As they scarfed down the hot pizza like it was the last one on a buffet, they took turns spitting out potential messages for the plywood. They'd decided to sit on the deck, supported by stilts, rather than eat inside because now that the windows were boarded up it seemed rather gloomy indoors. Outside, a set of floodlights were stationed on each corner of the treehouse, which lit the entire area very well. If a big buck were to walk anywhere within forty yards of the treehouse, they'd be able to count the antlers on his crown.

"Let's go out tonight," Mickey suggested.

Niles took a swig of soda from the can he'd been working on then sat it on the ring of sweat it had made on one of the boards at his feet. "We have to start work early in the morning," he reminded his partner in crime.

"So what? We're young, we're single, and we only live once."

"I'm up for it if we don't stay out too late."

"That's a deal, but if you get to pick when we come home, then you have to be the designated driver."

"I was the D.D. last time," Niles exclaimed.

"I'll be the designated driver tomorrow morning," Mickey offered with a wink.

"You'll probably be hungover tomorrow morning," Niles forecasted.

"Nah. I'm not planning on puking on lawns all day."

"You better not because I'm not planning on doing all the work again."

"Bro, that happened one time."

Niles pinched his lips and cocked his head.

"Maybe twice," Mickey added.

An hour later, each of them had taken a shower, and they were on their way to downtown New Bern in Niles's car, which now smelled like the cologne section at a department store. Niles wore a pair of jeans and a nice V-neck t-shirt, and Mickey stepped into khaki pants and pulled a pink shirt with a striped collar over his half-wet hair. The drive from Bridgeton took them across a high rise bridge, from which, during daylight hours, one could catch a glimpse of one of the most spectacular views in North Carolina. Beyond the passenger side windows, the massive Neuse River separated the small town where Niles and Mickey were headed from the even smaller town where they lived. Up ahead, an exit would take them to a drawbridge, which was part of the charm in the view as people peered into historic New Bern from this mountain of a bridge. Downtown New Bern sat in the mouth of where the Neuse and Trent rivers met. The smaller bridge crossed at the fork in the rivers and just beyond it sat Union Point Park, a neatly landscaped area with lush grass, bricked walkways, and gorgeous hardwood trees. Now, at nighttime, green poles with globe lights at the top lit the park, making it clearly visible from the top of the high rise. The rest of the downtown area was dotted with these same streetlamps causing a quaint glow to hover over the city.

Just beyond the drawbridge, Niles guided the car to the left down South Front Street, and both he and Mickey quickly noticed that the town seemed more alive than on a typical Monday night. They turned right onto Craven Street, but couldn't find a parking place near Prohibition, a bar and restaurant that people their age frequented. At the next stoplight they came to, City Hall sat on the opposite corner. Niles steered the car in that direction and eventually found an empty space in front of the Episcopal church, where stringy gray moss hung from trees as prehistoric-looking as the building itself. Protruding roots crawled along a dusty graveyard nestled on the church grounds being held captive by a black cast-iron fence. Between the tombstones and City Hall, a small playground seemed almost out of place.

Neither Niles nor Mickey thought about any of these things because they had walked along the brick sidewalks in the downtown area hundreds of times and had become numb to sights a tourist might find fascinating. On any given day, New Bern bustled with out-of-towners with cameras and maps highlighting the historic sites and fiberglass bears that represented the city's mascot. The two jaywalked then followed the sidewalk around a corner, soon making it to the outdoor entrance of Prohibition where a veranda the size of a large alleyway separated the restaurant from the bar. Music was floating through the air, growing louder as the guys made it inside the gate where a bouncer stamped their hands after taking a peek at their driver's licenses. Most nights, Mickey and Niles knew about half of the crowd and recognized some of the others. The faces that weren't familiar belonged to visitors, usually young Marines from the base at Cherry Point or people from surrounding towns who ventured in to check out the local nightlife. Niles found it easy to chat with the military guys because his dad had served and been stationed in Havelock, which was the reason his family moved to this area when he was a kid. He found it more challenging to spark conversations with the attractive women at the bar partially because he wasn't as outgoing as Mickey but also because many of them were friends or acquaintances with Eden. It seemed weird to flirt with someone who had always known him as Eden's guy, not to mention that he'd been with Eden so long that he really hadn't dated anyone else. He wasn't accustomed to trying to pick up women at a bar or anywhere else for that matter. Even now, people he didn't see often would come up to him around town and ask about Eden. Sure, news of their divorce had traveled like a wildfire in the nearby Croatan Forest during a dry season. Still, he had found out the hard way that not everyone knew, especially the older generation, like his former school teachers, people who had known his parents, and so on. In those situations, he always felt awkward and embarrassed. Most of the time, he would say, "She's doing good" rather than break the news. Then, he'd find himself hoping those people would find out about the divorce from someone else before he ran into them again. When Niles had said "I do" and walked down the aisle with Eden Franks hand-in-hand with shiny new rings on their fingers, he had never in a million years imagined a divorce would ever be possible. Not that the average newlyweds think such thoughts, but he and Eden had been happy for years on top of years. They'd grown up together, and they were the perfect match—*were* being the operative word. Prior to the accident, they *were* inseparable. Then, the accident happened, and those little pills crept into their lives. Eden had become a person he barely recognized, yet he still loved her and in some ways even more than before. If Niles was honest, he had to admit that he felt guilty about something, although he wasn't sure what. It wasn't like he hadn't tried to keep the marriage together. In their own ways, they both had. It just hadn't worked out, and now, here he was—single and picking at his ring finger again with his nail.

"Dude, this place is hopping," Mickey announced, the level of the music causing him to speak louder than normal. "There are babes everywhere," he pointed out as his eyes traveled from one female to the next.

Niles surveyed the area, too. "Yep," he said, watching the movement all around them. "The hurricane excitement has brought people out of the woodwork."

The place wasn't quite as packed as a weekend night, but there were probably seventy-five percent as many people. More guys than gals, as usual. Mickey never seemed to care that the odds weren't in his favor, but Niles knew this was because Mickey wasn't afraid of striking out. If one girl turned his buddy down, he'd laugh it off and move right on to the next one at the bar. Honestly, Niles didn't care either because he wasn't trying to take anyone home. In fact, he hadn't asked out a single woman since the divorce. For some reason, the thought made him feel like he was cheating on Eden. He didn't understand it, it just did.

"Want a beer?" Mickey asked.

"Nah, I'm good," Niles answered. "Remember, I'm driving us home."

"One beer isn't going to impair your vision or judgment."

On nights when he was the designated driver, Niles didn't like to drink even one. The reward wasn't worth the risk. The last thing he needed was a D.U.I., which would be ammunition for Eden when they ended up in court again. At some point, he was hoping to gain evenly split custody of Riley rather than only having him every other weekend and one weekday. When the judge denied that request in the first place, the ruling baffled Niles. Now there were times when he wished he'd listened to his attorney and allowed the man to attack Eden regarding prescription drug abuse. At the time, Niles didn't want to drag his son's mother's name through the mud. In a small town, titles like 'druggie' stuck to people like an ugly wart even if the person eventually kicked the addiction. This was one of the reasons he was always begging Mickey not to call his ex-wife such names. Thankfully, his friend honored that request in public but not so much in private.

"I'll drink a root beer," Niles teased.

"At least then it will look like you're drinking and having a good time."

"I always have a good time," Niles snarled.

"You need to let one of these ladies have a good time with you," Mickey suggested, pointing out a few that he thought were ripe for the taking. "At least get one girl's phone number tonight," he added. "Which reminds me, did you call Eden?"

Eden. Her name always came up—in Niles's mind and out of other people's mouths. "When could I have called Eden? You've been with me all night."

"I wasn't in the shower with you."

Niles bobbed his head side to side. "Yeah, I called Eden while I was in the shower," he responded with sarcasm.

"Hey, I've done way weirder things than that in the shower, my man."

To be funny, Niles covered his ears and began to hum,

although Mickey could barely hear him over the song that was bouncing off the walls. "I don't want to know anything about what you do in the shower," he said a little louder than usual since he could barely hear himself speak.

Nearby, a couple of their high school buddies overheard Niles's comment and turned to chime in with their own humor. Within a matter of moments, Niles and Mickey were talking with a group of friends about the storm and hurricane parties being planned. Bottles were being passed around at the bar, and the clanking sounds of empty ones being thrown into the recycle interrupted the beat of the music periodically. There seemed to be a pattern to everything, from the movement of people mingling to the way the bartenders danced around one another behind the main stage. A stool would become empty, and then within a matter of seconds, it was filled by a new body. People who couldn't find a seat were standing anywhere they could find the room, mostly in small clusters of three to six individuals. At the front of the establishment were a few couches and chairs in a more relaxed area with a coffee table and bookshelves that held magazines, novels, and board games. For a moment, Niles locked eyes with a cute blonde sitting on the leather sofa, but then he turned back to the conversation with his buddies. He thought about what Mickey had said but then decided not to waste his time. Life seemed much more comfortable right here within the circle of people whom he already knew.

8

When Eden and Riley made it home from the grocery store earlier, she had put away the groceries with Kirk on her mind and an extra pep in her step. Those jeans. That smile. Those eyes. When she and Niles had first split, she couldn't imagine being with another man. Once some time passed, her mind shifted, and she found herself enjoying the freedom of flirting with whomever she chose and hanging out with anyone in whom she found interest. After spending some time on the dating scene, she decided she no longer cared for the idea of marriage or even a long term relationship; she found living day by day and keeping her options open more appealing. She hadn't become easy, but she had learned how to let loose and have fun. Sometimes that required more alcohol than other times, but it mainly depended on how she felt at the moment. Pain pills, alcoholic beverages, and the arms of a welcoming man seemed to take the edge off what was otherwise a miserable life. Riley Cameron, of course, was the brightest ray of sunshine in her everyday world, and his smile and little arms healed her wounds many times, too. However, a five-year-old shouldn't have to rescue his mommy, she thought, and so she tried to find other ways to escape the pain so that he could have the best of her rather than watch her suffer.

Eden decided not to text or call Kirk right away. There was no reason to come across as needy, mainly because she wasn't. At this very moment, she could crumple up the receipt with his number on the back, toss it in the trash can beside the refrigerator, and never think about the man again. On second thought, maybe the not thinking about him part was an exaggeration. Those eyes—she would see them again, if only in her mind. However, that didn't mean she had to communicate with him, which was one of the pleasant aspects of being single. She didn't have to call Kirk or anyone for that matter. If her head started hurting worse and she didn't feel like talking, she could lie on the couch, pull a blanket over her shoulders, and let her mind rest. If she and Niles were still together, he would be hovering over her asking what he could do to make her feel better or giving her a hard time about being sleepy all the time. "Maybe all that medicine is having negative effects on your body," he'd probably say for the millionth time. Not having to answer to another adult was one of the fortunate parts about it being only her and Riley now. The little fellow would play in his bedroom or in the living room, and she barely knew he was there.

Eden was thankful that her son wasn't one of those rambunctious kids. He was all boy, but he didn't spend his days bouncing off the walls like a mouse in a maze. His daddy probably wore him out with all those treehouse toys and outdoor activities. Niles and Riley stayed as busy as beavers, and Eden knew her son enjoyed it, but when he was home with her, she felt like he wanted and probably needed to chill out. She played with him some when she felt up to it, but most times, it was hard on her body to crawl around on the floor. She would love to be like the average twenty-year-old mother who could scoot around the carpet as swiftly as a wrestler on a mat, but she had to be careful. She hadn't been able to let Riley crawl on her like a jungle gym ever since she'd been thrown through the front windshield of a vehicle. She still wasn't sure how she hadn't died after piercing through a sheet of glass like an arrow and then landing on the unforgiving ground.

At times, she wished she had died that day. Then she wouldn't have had to go through all the pain caused by the accident, the divorce, and the ensuing mental agony of having to deal with not having Cameron with her every day of her life. It made things better that Riley was there most of the time, but when he went to his dad's, Eden felt like she had lost her whole family. People often reminded her that she had plenty of things to be thankful for, even beyond breath. She could have easily been paralyzed or suffered significant brain damage. Still, on many occasions, Eden couldn't decide whether to thank God for letting her live or blame him for allowing the accident. Usually, blaming him felt best.

When dinnertime rolled around, Eden abandoned the couch and boiled a pot of water for noodles. Earlier in the day, she thawed a package of frozen hamburger meat, wanting to consume as much of the perishable food on hand as possible within the next couple of days. When the cold air from the freezer slapped her in the face, it felt refreshing, and she found herself standing there for a long moment. Eventually, she prepared the meat in a skillet and mixed in the noodles and sauce. Then she and Little Man ate Hamburger Helper while watching one of his favorite shows. After screaming at him for dropping a few noodles on the carpet, she felt terrible, but she still made him help clean up the mess, hoping it would teach him a lesson. Afterward, the two of them loaded the dishwasher, and she let Riley pour in the detergent because he found it mesmerizing for some reason. He always wanted to fill that little square container to the brim, and usually, it ended up overflowing. She didn't fuss at him for that, but she recalled the times when she forgot to let him pour it in; he'd pout about it until she sent him to his room.

After dinner, she cracked open a second beer and set it on the coffee table. The other twenty-two cans were squeezed onto the bottom shelf in the refrigerator. Upon fitting them in, she realized that she had forgotten to grab a couple bags of ice to place in the freezer temporarily. A cooler filled with ice was the back-up plan for when a hurricane caused the electricity to go out. Her cooler was in the garage, but she wasn't sure if it was clean. She'd have to check that out another time because she didn't feel like putting her shoes on, searching the shelves out there, and then cleaning the thing if need be. Who knows what was inside of it, maybe spiders or sand from a beach trip. Plus, she'd just taken a muscle relaxer and figured it would be best not to use her strength for anything other than picking up the beverage that was cooling her hand.

All evening, she had been receiving text messages from girlfriends out enjoying the nightlife or at least what was considered such in this small town. In all honesty, the downtown scene had improved in the past few years. A couple of new bars moved in as well as some restaurants that stayed open past nine o'clock, and there were often local bands playing. Typically, a Monday night wouldn't be the night to go out, but apparently, from what her friends were saying, everyone had gone out tonight for a pre-hurricane party, which she was sure would happen every evening until the streets and businesses shut down. Then, parties would continue at people's homes, but she doubted she'd be able to make any of them if she stayed in town because Riley would be with her. She didn't mind drinking around him at home and even having a few friends over, but she didn't want to subject him to many of the things that went on at parties—the drugs, the sex, and so on. A five-year-old didn't need to see certain situations regardless of whether he understood what was happening. This reminded her of Kirk and his offer to bring beer and hang out. She contemplated calling him but then became sidetracked when her friend Dana messaged her and said that Niles was at the bar. First, she wasn't sure why her friends felt the need to report to her when they saw Niles out and about. Secondly, she didn't know why it bothered her. Maybe it was the thought of him talking to other women. Women who he might eventually date and bring around her son. What if he brought home some trashy girl? Riley Cameron didn't need to be exposed to that. It also didn't seem fair that her son's father was out partying and she was stuck here on the couch in an oversized t-shirt and no bra.

Who's Niles there with? she couldn't help but ask after sending a few messages pretending not to care.

Who do you think? Dana responded.

A girl?

No, he's with Mickey.

Oh, yeah, of course, Eden replied.

But there is some random blonde chick over on the couch that keeps giving him the eye.

Who is it?

Don't know. Haven't seen her before, but she's cute.

Oh, okay, Eden replied nonchalantly.

She clicked away from the string of messages and then tapped the *new message* button, thinking of texting Kirk. Talking to him might be an excellent way to get her mind off Niles and some girl who was eyeing her ex.

9

Reese glanced down at the digital clock on her phone, surprised that there was less than an hour left before Monday would become Tuesday. When scheduled to work the following morning, she rarely stayed out anywhere close to midnight, but one glass of wine had turned into three. She was thoroughly enjoying the soothing sounds of classical music at a piano bar she frequented in downtown Chattanooga. It was by no means the typical cop hangout. Prior to heading here, she'd traded in her uniform for a simple black dress and heels that almost made her feel tall. The lights were dimmed, and the level of conversation was just above a whisper. Other than the few times Dominguez and his wife had met her here, she couldn't recall ever seeing a single police officer in this place. Not that she knew everyone who wore a badge in this county, but between her time in law enforcement and meeting so many of the men and women with whom her dad had served, she probably knew as many as anyone in the area. No one in this bar looked remotely like a cop, and thankfully no one looked like a criminal either. Most people were sitting close to a significant other, but there were a few like her who were flying solo. None of the apparently single folks hit on her, which was one of the reasons she chose to come here for drinks and entertainment. The gentleman nestled behind the black grand piano was wearing a suit jacket and looked as though he'd been playing similar engagements for decades. His voice reminded her of melted butter, smooth and soft, leaving her wanting more every time she considered sliding backward in the chair she'd been occupying for hours.

Tonight, as Reese took in the music and the scene around her, thoughts of her dad weighed heavily on her mind, enough so that she was glad she had paid for a ride rather than driving. If the police department had a profile on her like the ones in the suspect database, it would classify her as a social drinker. Yet, on the days when she pulled her firearm, she ended up feeling more like a moderate drinker. This time, she felt like she could quickly become a heavy drinker.

The last thing that an officer of the law wanted to do was shoot a perpetrator. Closing her eyelids as that thought shifted across her mind like a black cloud, Reese immediately took it back. More accurately, the last thing a cop wanted was to *be* shot. However, firing on another human being neared the top of the list of possibilities that neither she nor her comrades wanted to transpire. Almost everyone who ran in the circles in which she ran knew that her father had been shot by a man who deserved to be shot himself, quite honestly. This particular criminal tortured innocent women and children and even killed an officer of the law.

A little way down the city street outside of the piano bar was a more boisterous bar filled with off-duty cops. Bright streetlights, installed to help keep the town safe, led the way there. Reese thought about leaving the comfort of the subdued tones dancing off the ivory keys for the reassurance of familiar faces and music capable of drowning out thoughts like the ones she was battling. People there would understand the adrenaline rush of pulling a gun from a holster and pointing it at someone with the intention of firing. Officers didn't pull their weapons for any other reason, and today she'd felt more pressure than any other time. Pointing a firearm at someone wasn't a scare tactic, it was a method of self-defense and reserved for the protection of others caught in harm's way. The person Reese had aimed the nozzle of her nine millimeter handgun at had his own pistol tucked into a pair of sagging jeans and she'd highly doubted he possessed a conceal-carry permit. She spotted the weapon as soon as she jumped out of her patrol car and began to run toward the park where a man had been seen striking a woman. Immediately, the scene reminded her of the shooting in which her father was involved. As she sprinted through an open gate toward the perpetrator, kicking up blades of grass beneath her black boots, she saw her dad's face. She could even feel his presence when the man's hand reached toward his belt. She halted in mid-stride and hollered out, "Police—don't do it!"

"This ain't your business," the man shouted back, letting his hand linger at his hip as he stood as still as a statue, glaring at her with two of the evilest eyes she'd ever seen as if he had been looking forward to this moment his whole life.

As soon as Reese noticed his arm lower, she'd popped open the cover of her holster and drawn her weapon like clockwork. Immediately, she found herself standing firm in the exact stance she had taken so many times at the indoor gun range that her department used for practice, but this target was real. It wasn't a thin sheet of paper with perfect circles and bright colors.

"Put your hands above your head," Reese demanded. Backup would arrive at any moment which made her feel more confident.

The man guided his hands out from either side of his body, like a gunslinger in a western movie. "You ain't the first person that ever pointed a piece at me," he revealed with a snarl.

If you reach for that weapon, I'll be the last, Reese thought, but she decided not to speak her mind. As usual these days, bystanders had already begun to pull out their phones to record video. This didn't make her nervous, but she knew many of them were probably waiting for her to make a wrong move or say something out of line so that their video might go viral on social sites or maybe even be sold to the news media. It didn't really matter because the bodycam on her chest recorded everything that was going on anyway.

"Please, place your hands on your head so that you and I can have a talk," Reese insisted rather than responding directly to the comment.

"Why don't you put away your gun and run your hands through that pretty black hair of yours," he suggested, snickering between a few missing teeth. "Then we can all go home happy."

Why did so many people go there, Reese thought to herself, wanting to walk up to the man and kick him right between the legs. It was sad enough that a grown man didn't respect a police officer but even worse that he had no reverence for a woman. This behavior shouldn't come as a surprise to her since he had been reported for beating on the woman near his feet. She looked as though she wallowed in the dirt then ate some while lying in it. Reese had even witnessed him kick her as she'd shifted the patrol car into park. It did somewhat surprise her when the apparent victim glared up as if jealous of her for the provocative comment the man had made. *Believe me, I'm not the least bit interested in this dirt bag*, Reese wanted to announce, but that was another comment she knew to keep private.

"Why can't y'all pigs just stay out of my business?" the man asked.

Reese took a step toward the perpetrator, placing her about fifteen yards away—enough room where she wouldn't miss if she had to fire, but not close enough where he would have any chance of lunging for her weapon before she could squeeze the trigger. For some reason, this made her think of the first time she'd taken target practice with the officers at her station.

"When you hit a woman, you make it our business," Reese informed him.

Each of his hands remained about a foot from either hip, and his fingers were dancing as if playing saxophone keys. It was evident to Reese that this man wasn't afraid of her or the weapon pointed at his chest. Without taking her eyes off him, she surveyed the area as best as possible and listened to the sounds around them: children playing nearby on a rusted swing set, a hinged door slamming at the housing complex across the street, and sporadic shouting from bystanders. Some people called for others to come out while the wiser adults attempted to shew people away, especially the kids. It bothered her that this scene barely seemed out of the ordinary to many of the people watching. The most frightening part was that in these situations, stray bullets sometimes ended up in innocent bystanders. This was one of the reasons her dad had spent countless hours with her at the range from the first time she shot a gun to the final opportunity they had to target practice together. He never wanted one of those stray bullets to come from her firearm . . . or from the perpetrator's weapon. "But how can a police officer keep the bad guy's bullets from hitting innocent people?" she remembered asking at a young age one day at the range. At that moment, her dad helped her hold a small twenty-two caliber pistol steady then let go of the training wheels as her little finger weighed in on the trigger an instant before a bullet she'd slotted on her own poked a hole through the target. "Don't ever miss," he whispered.

In her peripheral vision, Reese could see two young women sitting idly on a park bench, both wearing miniskirts and one with a purse atop her lap. They appeared interested yet unafraid. Out of the corner of her other eye, Reese watched a group of three men who didn't seem bothered by the presence of an officer with a firearm in hand. They'd been laughing and joking the whole time, even spouting out perverted comments such as, "She can handcuff me any day," "I'd hit that," and so on. In the distance, she began to hear the faint sound of sirens.

"Your buddies are coming to help you out," the perp announced real cute like. "You mind if I reach my hand into my pocket to get my cell so I can call my crew, and we can keep the numbers at this party even?"

"I wouldn't recommend that," Reese suggested, feeling the curve of the trigger touching the skin beneath her finger. For now, both eyes were open so that her vision could remain as wide as possible. If he made a move, the right eyelid would instantly collapse, and she would exhale, allowing her body to relax. She practiced these techniques frequently at the range, mannerisms she understood the day when her fellow officers watched on as the newbie, a woman, sunk five holes in the target but not a single one anywhere close to the bullseye.

The man suddenly lifted his arms above his head, but then he took a small step in her direction.

"Don't move another inch," Reese shouted firmly, knowing precisely how many pounds of pressure it would take to stop this man in his tracks.

"Whoa! You told me to put my hands in the air."

"Yes, and keep them there, but keep your feet right where they are."

"You have pretty eyes," he announced loudly, laughing under his breath that most likely smelled of alcohol. Reese had taken note of the brown bags laying on the ground beside the victim. It appeared that they'd both been drinking, but that wasn't a concern at the time being even though it wasn't permitted in the park.

A few moments later, the sound of sirens overshadowed the conversation. Dominguez quickly angled his vehicle so that the right front corner of the patrol car was pointing at the man at which he noticed Kirby's gun aimed. There was a fence between the parking lot and the park, but just in case shots were fired, he'd have cover. However, as soon as he hopped out of the driver's side door and realized his presence hadn't escalated the situation, he scurried toward the perpetrator, coming in at a slightly different angle than his one-time partner. As he moved, he made sure to take a line that was clear of bystanders beyond the man with his hands lifted toward the sky. Instinctively, he flipped open the latch on his holster but didn't yet draw his gun.

"Welcome to the party," the perp shouted out of the corner of his mouth, spit falling as he slurred the words.

"The party is over," Dominguez clarified then spoke to Reese. "Are there any other potential threats?"

"Not any that have shown themselves," she explained.

Like Reese, Dominguez was watching every movement in the park while keeping his focus on the perp.

"Sir, clasp your hands together, place them behind your head, and then drop to your knees," Dominguez instructed, moving toward the guy as he spoke. He wasn't trying to take over the situation, and he knew Reese was wise enough to understand that a single officer shouldn't do this on their own, which was precisely why she was standing where she was when he'd arrived. Ever since that first day when he'd watched carefully as she shot at the range, he'd known she was different. He recalled another officer saying, "I wouldn't want her as my partner, she can barely hit the target."

Thankfully, the man in the park did as Dominguez ordered, and a few moments later, Dominguez had a pair of handcuffs wrapped snugly around the guy's wrists. Reese remained in the ready position, holding her handgun, covering her fellow officer until Dominguez snatched the gun from the man's belt and tossed it toward Kirby's feet. Reese carefully knelt down to pick it up, making sure not to take her eye off the scene, then walked toward the victim to check on her as Dominguez patted down the suspect.

Within moments, several marked patrol cars swarmed into the parking lot, and each officer took on a task without needing instruction.

At the piano bar, Reese tried to let the vivid memories of what happened today float out of her mind, replacing them with the sounds of jazz currently sifting through the air and into her ears. The wine and calming music were relaxing the tense muscles which had been pulling at her neck all evening. Feeling much looser than when she walked through the front door, she held up her hand and asked the waiter for another glass. One more, and then she'd call it a night, she decided.

10

The morning sun trickled its way through the canopy of treetops and into Niles's bedroom, spraying an assortment of laser-like rays across the flat wood walls surrounding his small bed. Every item inside the treehouse had been carefully selected to fit into the compact space. Most of the furniture was handcrafted by Niles and Mickey using hardwoods from the property. Every time they cut down one tree, though, they replaced it with ten saplings, which had been ingrained in Mickey's mind from an early age. His family had owned a tree farm in the North Carolina mountains for generations and always aimed to be friendly to the environment. Making items from wood was something both Niles and Mickey casually enjoyed. The finished products weren't anything fancy enough to attempt selling as merchandise, yet they were practical and decent looking pieces, especially for two single guys and a five-year-old living in the middle of the woods.

Niles was accustomed to waking early and heading out to work while the dew was still dancing on the grass blades. Of course, his lawn was made up of pine straw and sand-like dirt, which saved him from having to mow outside of work. Prior to becoming an adult, he had to be up for school every morning like other kids. He hadn't loved school, but he hadn't hated it either. The best part had been spending the days there with Eden, his girlfriend at that time. During their high school years, they would meet in the student parking lot as early as possible and chat until the first bell rang. When it was warm outside, they'd sit on the hood of one of their vehicles or in the bed of Mickey's truck with a group of friends. When it was cold out, Niles and Eden would typically sit alone in his car and often fog up the windows. In between classes, they met at rendezvous points and made the most of the minutes that seemed to pass like seconds. Every day at lunchtime, they waltzed into the cafeteria hand-in-hand and sat side-by-side, much closer than those around them who weren't in a relationship. During most semesters, the two of them would end up having at least one class together, and if the teacher would permit it, they'd sit next to each other. In their younger years, before their parents allowed them to have cell phones, they passed handwritten notes back and forth. As they grew older and were able to have their own phones, they would sneakily type text messages to each other.

Even though he hadn't realized it at the time, if Niles was honest, he'd have to admit that he missed those days when responsibilities were fewer, and he and Eden were head over heels in love. These days, what he missed most were people. He wished that after graduation his mom hadn't moved to California to be closer to siblings, although he realized why she did. At the time, he was preparing to embark on military life with his family. Niles also wished he could have one more hug from his dad. His father was one of those parents who gave tough love, and the burly man would have been absolutely irate if he had been around when Niles was kicked out of boot camp. However, part of the reason Niles ended up back at home with his new wife and their offspring was partially because of the things his dad taught him. He vividly remembered sayings like, "Never let a man put his hands on you," "Never let a man hit a woman," and "Never let anyone harm your children." In hindsight, Niles realized that the advice given probably hadn't fully pertained to boot camp, but at that time, he'd heard his dad's voice loud and clear.

These thoughts were interrupted by the sound of Mickey peeing in the bathroom between their two bedrooms, and it sounded like a water hose was filling a pool. The inner walls of the house were barely insulated, which Niles kind of regretted now. They'd made that decision to shave off a few dollars from the cost of the project. Thankfully, the bathroom kept noises from Mickey's room at bay, especially on nights like last night when he came home with a woman and a handful of beers in him. Now, Niles was confident that the alcohol was in the toilet, or more specifically, traveling through pipes or maybe even at the wastewater management plant since his roommate had made several trips to the restroom overnight. This reminded Niles of other nights when he randomly found himself hoping that the girl who'd come home with Mickey had checked the toilet seat before sitting down. As this thought trickled through his mind, he couldn't help but laugh at the idea of Jenny—the girl from the restaurant who'd also ended up at the bar last night—possibly landing on a wet seat. As he continued to laugh all over himself, he knew he shouldn't, but the thought was just too funny not to find humor in it at the moment. He doubted that such had happened because he would have probably heard her yell out a word or two of profanity, which had occurred in the past under similar circumstances.

Thankfully, Mickey didn't bring home women when Riley was at the house. Niles had never made such a request, but it was something he appreciated, although he and his best friend had never even discussed the matter. Mickey spent a lot of time with Riley, and truth be told, the little guy looked up to him just as much as he did his dad. Mickey was like the fun uncle, and Riley even called him Uncle Mickey from time to time, which Eden despised. Of course, that only encouraged Mickey to say things like, "Uncle Mickey loves you, Riley!" and "Come outside with Uncle Mickey and climb on the ropes."

The ropes course Niles and Mickey personally designed and created weaved from tree to tree throughout the wooded area, and every pathway connected and ended up back at the treehouse. Beneath every obstacle, there was a safety net in case either of them or Riley fell. Niles and Mickey used the course for training to help with balance, agility, and other facets of strength and endurance that helped them excel at mixed martial arts. Riley loved monkeying around with the men, and he was pretty good at climbing and jumping. He'd even learned some self-defense tactics, but he hadn't taken to the sport as Niles hoped he might. He was still young, though. Like his dad and Uncle Mickey, Riley had endured a few bruised elbows and knees, but there had been no injuries requiring an emergency room visit. "It's nothing worse than what his skin looked like when he fell off the bike at your house," Niles had reminded Eden when she complained about the first battle wound from the ropes course—an ugly scrape on their son's left arm. Riley's favorite part of what his mom called the big kids play area was the suspension bridge. It was about twenty yards in distance, and it swayed when the soles of his little shoes ran across the planks of wood.

Niles heard two voices coming from the living room and kitchen, which was combined to make a decent-sized area that took up most of the square footage inside the treehouse. A wall of windows had been installed to let the light in and give the space a more open feel. The skylights in the vaulted ceiling were one of Niles's favorite features inside the treehouse. Of course, the view today was unavailable since every window was covered by a sheet of plywood. The bedrooms had been purposefully made small and, for the most part, were only used for sleeping. "Hence the name 'bed' room," Niles often explained when people asked him how he could stand having such a tiny bedroom. Mickey was often a bit blunter and would reply with a comment such as, "How can you stand having such a large house payment?"

Before Niles literally opened the door to the conversation between Mickey and Jenny, he thought about giving Eden a call to discuss plans for a possible hurricane evacuation. Last night, as he lay in bed, periodically hearing the clanking of a bedframe slapping against a wall, he'd tuned it out by thinking about the best approach for convincing his ex to let him take Riley to the mountains for a few days. Technically, the only way Niles found to silence the noise coming from his friend's room was by inserting a pair of earbuds connected to his phone. He played a collection of John Coltrane jazz songs that helped him relax on nights when he was missing his son and even Eden. He would be lying if he said he didn't miss her, too, especially the person she used to be. At the same time, he couldn't help but remember when the two of them were the ones rocking the bed. Of course, his buddy wasn't in the house back then. As the music had calmed Niles last night, he thought about the upcoming conversation. He definitely wouldn't mention that Uncle Mickey was going with them. He would make sure to offer to let Eden have his next scheduled weekend with Riley once they returned home, maybe even his weekday visit, too. Other than that, he knew he would need to be polite and pray that he caught her in a good mood. This thought suddenly reminded him that if he called this early in the morning, she would be irritated. She didn't get up as early as she used to, he recollected. "Mommy stays in bed a long time in the morning," Riley had informed his dad on several occasions.

"What do you do when Mommy is in bed?" Niles would ask his son.

"I play in my room, usually."

"Why don't you wake up your mom?" Niles queried.

"She shouts at me if I go in her room when she's sleeping,"

Riley snarled, forcing his cheek to rise without realizing the way it caused his eye to squint.

In a way, it was a cute face, Niles remembered thinking, but the reality behind the comment later caused tears to trickle down his own face. He'd once said something to Eden about screaming at their son, but bringing it up only seemed to make things worse for everyone. "Riley is just trying to pit us against one other," she assured. "I may have raised my voice at him for waking me up, but he's being dramatic about the whole thing." Niles didn't buy that; the kid was as tough as nails, but what could he do about it? Call the judge who was basically in the back pocket of the attorney who represented Eden and for whom she worked? When Niles had talked to his own lawyer about his ex-wife's behavior, the man who'd faithfully represented him in court had said, "Parents yell at their kids every day, Niles. It's unfortunate, but there's not much lawyers or judges can do about that."

"What about her abuse of prescription drugs?" Niles probed.

"That's extremely difficult to prove," explained the attorney. "Unless she is caught buying pills illegally, we won't have much of a case. It will be your word against hers."

Niles knew Eden was as smart as possible about covering up her addiction, which she didn't technically admit to having. She always had a good reason or, in his opinion, an excuse for why she needed more medicine. After the accident, when they were still married, it had taken him a long time to figure out why her moods were changing. She could go from sweet to sour in no time flat. Sometimes she would seem perfectly coherent then an hour or so later, distant and loopy. One day, while he was on a medication for an infection, he realized a pill was missing. At first, he didn't think anything of it; he figured maybe he'd forgotten exactly when he'd started. Then near the end of that prescription, he noticed that he was another pill short. At that point, he knew for sure that one was missing. He figured he could have possibly dropped it, but other than that, he had no idea how it could have disappeared. That day, he asked Eden about it, not even thinking that she might have taken the medicine, and he would never forget how she wouldn't look him in the eyes. She didn't admit to knowing anything about it; she just brushed it off by mentioning that maybe he'd taken more than he thought. That was one of the first red flags. A month or so later, he began to notice that they were having to replace over-the-counter medications like cough syrup and ibuprofen more often than what seemed reasonable.

A knock suddenly erupted on Niles's door, echoing through the room like a bomb had gone off. Startled by the sound, he flinched hard enough that it caused a kink in his neck.

"Wake up, sleepyhead," Mickey shouted through the door. "We have a lot of work to do today."

Massaging his neck with his short, thick fingers, Niles said, "I'll be right out." All along, he thought he'd be the one dragging Mickey out of bed this morning.

A few minutes later, Niles ran his toothbrush across his teeth and used the bathroom. Then, he ate cereal at the bar that ran along the wall, where the elongated window usually offered a decent view of the river through the cluster of trees on the backside of the house. The shoreline was approximately fifty yards from their place, and the only reason they hadn't built closer to the water was because of the marshy area where the river sometimes crept into at high tide, especially when storms passed through. When plotting the treehouse placement, both Niles and Mickey were afraid that the ground closer to the water would be too soft and that the structure wouldn't be sound enough if built there. That decision compelled them to construct a long dock that led to the river, and at the end was a square platform with two benches and a ladder for climbing in and out of the water. A small rowboat attached with a loose rope sat on the left side of the dock leaving the other side empty where Riley's ark usually parked. After everything was finished, Niles remembered Eden's father studying it all and then saying, "I'm proud of you boys for realizing where not to build. I can imagine it was tempting to slap this treehouse up as close to the river as possible. That would be one heck of a view from this height."

The river would never rise into this structure, Niles knew that for certain. It was fifteen feet above ground level and probably close to twenty above the water level of the Neuse River. If the river reached the treehouse, then that would mean God had flooded Earth again, and they would all need to pack into Riley's ark and pray for the best. In that case, the stuffed animals would have to substitute for live ones because Niles certainly wasn't rounding up two of every animal and living in a boat with them while they pooped and peed all over the wooden floor. It was tough enough living with Mickey, who had access to a functioning bathroom. With three boys in the house, that room probably needed to be sterilized more frequently, but a proper cleaning rarely made the priority list. Basic sanitation and straightening seemed to work just fine. As far as Niles knew, the women who Mickey had over never complained about the place being dirty. Not that his best friend always chose the classiest women, but they weren't trashy girls either. Niles actually liked what he'd seen from Jenny so far but doubted that she'd be around too long, so it didn't really matter.

"Dude, guess what I found out about Jenny last night?" Mickey asked after they dropped her off at her parent's house.

"That she's good in bed," Niles teased.

Mickey snorted, and it took him a moment to catch his breath. "I already knew that," he exclaimed.

"What did you find out?"

"This chick is into video games," he shared excitedly.

"When is the wedding?" Niles asked as straight-faced as a poker player.

11

*E*den slept better last night than she had in months, although she fell asleep much later than anticipated. After fifteen minutes of texting back and forth with Kirk, exchanging flirtatious comments with a man she barely knew, she surprised herself by inviting him over. He ended up sitting next to her on the couch until nearly two o'clock in the morning. Granted, he hadn't arrived at the house until ten o'clock because she wanted to make sure Riley Cameron was sound asleep before she let a strange man show up at their door. The last thing she needed to deal with was her son running off to his daddy's house talking about a man being over late at night. Not that who she spent time with was any of Niles's business, but it made life simpler if her ex didn't know the details about her personal life. Plus, she didn't think it was good for Riley to see men come in and out of her house.

As promised, Kirk brought a case of cold beer, and they worked their way through it as they got to know each other. She found out that he was a drummer in a local band that traveled throughout Eastern North Carolina, playing gigs at bars and private parties. He made a little bit of money following that passion, but during the day he worked at the local music shop. Eden explained her position at the lawyer's office and shared her plans of becoming a paralegal. She'd once thought about going to a prestigious university to pursue a law degree, but when she got pregnant in high school, that pretty much threw the idea out the window. Her parents offered to help make it happen, and Niles had always been supportive of her dreams back then, but in the end, she decided it wasn't feasible. At the time, she felt the need to focus on being a mother. A career and money weren't as important as raising children. While she and Niles were still in high school, he worked in construction with her father to pay for diapers, wipes, and all of the endless products needed to take care of newborns. During the months when the sun was up early, he worked for an hour or so before school, then after school, he would work until sundown. On the weekends, he picked up a job with a landscaper. Following high school, the plan was for him to join the military like his dad, and Niles had gone through with the initial part of that plan, but like an idiot, he got kicked out. That was the first time that Eden recalled being truly disappointed in Niles. She hadn't wanted him to have to work a blue-collar job for the rest of his life to support their family. She'd seen how rough life was for many of the guys who worked full time for her dad, and she wanted a simpler life. Once Niles was booted out of the service, it really limited their options. Like her, he couldn't go to college and get a degree without major sacrifices. The truth was, they didn't have the money or the time. At that point, her parents were still willing to help either of them, but neither she nor Niles wanted to accept handouts. They planned to make it on their own, defying the odds which say a couple who got pregnant in high school couldn't be successful and raise a happy family together. Giving birth at the age of fifteen wasn't ideal, but it was a reality in their case, and the two of them made the best of it until life suddenly went downhill. One mistake had changed the entire course of their lives.

Last night, when Kirk inched closer on the couch and slowly dropped the tips of his fingers onto her knee, her body felt more alive than it had in ages. With those blue eyes, he gazed at her as if asking permission to touch fine china. She let a smile stretch across her face, and his hand lingered on the soft fabric of her worn-out pajama pants as the warmth of a strange man's fingers traveled through her bones. It was perplexing to her how a stranger's affection could temporarily cure pain.

As the television played a late-night talk show, Kirk's hand had rested motionless for some time. Eventually, his fingers began to glide across her quad and toward her thigh, causing more friction beneath her skin. She wondered if he was feeling the same jitters as she was feeling. Wondered when he'd last touched a woman this way? Last year? Last night? Did it matter? Maybe, maybe not, she decided. If she let things progress further, would he come back tomorrow wanting more? Better yet, what if she allowed him to have everything he wanted? Then, would he come back tomorrow? Most times, she felt like all men were pigs, and all they wanted was sex, but it didn't stop her from letting her palm rest on the top of his hand. Moments later, her fingers were tracing through the hairs on his arm. Eventually, he turned his body into her and kissed her softly on the lips. She could taste the remnants of beer on his tongue and see the desire in his eyes. Surprisingly, even though he had that rough look about him, he wasn't forceful at all, and in time she let him guide her down on the couch and settle in on top of her.

This morning, as Eden lay in bed with the grin she'd woken up with still covering her face, she wondered if she had made a mistake last night. Would Kirk really come over again this evening like he said he would? He seemed genuinely interested in her, not just in her body. He'd asked meaningful questions, like "What is your favorite movie?" and "If you could visit any place in the world, where would you travel?" He'd shared stories with her about the summer his band played a string of shows in Switzerland. The lead singer was from the mountainous country in South Central Europe, and while the group toured through the region, they bunked with his family and friends that lived there.

"The humans over there are terrific," he advertised.

Eden laughed when he used the word humans instead of people. She began to notice that his choice of words was often unique, and she liked that about him. "I've always heard that Switzerland is a safe and clean place."

"The Swiss are definitely a peaceful population. We were in the bars late at night playing gigs and socializing with the locals, and never once did we feel threatened. No one slung beer at us or approached us in the alleyway when we were loading up our gear."

"Does that type of stuff happen here?" Eden inquired with a furrowed brow.

"In Eastern North Carolina?" he questioned for clarification purposes.

With her hand on his jeans, Eden nodded her head up and down.

"Not often," Kirk explained. "But it has happened a time or two. When we play in some of the bigger cities where the crime rates are higher, we have to be cautious of where we will be packing up late at night with a guitar case full of cash."

"Have you ever been robbed?"

"Once, in Fayetteville," he shared. "Two men in ski masks with switchblades cornered us behind a dive bar and took our money and some of the equipment."

"Oh, gracious. Was anyone injured?"

Kirk shook his head east to west. "No, thankfully we escaped unscathed, but we forfeited a guitar and several hundred greenbacks."

"That's terrible."

"The positive spin was that the perpetrators didn't have enough hands to plunder my drum set," he said, laughing at what had been a frightening incident at the time.

This morning, Eden could still hear his voice crawling between her ears. It was unique in a refreshing way, kind of scratchy. He sounded like a drummer, whatever that meant.

"You should come to watch us play," he invited.

"I'd love that," Eden agreed. She'd never dated anyone who was part of a band, but the lifestyle seemed alluring nonetheless. Not that she and Kirk were dating since this was their first time hanging out.

Back in reality, Eden wondered what Riley was up to as she peered out of her bedroom window at the bird feeder that hung from the eave. Since waking, she had been watching a finch bounce back and forth from the feeder to the ground to a nearby tree. He was singing all the while, although she wasn't sure which song. His colors were magnificent, a bright orange beak and feathers painted with grays, a mild orange, and a lone strip of brown dotted with white spots reminiscent of a fawn. The scene playing outside her window reminded her of mornings when she and Niles were a newly married couple. Both of them would head to the nursery and come back with a baby in their arms. They would all lie in bed and watch the birds frolic and listen to the complimentary concert the winged creatures put on without fail. Although Niles insisted that it wasn't free: "The birds will sing for food" was the way he put it, as if their feathery friends showed up on the other side of the windows holding cardboard signs. Regardless, it was pretty inexpensive entertainment, and she missed those days. Not because Niles was no longer occupying the empty spot next to her on a set of sheets that needed washing, but because of the precious baby moments she could never have again. She wished she could hear the soft cries one more time, see those tiny eyes that appeared more and more as they grew, and trace all those little body parts with her fingertips. Babies were the greatest gift in the world. She was so thankful to have had that opportunity even though now someone was missing from the family picture they'd updated every six months up until the divorce. "Do you think it's healthy to have those photos displayed?" Niles had asked several times. In her mind, the images were treasures, and she knew that Riley Cameron would appreciate them one day. Even now, she would catch him staring at the portraits from time to time, and he would often ask questions. It was sad to watch how quickly he forgot how things once were, but Eden felt it was vital for him to know his past and deal with it in his own way. Sometimes she forgot how different things had been, but often the memories came rushing in like a flood.

Eden found herself hoping that New Bern wouldn't flood when this hurricane barreled into the town. Upon turning on the television sitting atop her tattered brown dresser, she found that the forecasts were narrowing the areas of greatest impact. "Elevated water levels are expected to be the biggest threat," the weatherman warned. Today was decision day. Should she and Riley stay or should they go? Her mother had sent a text message first thing this morning stating that the storm could likely strengthen to a category four or possibly a five. She went on to say that she and Eden's father had made the decision to leave town tomorrow morning.

Yesterday morning, Eden was prepared to evacuate with her parents without thinking twice. But now . . . now she couldn't get Kirk off her mind. She realized that she shouldn't allow a man she barely knew to sway her decision one way or another, but she also wanted to see him again—and hopefully again and again. If she left, she might not see him for a week, or by the time she returned, he might have moved on. Last night, he'd mentioned that he was staying in town no matter what.

"I've never left for a hurricane," Kirk had sneered. "These weather junkies juice up the storm's potential and make it sound like we're all going to blow into the next state, but then the storm weakens. A few trees fall, the homes on the riverfront sometimes flood, and the electricity will go out for a little while," he reminded Eden as he ran a hand through his long hair. "My lawn is free of gigantic trees, and I haven't managed to collect enough loot to acquire a dwelling on the river, so I'm good," he chuckled.

"You're probably right," Eden realized.

"Do you have much timber surrounding your place?" he inquired. "It was dark when I arrived, so I didn't particularly notice."

"Not really," she confirmed. A few small trees dotted the backyard, but none that would do significant damage.

"Then you're good, too," he ensured. "I know you're only a few blocks from the river, but there's no way the water will surge all the way to your house. I'll wager a case of beer on that," he chuckled, holding up the can in his hand as he spoke, then chugging it.

Both last night and this morning, Eden had been thinking about what Kirk pointed out. He was probably right, she had decided. The forecasters did always talk up the hurricanes, presumably to keep viewers glued to the television. It worked. She'd had her TV playing one of the weather channels pretty much around the clock, or at least until Riley begged long enough for cartoons, and she gave in.

Regardless of what she decided, she needed to get out of bed and go to work since she hadn't gone yesterday. Also, the office might end up being shut down at the end of the week, or she might be out of town. Court would probably be canceled, too, which meant she'd have to contact the clients who were on the docket.

A few minutes later, Eden waltzed into Riley's room, but he wasn't there playing or sleeping. On her way up the hallway, she glanced into the bathroom, but he wasn't on the toilet either. She knew he wouldn't be brushing his teeth, washing his hands, or taking a bath. Those were all things she had to force him to do on any given day. Once in the living area of the house, she found her son sitting at the bar behind an open box of cereal, the plastic sticking out the top like tissue paper from a gift bag. It quickly became evident that the little fellow had poured his own milk. Although a good portion of it had made the bowl, there were splatters of the white liquid across the counter. A dozen or so flakes were scattered on the bar and near the legs of the stool, atop which Riley's knees were nestled.

"Riley, what are you doing?" she asked, wishing he would have gotten her to pour the cereal.

Noticing her presence for the first time, he peered over the cardboard box. "Eating cereal," he answered matter-of-factly.

"I know that," she responded matter-of-factly, placing her hands on her hips.

"And watching cartoons," he added, using his spoon to point at the television, milk dripping off the end of the utensil and onto the floor.

"Riley, watch what you're doing!" Why did their mornings always seem to start off poorly, she wondered? At least he was eating breakfast, which would be one less thing she'd have to worry about, she finally decided. Cleaning up was another story.

"Sorry, Mom," he said, realizing that he was spilling milk. "I'll clean it up."

"Just finish eating and sit your bottom on that stool rather than your knees so that you don't fall off and hit your head. How many times do I have to tell you that?"

"Okay," he agreed, not answering her question, but doing as she asked.

Eden left him there with his mouth full and headed to the bathroom. She didn't feel like she needed any of the pills from the cabinet, she was still on a high from last night. After popping her regulars into her mouth anyway, she then brushed her teeth. A few minutes later, she let Riley know she was hopping into the shower and asked him to put away the milk and cereal.

After showering and then blow drying her hair with a towel wrapped around her body, she climbed into a pair of black dress pants and put on a burgundy blouse. The high heels she stepped into felt awkward, as always, and she wasn't even sure why she wore these things. Niles had never liked for her to wear heels because it made her taller than he was. Now, she sometimes wore them on purpose when she knew she would see him, just because she could. She wasn't planning to see her ex today, but she often wore them to work because her boss had made mention several times that heels looked professional.

Prior to walking out the front door, Eden applied a thin coat of makeup, got Riley ready, and grabbed a granola bar to scarf down on the short drive to her parent's house. She was thankful that their residence and her office were all within a mile or so of her home. During the week, her mom always watched Riley, which was helpful, and it saved her money because, otherwise, she'd have to pay daycare. Of course, Niles would be required to help with such an expense, but she knew he didn't have much money either.

As usual, she walked Riley to the front door, where he hopped on Grandyma's leg like it was a pogo stick. With roughly fifteen minutes to spare before work began, Eden chose not to go inside, and she was hoping to spend the time on the phone with Kirk. Unfortunately, her plans abruptly changed when she made it back to the car and picked up her device. Someone else was calling.

12

Reese dragged herself through the front doors of the station at a slower pace than normal this morning, feeling the effect of a less than perfect night's rest. The alcohol had worn off, but the consequences of a late night out hadn't.

"Kirby, you look like crap," Dominguez said when his former partner walked into the conference room.

"Thanks," she responded, accustomed to the fact that most cops seemed to have a way of sharing the bitter truth with one another.

"Let me buy you a cup of coffee," he offered.

Reese snickered lazily as she watched him waltz over to the coffee pot in the corner of the room near a row of windows. The adjacent wall held a large marker board that was used for a variety of communication purposes, and the wall directly across the room featured several large flat-screen televisions. Those were used for watching anything from training videos to security camera feeds used to aid in investigations. Thankfully, video technology improved drastically over the past decade, making it much easier to solve crimes caught on tape.

"You're so sweet," Reese said sarcastically when Dominguez returned with a steaming cup of coffee. Maybe it would help, but she highly doubted it because the twelve or so ounces she'd inhaled on the way to the station had barely kept her eyelids from collapsing.

The other team members filtered into the room within the next few minutes, and, as always, everyone was settled before Captain Lawson graced them with his presence. "If you're on time, you're late," was a motto he made perfectly clear each time a new recruit joined the force. Then, he'd follow up with, "I better be the last one to step into this room every morning." Reese knew from experience that she'd rather be tired than late. The captain had a list of what he called 'dirty jobs' waiting for anyone who didn't follow his rules.

This morning, she listened as best she could as Captain Lawson went through the daily rituals, tossing out tasks and catching the team up on events that happened overnight. There was a box of bagels set in the middle of the table again, and Reese munched on one since she hadn't been able to eat breakfast at home. When it came time to discuss her assignment, the captain slid a packet titled *Kirby* across the table like a paper football. After reading the opening document, her eyes opened twice as wide as they had since waking up on her soft pillow to a screaming alarm.

"You want me to go home right now?" Reese asked as she thumbed through the rest of the papers and the additional contents.

Suddenly, all eyes in the room began to dance between Kirby's and Captain Lawson's. Dominguez held a gaze on his superior, fearing that Kirby was being sent home because she appeared to have a hangover. He was trying to remember if he'd made a joke about that when the captain was in the room, but he didn't think he had. The other two detectives had asked Kirby which bar she'd stumbled out of last night, mentioning that they didn't see her at the typical hangout. Still, Dominguez didn't think Captain Lawson was in the room then either.

"Yes, head home as soon as we adjourn, and I'll see you in a week or so."

A week of suspension for showing up tired, Dominguez thought to himself, *that's crazy?*

"Yes, sir," Reese responded.

A few others asked follow-up questions regarding the assignments in their specific packets, but everyone seemed more concerned about what was going on with Kirby. Then, when the captain opened the door, he turned back in the doorframe and let out a subtle laugh.

"You all can close your gaping mouths now," he instructed. "Kirby is heading home to pack her bags for the hurricane trip to the Carolinas," he informed them, realizing what they had been assuming. Then, he glared at Reese. "You picked the right day to be sleepy, but you sure as heck better not let it happen again tomorrow," he recognized out loud. "You'd have to pick up a caffeinated beverage the size of the Humvee you'll be driving; if that happens, don't charge it to the station." Inside the packet, she had found a credit card and two sets of keys. "If you wreck that vehicle and the search and rescue boat, you'll be going home for good," he added before walking out.

Reese couldn't tell if the last comment was serious, but she knew she would do everything in her power to get a better night's sleep tonight. If she had to drive a long distance today, she wasn't sure she'd be able to stay awake; she might even have to pull over on the side of the road and take a catnap.

When the conference room door shut, everyone on the inside let out the breath they'd been holding for their fellow officer. Reese snickered because she'd somewhat played up the situation on purpose because everyone had been giving her a hard time before the meeting began.

Dominguez shook his head. "I thought you were toast, Kirby," he uttered.

Brown chimed in with a joke. "If the captain was sending you home for a week, I was going to offer to take your spot driving the

Hummer to the coast. Maybe find me a cute Carolina girl over there," he added with a wink.

Johnson chuckled. "Kirby is a better driver half asleep than you are with eight hours and a Humvee-sized coffee."

A roar of laughter instantly echoed inside the walls of the room. The detectives knew that when the rookie Brown trained with Johnson, he'd backed a police vehicle into the fence behind the station the first day on the job. Luckily for him, the veteran had accepted the blame for the accident, knowing the captain would only slap his wrist. Even though Johnson had taken the heat, he'd never let Brown forget about it. A week after the incident, he spray-painted the fence brown in that section, and it was still that color and probably would be as long as Johnson was on the force.

"I run into one fence, and you guys tag me as a bad driver," Brown defended himself. "I'm a better driver than any of you," he spouted with confidence. "A better shooter, too."

"So, you think you can beat Kirby in a shooting contest?" Johnson asked, recollecting the day he was assigned to show Kirby the ropes at the range. As the bullets from her firearm struck everywhere except inside the target, he remembered the remarks from the team, especially the one that sounded the loudest.

"She shoots like a girl," the cockiest detective on the force had clamored after the third target was removed from the clip.

Out of the corner of his eye, Johnson watched Dominguez waltz across the cement floor and confront the man. "That's my partner you're talking about," he warned.

"Good luck, brother," the detective snarled. "She's so bad, Johnson hasn't even given her a single instruction since she began firing. He's the best shooter this range has ever seen, and he hasn't given her one tip. He's watched target after target being pulled from the line and doesn't know how to help her."

"That's because he's wiser than you'll ever be, detective," Dominguez offered.

"That might be true, but the fact is that Johnson realizes your partner might miss an elephant if it was charging at her." By this time, everyone in the range had wandered over to see what the fuss was about, and a stream of laughter echoed inside the cinder block walls as the two went back and forth.

Before that day, Dominguez had never seen Kirby shoot, but he followed his instincts. "I'll bet you a month's salary that Kirby can outshoot you."

Johnson eyed the two detectives, listening carefully as they debated about Kirby's accuracy. However, what stood out the most was how Kirby continued firing as if she wasn't the topic of conversation. Even though she was wearing ear protection, he knew she'd heard every word that had been uttered.

"That's not a fair wager, everyone here knows I make way more than you," he snickered.

Pressing his lips together, Dominguez nodded his head up and down. "Then I'll bet you your badge," he proposed, his eyebrows rising with the wager.

Along with everyone else in the range, the detective's eyes widened. "My badge?" he sneered.

"Exactly. You outshoot Kirby, I'll turn in my badge," Dominguez offered as the room fell silent. "She outshoots you, you turn in your badge." Dominguez had never cared for the guy, and the insults he'd be slurring about his new partner only added fuel to that fire.

"That's a win-win for you, Dominguez."

"How do you figure?"

"If I outshoot her, which I will, then you don't have to trust her with your life out in the real world," he pointed out. "If she outshoots me, then you get rid of me."

"I see your point, but if you outshoot her, you won't have to deal with me anymore," Dominguez combatted. "And I'm sure that's a win for you."

"I'll take your bet," the seasoned detective responded without hesitancy.

13

After trimming a row of bushes, Niles climbed into the truck with sweat slithering down his back. Before putting his phone to his ear, he brushed over it with his free hand then waited for Eden to pick up on the other end. Through the cloudy window on the passenger side, he halfway watched Mickey cruising on the riding mower like a NASCAR driver. As usual, his partner had parked the truck on the edge of the street rather than in the driveway. At some customers' houses, parking the truck and trailer in the drive was the only option, but that could cause issues with homeowners coming and going while the two of them were working, so they preferred the roadside. Anytime they had to stop mowing, it slowed progress and inevitably cost them money. Their old boss had been a stickler about such things, and it had proven to be a good lesson learned on his dime. "There isn't time to stop and smell the roses, only to trim the rose bushes," he would often remind the guys with a smirk on his chubby face. The only reason Niles was taking a break so early this morning was because he really needed to discuss the hurricane evacuation with Eden. Honestly, he'd already put this conversation off too long. On the way to the first job this morning, he had made sure to let Mickey know he'd be stopping his task around the time that he knew Eden regularly

JOEY JONES

dropped off Riley at her mom's house.

"Good morning, Eden," Niles greeted when his ex-wife answered the phone. The moment she'd said, "Hello," he'd picked up on a sense of disgust in her voice, although he wasn't sure if her tone had something to do with him calling or an unrelated factor. Either way, he figured her mood didn't bode well for his intentions.

"Hey," she offered simply, hurriedly, holding the phone against her shoulder as she backed out of her parent's driveway, noticing the choppy river in the rearview mirror. The waterways always told the story that a hurricane was heading inland, even when it was hundreds of miles away. Currents were one of the first visible signs of any approaching storm. Her grandfather had once told her that before weathermen existed, natural occurrences like water patterns and the activity of animals helped people know when a storm was brewing.

"I hope I didn't catch you at a bad time," Niles checked, wondering if maybe he should offer to call back later in the day.

"Is there ever a good time to talk to your ex, Niles?"

Niles shrugged his shoulders but said nothing as his thumbnail began to draw on the bottom of his ring finger.

Sensing the hesitation on the other end, Eden continued. "I just dropped off Riley Cameron. Now, I'm heading to work, and I have something else I need to do before I get there, so make it quick," she suggested.

Niles furrowed his brow. "I want to talk to you about the hurricane," he announced. The sound of the mower invaded the truck's cab, and he suddenly realized it would continue to do so every time Mickey rounded the yard near the curb.

"What about it?"

"Well, it sounds like it's going to be a bad one."

"They always sound bad," Eden pointed out, remembering the words Kirk had spoken last night and wanting to end this

88

conversation as quickly as possible so she could call her new friend before work.

"I'm planning to evacuate," Niles shared. He figured he'd make that clarification upfront before he brought up the fact that he'd like for Riley to go with him. He wanted Eden to understand that he was leaving regardless.

"Niles, I don't need to know whether you're staying or going." Eden didn't want her ex thinking that she tried to keep up with him.

That response didn't sound encouraging, Niles thought as he stared at the dirty rubber floorboard beneath his shoes. "I would like to take Riley with me," he revealed.

"Why?" Eden snarled.

"So that he will be out of harm's way."

"Do you think he's going to be in harm's way with me?" she huffed.

Niles could feel his blood beginning to boil. "I'm not saying that, Eden."

"Then what are you saying?"

Trying to keep his calm, Niles took a deep breath but made sure not to exhale into the mouthpiece. "I'm just asking if you would be okay with Riley going with me, that's all."

"Where are you going?"

"To the mountains."

"Where Mickey's family is from?" Eden inquired, nodding her head as she thought about her son traveling across the state of North Carolina with her ex and his immature roommate. Mickey would probably let him drink Mountain Dews and feed him Skittles in his car seat.

Niles had a good idea where this question was leading, so he decided to try to push the thought in another direction. "I'm not exactly sure where we're going."

"We?" she inquired.

"Me and Riley," he clarified. "If Riley goes with me," he made sure to add.

"Is Mickey going?" Eden asked bluntly.

Niles's nostrils flared. It was inevitable, he should have known she would ask that question before she would provide any type of answer. "I'm not sure," he answered. Technically, he hadn't told Mickey whether he could join in on the trip.

"Well, I'm sure Mickey isn't going to hold down the tree fort while you leave town to escape the hurricane."

Niles wasn't sure how to respond kindly to that comment. Eden was always poking fun of his home, and he didn't appreciate it. Anyways, why did he need to provide information about Mickey's plans? He didn't, he decided. "I'm not sure what Mickey has planned," he eventually said, the tone of his voice rising a tad.

"My parents are evacuating, too," Eden mentioned.

"I think that's a wise decision," Niles announced. "How about you?" He was hoping she would say that she was staying in New Bern, which would help support his reasoning to have Riley evacuate with him.

"I am not one hundred percent sure, but Riley and I are probably going with them." It wasn't the whole truth, Eden realized, but if she decided to leave town, then she had all intentions of her and Little Man traveling with her parents to her aunt's house.

"Oh, I see," Niles responded, wishing now that he had made the phone call sooner, before any plans were made on her end. "How would you feel about Riley going with me?" he asked. "Since you're not sure whether you're evacuating?"

"Like I said, I'd like to have him with me."

"What about if you don't evacuate?" Niles inquired. "Don't you think it would be best for Riley to leave regardless?"

"Are you saying that I won't make the best decision for our son?"

"Eden, I'm not saying that. I'm just asking if he can go with me. I know I'm leaving, and I think Riley would enjoy getting away. I'll take him to do some fun things, make a vacation of sorts out of it."

"So is this trip you have planned about a vacation or doing what is safe?"

Niles huffed, wondering why the two couldn't coexist. "Primarily about evacuating," he answered, "but I don't see any reason not to make the most out of the trip."

"I don't know, Niles. Why didn't you ask me about this sooner?"

Wishing he had, Niles felt his eyelids collapse. Although in all honesty, he didn't know if this conversation would be going much differently if they'd had it yesterday or any day prior to that. "I wanted to know for sure that I was leaving before I asked about taking Riley," he answered. "I thought it would be best if things weren't up in the air."

"Are you saying that I am wrong for not having made a final decision?"

"No, not at all. I'm just saying that I have." Nearly the entire time he'd been on the phone, his head had been shaking, and his mouth was gaped open in disbelief of how difficult Eden made things.

"And that means Riley should go with you?"

Niles let out a steady breath, trying not to push it into the phone's receiver. "I'm just asking if you'd be okay with that," he responded firmly.

"I'd like him to be with me if I leave."

"What if you don't leave?" Niles debated.

"Then, we can cross that bridge once I decide."

"Why do we have to wait for you to decide?"

"So, this *is* about me making a decision?" Eden clamored.

"No, I'm just saying, maybe he should go with me this time,

and if another hurricane forces an evacuation, he could go with you," Niles suggested, somewhat proudly. That was one of the things he'd planned to say, and he was glad he remembered it. "We could take turns." That sounded fair, he thought.

"Niles, I have primary custody," Eden reminded him.

"I know that." He remembered this fact every single day that he didn't have his son and even on most days when he did. On the weekends, when Riley was with him and Sunday rolled around, the evening felt like it used to when he was a kid and realized he had to go to school the next day. The mood seemed to melt into a somber reality.

"So, Riley should be with me."

"Will you at least think about it?" he pleaded, disgusted.

"Sure, I'll think about it," she said sharply.

That's where the conversation basically came to an end. Eden said she had to get into the office, that she had a lot of work to do. Feeling defeated, Niles lowered his head. He needed to get back to work, too, but what he really wanted to do was lean back onto the headrest and cry. Better yet, he felt the urge to slide over to the driver's seat and head to Eden's mother's house right now, pick up his son, and leave town. But that wasn't an option. The police would be hot on his trail by the time he reached the next town. He wished he hadn't let his temper show, but it was hard to hold in his emotions when Eden wouldn't reason with him. She wanted things her way, and that was all there was to it, which made him mad.

"Did you offer to give up your next weekend with Riley?" Mickey asked. When his best friend stepped out of the truck looking like he'd been beaten to a pulp in the octagon ring where they often sparred, he shut off the mower and walked over.

With his head lowered and lips pursed, Niles shook his head side to side. "I forgot."

"Dude, if we were chicks, I'd give you a hug right now," he said earnestly but then couldn't help but snicker. "You look like you need a hug."

Niles fought against a chuckle that began to bubble up inside of him, but even Mickey couldn't make him laugh at the moment. "This just sucks," he exclaimed. "Riley is our son," he said, referring to Eden. "This should be our decision. Not just hers."

"Call your lawyer," Mickey suggested, wiping sweat from his cheek.

Niles shook his head again. "It won't do any good."

"Why not?"

"Even if my lawyer reached out to her lawyer, the other guy would just put him off until it was too late for a decision to be reached. Everything involving custody issues is a process and usually a long one."

Mickey placed his hands on his hips. "That sucks."

Niles worked like a madman until lunchtime. He couldn't get the hurricane evacuation dilemma off his mind; however, he let the anger he felt fuel his fire so he and Mickey could accomplish the impossible workload that was continuing to pile up. Throughout the morning, call after call had been coming in from people requesting help with hurricane preparation. Apparently, word had gotten around quickly that in addition to landscaping, the two of them were willing to board up windows, carry patio furniture indoors, cut tree limbs, and do pretty much anything and everything in order to make a home in Hurricane Florence's path as safe as possible. They dashed from one house to the next, jogging to and from the truck at every stop and moving as quickly as possible while tackling each task. Niles had scrapes up and down his arms, and his back was already sore from all of the heavy lifting. One homeowner suggested wearing back braces, but there hadn't been time to run to the store for anything like that. "We're too young and strong for such things," Mickey had teased after the individual walked away. They made a few trips to Garris Evans for plywood, where an employee they knew relatively well from high school informed them that the place was beginning to run out of wood due to everyone in the county boarding up homes and businesses. So, on their last trip there, they'd filled the entire bed of the truck with plywood and moved all of the tools to the trailer, strapping everything down with bungee cords. Thankfully, they'd disposed of all of their loose trash at the local dump when hauling off items from a customer's garage to fit his vehicles inside and avoid damage from flying debris.

"Bungees have to be one of the best inventions ever," Mickey mentioned when he and Niles finally sat down on the truck bed for lunch. It was the first time either of them had stopped moving, except when riding, since Niles called Eden. They just finished boarding up windows at five different shops in the downtown area and decided to call in a to-go order from The Country Biscuit. "We're close by, so we might as well grab something to eat," Mickey had suggested. Although when the two of them were standing in the pick-up line and Jenny dashed over to give his partner a kiss, Niles realized Mickey had an ulterior motive. While the lovebirds chatted, Niles listened intently to the local weatherman who was still on-air on the television in the corner of the restaurant. He nearly fainted when the guy announced that Craven County—which included New Bern, Bridgeton, and a couple handfuls of other small towns—had issued a mandatory evacuation as of two o'clock today. In Niles's lifetime, the county had never made that decision. *This storm is the real deal*, he thought to himself. As he listened, he discovered that the community shelters wouldn't open, and shelter sites further inland would be determined soon. It also meant that the local hospital would suspend ambulance services when sustained winds reached thirty-five miles per hour. Across the bottom of the screen, the information bar was flooded with notices of schools' and businesses' closings. Niles instantly found himself thinking of Riley's safety, even more intently than before. Now that a mandatory evacuation had been put into play, he knew without a shadow of a doubt that his son needed to be out of this area when the storm rolled in, and he was determined to do whatever it took to make that happen even if that meant breaking the law.

14

Not long after arriving at work this morning, Eden took a phone call from the courthouse, informing her office that Craven County would soon be announcing a mandatory evacuation. An exciting perk about working for one of the most prominent lawyers in Eastern North Carolina was being privy to insider information across the board. The advanced notice on the news today not only helped in regards to making business decisions but also gave Eden an edge with considering plans regarding her personal life. A mandatory evacuation meant that Niles would now have more incentive to pressure her about Riley leaving town for safety reasons. Prior to the evacuation being implemented, she'd known that her ex had relatively no chance of leaving town with their son legally without her permission regardless of her decision whether or not to ride out the storm. He could have called his attorney, which he probably already had, but that would get him nowhere. When his lawyer's office called to leave a message for her boss, who also conveniently represented her custody case, she could simply make sure the note remained in limbo until it was too late for anything to be done. Every message, letter, fax, and email for her boss crossed her desk before making it to him. Regardless, even if correspondence reached her attorney, he would ignore it for the same reason. In essence, the request wouldn't be deemed a priority by the judicial system. Any judge would say that this was something Niles should have considered adding to the initial custody papers and that if he was interested in pursuing such terms, he'd need to take the proper actions. That would take months, even longer, if Eden wanted to draw out a decision. However, now that a mandatory evacuation had been put into play, things were different. If Niles's attorney could get into the ear of a judge, he or she would be more inclined to look into the minor child's safety. If that were the case, Eden would definitely want her attorney involved, which meant that she needed to make a decision promptly. If she made plans to leave town, the mandatory evacuation would give Niles very little leverage with the idea of taking Riley with him. If she chose not to evacuate, that might be a different story. In her mind, this left three choices: Go with her parents and take Riley; stay and risk a judge siding with Niles; or just say she was leaving but make a final decision when the storm drew closer. Her gut told her that the mandatory evacuation was a hasty decision based on hype from national weather forecasters and that the storm would blow over without causing much damage. Even the representative from the courthouse had mentioned in a roundabout way that she thought the decision had been made for legal reasons regarding the potential for increased flooding in low-lying areas. Basically, the county didn't want to risk being sued for not looking out for the best interest of its residents.

Since receiving that call from the courthouse, Eden had been on the phone all morning with dozens of law offices as well as clients who were on the court docket this week. Court was going to be canceled for at least the next three days, maybe longer, depending on what happened when the storm came through. "I expect we'll be back in session on Monday," her contact at the courthouse assumed. Once Eden relayed the news to her boss, he began to pace around like a chicken with his head cut off, trying to meet deadlines that had now been moved up. This meant that every employee in the office had an increased stack of paperwork on their desk as well as more phone calls, emails, and all the rest. When time permitted, Eden had been texting Kirk back and forth. After Niles took up most of her free time this morning, she'd only been able to talk on the phone to Kirk for about five minutes. When he'd answered, he'd sounded half asleep.

"Are you awake?" Eden had asked early on in the conversation.

"Barely," he responded with a mumbled chuckle. "I hung out with this super hot chick last night who kept me out really late."

Eden couldn't help but blush. "She must be quite the catch," she responded in the third-person point of view, playing the game Kirk started.

"I'm not an avid fisherman, but she's the best thing I've ever reeled in," he complimented.

"Sounds like you're a lucky guy," Eden said with a smirk.

"I completely agree."

"She's pretty excited about seeing you again," Eden revealed. She knew it was silly for two adults to talk about themselves like this; nevertheless, she was enjoying every moment of it. She was also savoring the cup of coffee that she was touching to her lips while absorbing Kirk's voice. Honestly, the early morning caffeine boost was probably the only reason she didn't sound as tired as her new friend.

"You think?"

"Well, that's what I've heard anyway," Eden said with a grin covering her face.

This flirtatious banter carried on for a bit longer, and then they talked in more detail about getting together again this evening. Eden found out that Kirk's band had scored a pre-hurricane party gig in town. Still, he promised to come over afterward, which would work out perfectly because Riley would be sound asleep by then. She figured that she could take a catnap soon after putting the little guy to bed then wake back up when Kirk was heading over. He offered to bring beer again, and she teased that he might need to bring something with caffeine, too.

Now, sitting at her desk with a fresh cup of coffee, Eden hoped that the headache brought on by a lack of sleep and a crazy morning would dissipate well before the time Kirk came over. The handful of pain relievers she popped in about an hour ago was beginning to help, and the coffee was keeping her eyelids open although the abnormal buzz around the office was enough to prevent anyone from focusing. Her coworkers brought in doughnuts, pretzels, and all types of other snacks like they were having a holiday party. No one was hanging out in the breakroom, but everyone had been dashing into that area all morning. While in the office, she ditched the heels except when a client popped in and required her presence. Her boss ordered subs for the entire staff for lunch since he asked everyone to work through their breaks. During busy times like this, associates would typically eat at their respective desk while continuing to handle clients' needs. Eden's work was interrupted, however, when her personal cell phone rang.

"Yes, Niles," she answered hastily, feeling like she needed to take the call.

"Have you heard about the mandatory evacuation?" he asked.

"I have, thanks," she responded simply, knowing what he was getting at.

"I'm not trying to rush you to make a decision," he began, "but have you thought any more about whether you'll leave town?"

"Of course, I've thought about it," she acknowledged. "I think everyone in the county is trying to decide what is best for them and their family." She paused for a brief moment as she glared at a long list of unread emails on the computer monitor that sat atop a desk made of solid oak. "I've been absolutely slammed at the office, so I don't know exactly what my plans are yet because I haven't even been able to take my own mom's phone calls. That said, I suppose Riley and I will plan to leave with my parents." Eden knew that was the best response for the time being because it would give her ex very little ammunition.

The line fell silent for a moment.

"Niles?" Eden said, emphasizing his name.

"I'm glad to know that you think it's in yours and Riley's best interest to evacuate, but why does he have to go with you?"

"Because he's with me."

"Yeah, but tomorrow night is my night to spend time with him."

On Wednesdays, Niles ordinarily picked up Riley from Grandyma's house and kept his son overnight as well as the following day until after Eden got off work.

"My parents are planning to leave in the morning, Niles," she reminded him. "You're more than welcome to drive to Kentucky and have your overnight visit with Riley if you'd like," she offered, knowing no one in their right mind would do that.

Niles didn't even see a reason to respond to the absurd comment about traveling all the way to Kentucky. "So then you're saying that whoever has Riley when they decide to leave for a hurricane gets to leave town with him?"

Before spouting out something she might regret, Eden thought about how to best answer her ex's question. "I'm just saying that this time, he's with me, and I have primary custody, so I think it is best that he stays with me."

"So, you get to make all of the decisions?" Niles combatted.

"The court made that decision, Niles, not me."

A wrinkle quickly formed in Niles's brow. "The court said that you get to take Riley if a hurricane evacuation happens?" he challenged.

"Niles, I don't have time to debate this with you," Eden huffed.

"Like I said earlier, I'm swamped with work, and I'm sure you need to be working, too, if you're planning to leave town tomorrow."

It pushed Niles's buttons when she suggested what he should be doing with his time as if working was more important than figuring out what was best for their son. "Fine, if that's how it's going to be, but I get to take him next time," he argued.

"I'm not agreeing to that," Eden snarled.

"Why not?" he pleaded. "That's only fair. He's our son, not just your son."

"If that's the way you want it, Niles, call your lawyer," Eden suggested then hung up the phone without speaking or hearing another word.

A minute later, she clomped to the breakroom in her heels and snatched up a sub, feeling hungry all of a sudden. As expected, most everyone else had already taken their pick of the sandwiches, and the only thing that was left was roast beef and cheese. She didn't hate the option, but it wouldn't have been her first choice. She snatched a few napkins from a pile, causing several others to float off the table in her haste to get back to her desk. Two bites into her lunch, she decided to text Kirk, hoping to let off some steam.

You won't believe the audacity that my ex has . . .

A few moments later, she received a response: *What???*

He thinks he should be the one who evacuates with our son!

Didn't you tell me that you have primary custody? she read as she held the sub near her mouth.

YES!!!

I don't have kids, but I'd assume that means you have primary responsibility in making decisions.

Exactly!

Wait, does this mean you've decided to evacuate?

Eden began typing a response, then deleted it, and wrote another. *I'm not sure—*

15

On the same parking lot where Brown smashed a patrol car through the fence, Reese transferred a handful of personal items from her vehicle to the Hummer after the meeting this morning. It was bittersweet to think about the fact that she wouldn't be driving her own car for a week or longer, but this produced way more positives than negatives. Not having to pay for gas was a big one. As detailed in the assignment packet, the captain had already taken the liberty to have the maintenance guy fill-up the HMMWV, which stood for High Mobility Multipurpose Wheeled Vehicle, for which the colloquialism Humvee had been created. Reading the specific title of the vehicle on paper drew a smile on Reese's face. The man had also been assigned to attach the trailer atop which the boat sat. Both the Hummer and watercraft wore the same design as the station's police cruisers: primarily white with a thick black stripe that stretched across the side, front to back, with the word POLICE in large white lettering. Beneath that, the words EAST RIDGE were written in black and traced with a thin red outline.

When Reese literally climbed into the vehicle after double-checking the trailer hitch and boat straps, she felt even smaller than the stats listed on her driver's license. Everyone on the special operations team had been trained to operate the specialized equipment, but this would mark the first time she'd taken this particular vehicle on an assignment. As she shifted the gear and pulled out of the fenced-in lot at the rear of the station, it felt like she was driving a school bus. When she pressed the gas pedal toward the rubber floorboard, the engine immediately flexed its muscles, letting out a steady roar as it tugged the boat along with ease. Reese felt privileged as she drove through East Ridge behind the steering wheel of a police vehicle rarely allowed on the road. In no hurry, she cruised slowly as if on a Sunday morning leisurely drive. Upon reaching the street where she lived, she opted to park at the curb rather than back in the driveway although her dad had taught her how to maneuver a trailer like a pro by the time she turned fourteen. The two of them fished together at Chickamauga Lake for as far back as Reese could remember. After giving her driving lessons in his truck on some of Chattanooga's finest red dirt roads, he began to let her back the family's small bass boat into the water. She loved it then which in turn had made her good at it now. Although her love for hunting, fishing, and guns seemed to intimidate the city boys, every guy she ever dated was impressed that she knew how to do such things. She could disassemble and reassemble a firearm in no time flat, even build a gun from scratch—another skill her dad passed along.

Inside her place, she pulled clothes from the closet and dresser, setting each article on a cast-iron-framed bed that she neglected to make this morning. The pillows were crooked and the sheets were wrinkly, but she straightened everything swiftly in order to focus on the task at hand. Once the entire surface of the bed was dotted with an assortment of clothing, she started the process of carefully placing each belonging into a large suitcase, fitting them in delicately like puzzle pieces. Even though she didn't mind not knowing how long the trip would last—in her line of work, she had somewhat become accustomed to the unknown—it definitely made packing more difficult. She greatly appreciated the captain allowing her the extra time to prepare by basically giving her the day off. "Kirby, you better pack your undies fast and get to the range early to practice," Brown had spouted out when the team had lined up a shooting competition for later this evening once everyone was off duty. Honestly, Reese didn't like that she had been dragged into the feud, but once the rookie said he could take her down, she decided to accept the challenge. This time, though, a badge wasn't at stake. Also, all of the detectives actually liked Brown. He was just a little too eager for a newbie, and sometimes needed to be reeled in a bit.

In addition to being sleepy, a feeling that temporarily dissipated due to the excitement of driving the Hummer, Reese realized that she hadn't taken adequate time to plan for this trip. She figured she should probably check on things like expected temperatures. However, she wondered how accurate the forecast would be with the unexpected weather patterns a hurricane was sure to bring. She now knew that plans were for her to end up in Wilmington, North Carolina. The schedule had her arriving in the coastal town as soon as the hurricane blew over, which was up in the air—the thought of that pun made her chuckle. Basically, she was part of the second wave of first responders that would be showing up to give the initial team a short break after handling around-the-clock emergencies such as flood rescues and other situations that popped up during the brunt of the storm. The captain's administrative assistant had booked her a hotel in Hickory, North Carolina, where she was supposed to spend a couple of nights after picking up hurricane supplies from the local police department. "They're not able to send officers, but in preparation for the storm, they have been collecting water, clothing, toiletries, and other supplies over the past few days that you should have plenty of room for in the back of the Humvee," Captain Lawson had instructed. All of the details were in her packet. Thankfully, Hickory was about the halfway point between

Chattanooga and Wilmington, and a quick internet search told her the trip to her first stop would take about four and a half hours. She'd never been to that area, so she was beginning to look forward to exploring the place while waiting on the hurricane to do whatever it was going to do. With the storm at the top of her mind, she flipped on the television to one of the weather channels and listened to the experts make predictions. As she rushed around the house, she kept hearing about the expectation of catastrophic flooding and a growing wind field. The news anchors were also talking about essential items people in the path of the storm needed to have on hand: water, flashlights, batteries, first aid kits, essential tools, cash, and plenty of dry and canned foods. All of these items and then some—except for money—came loaded in the vehicle she was driving. She remembered a bag the team packed with random things like duct tape, mosquito repellant, rope, matches, and more. There were also MREs to eat, but after trying a few of those in training, she sure hoped other food would be available. Dominguez, who'd served in the Army prior to joining the force as a detective, had advised adding hot sauce. "It makes the MREs edible," he shared from first-hand experiences encountered in the Middle East. Her partner had some great stories and some sad ones, too. He'd once watched a highly decorated officer dive onto a grenade to save the rest of the platoon. He'd also stitched up gunshot wounds and dragged a dying friend over one hundred yards to a helicopter while under gunfire. Second to her dad, Dominguez was the bravest man she'd ever known.

Before zipping her suitcase, Reese made sure to pack the shadow box on her nightstand, positioning it carefully between articles of clothing to help prevent damage. She loved the photo of her dad that was next to his badge. He was wearing his dress blues and one of his patented half smiles. It was like he made the decision that a tough officer couldn't show teeth in a picture, but a pure heart couldn't help but shine through when the flash went off. Remembering that she wasn't leaving until morning, she unzipped the case, kissed the glass, and set the box back on her nightstand. She hadn't slept without it being visible since having it made. It went on every single trip that she took.

After flipping off the bedroom's light switch, she began searching the refrigerator for items that might spoil while she was away. Unlike people in the Carolinas, she didn't have to worry about the electricity going out while she was gone. However, some items wouldn't make it until she returned. So, she made a list of things to bag and carry to her elderly neighbor's house tomorrow morning before leaving town: milk, eggs, cheese, strawberries, cantaloupe, yogurt, and bread. Those were the ones that made the most sense. Everything in the freezer other than the ice cream would be fine, she determined, after opening that door and peering at the contents for a few moments. She knew the lady next door would be pleasantly surprised to receive the groceries. On a fixed income, the woman rarely purchased anything other than the bare necessities at the grocery store. Reese had taken her there a few times when the woman's daughter had been sick or out of town. She was one of those funny little old women who spoke her mind, and because her hearing was terrible, she spoke loudly. When making a comment, everyone within earshot of a bullhorn heard it. One day in the middle of the market, a young woman had strutted by their cart wearing an extremely short mini-skirt with a halter top, and the frail woman had balked, "Look at that hussy!" Knowing the girl and everyone else around heard the comment, Reese couldn't help but snicker. Her neighbor ended up being great entertainment and a breath of fresh air in a world where politically correct statements had become expected.

Reese's dad had always kind of been that way, too, and she was surprised his mouth didn't get him into more trouble on the force. She knew he was careful about what he said when in uniform, but on personal time he didn't have any problem speaking his mind about hot topics like politics and religion. He loved God and guns, and he made sure everyone knew it. He hated the government doing irresponsible things with his tax money, and he didn't care for lazy people. At the end of the day, though, he loved everybody. It didn't matter whether they agreed with him or not, he respected their beliefs and opinions regardless of if they lined up with his own. Reese could remember some of his last words as if being breathed into her ear at this very moment. "Tell him I forgive him," he'd whispered, "and that God does, too."

16

Niles was so mad and tired and hot that he was only nibbling at his lunch, much like the birds that used to pluck seeds from the feeders outside of his bedroom window. He knew he should be hungry, and he realized his body needed nutrients to give him enough energy to work until sundown, maybe later. Still, he was having a hard time forcing a meal into his mouth right now.

"Call your lawyer, dude," Mickey suggested after Niles finished telling him about the phone conversation that he darted out of the restaurant to have with Eden.

"What good will it do?" he argued, slamming his sandwich on the wrapper that had been folded around it when Mickey brought their food out in a white paper bag.

"It can't hurt," Mickey offered with a shrug of his bony shoulders.

Niles wanted to punch something, anything: The truck; Mickey; the brick wall of the building. "She pisses me off so bad," he declared. "She wasn't like this when—" He paused, realizing he was about to say *when things were good before the accident.* He'd spoken that phrase a thousand times, and he knew he eventually had to realize that Eden was no longer the person he had once known.

"When the two of you were in love before the accident," Mickey said, finishing the sentence for his best friend.

The bones on Niles's face began to poke through his skin as he fought to keep from shouting or crying or letting out some sort of emotion in the middle of a busy public parking lot. "Yes—back then," he finally uttered.

"She's not that person anymore," Mickey pointed out for the hundredth time. "You have to get that through your skull."

"It sucks, Mickey. Divorce where kids are involved absolutely sucks."

"Kid," Mickey corrected in an attempt to add a dash of humor to a touchy subject. Then, he saw Niles's face immediately drop into his calloused hands, and Mickey found himself wishing he could take back the comment. Without saying another word, he stretched his arm across the truck bed and let it hang around his best friend's neck. "I'm sorry, buddy, I was trying to be funny, but I failed this time. Forgive me?"

Niles eventually came up for breath but decided not to talk about the situation anymore. He finished about half of his sandwich while Mickey kept apologizing. Niles shrugged it off and declared that the comment wasn't a big deal. Mickey finished every last bite of his lunch, then went back inside the restaurant for a refill, gave Jenny a kiss, and told her he'd call her later. Niles waited in the cab of the muggy truck and spent the alone time seriously considering the idea of stealing his best friend's vehicle, driving it a mile down the road to pick up his son, and leaving town. But he couldn't. He knew that was the dumbest option on his plate, and so he took his best friend's advice. After scrolling through the contact list in his phone, he let his pointer finger hover over the name of his lawyer for a short moment then tapped it. A few rings later, Niles heard the squeaky voice of his attorney's receptionist on the other end, and he did everything short of begging her to have George Billings call him back as soon as possible.

A few moments later, Mickey returned with a smile on his face and drove them to the next address on the list they had been crossing names off as well as adding to all day. Then, as the two of them were hopping out of the truck, Niles's phone began to sing. He glanced at the screen and immediately touched the green answer button.

"Hello, this is Niles North," he stated as professionally as possible, fingers trembling as he held the device flush with his ear. He stopped at the bed of the truck and rested his elbows there as Mickey peered across from the opposite side.

"Niles, this is George Billings, what's going on?" his lawyer asked with a tone of concern lining his voice.

Niles went through the spiel, explaining his decision to evacuate from Hurricane Florence and filling in the attorney on the two conversations he'd had with Eden about the possibility of taking Riley with him.

After taking in all of the information, Mr. Billings responded. "Eden stated that she plans to evacuate with Riley, correct?"

"That's what she said," Niles acknowledged. "But I'm not sure if I believe her," he added.

Mickey wandered a few feet away and fiddled with the bungees on the trailer.

"Niles, the primary concern here is Riley's safety, correct?" his attorney clarified in a calm tone.

"Yes," Niles agreed.

A cool breeze was drifting across the bed of the truck, pushing the smell of lumber into his nostrils as he hoped for an inkling of good news.

"Let's focus on that," George Billings pointed out. "Based on the custody papers, the court determined that both you and Ms. Franks are fit parents. As we both know, Riley's mother has primary custody. Based on what you've told me in this conversation, the minor child will also be in her care from now until the time of the evacuation, correct?"

The words *minor child* were used repetitively in the custody papers, and Niles's attorney often referred to Riley by that title. "That's right," Niles concurred, growing discouraged by where this conversation seemed to be leading.

"With this being the case, Ms. Franks has every reason to evacuate with Riley, and unfortunately, at this point, we can't make a case for why the minor child should evacuate with anyone else."

Niles recognized how George said *anyone else* rather than naming him specifically. Even though Niles didn't like what he was hearing, he appreciated his lawyer trying to be considerate of how hard it was for a father to swallow the fact that he couldn't evacuate his own son from a dangerous hurricane. The man was right just like Eden had been—she had primary custody. She held the power. Niles suddenly realized that his problem was deeper than the judicial system; his issue was with how Eden treated the situation and how he no longer had much say in his own child's life.

"Okay," was all Niles uttered in response.

"Niles, I believe you are a good father. You want what is best for your son, and I applaud that. I even appreciate your reaching out to me to ask for help in this situation," George shared. "I am planning to evacuate with my family, too, and I can't imagine not having my children with me. But, even though you have concerns about Eden's past choices and behavior in response to said choices, you have informed me that you believe this woman is a good mother who loves your son very much." He paused for a moment, and Niles said nothing. "If Ms. Franks evacuates with Riley, he will be okay. Plus, remember you told me that his grandparents will also be with him. I know Mr. and Mrs. Franks personally; they're great people. Based on previous conversations you and I have had, I know you agree with that," he reminded Niles. "Riley is in good hands."

"I know," Niles admitted as he thought about how much Riley

loved Grandyma. Processing reality, he let his fingers fall to the top rail on the rusty trailer and unintentionally began tapping on the metal as if it were push buttons on a keyboard.

"If circumstances change, let me know," the attorney mentioned as the call seemed to be coming to an end.

Niles was sure that the man had more pressing issues to tend to, but the comment he'd just made caused his mind to wander.

"What do you mean?" Niles inquired, his brow furrowing as he sought clarification.

"If Ms. Franks informs you that she has decided not to evacuate, I need to know that immediately. Such would be a justifiable cause to submit an urgent request to the court that the minor child be permitted to evacuate with his father."

With his ears perked, Niles suddenly stood a little taller. "What are the chances that would be granted?"

On the opposite side of the truck bed, Mickey lifted his head and, for the first time since they'd climbed out of the cab, stared directly at Niles.

"In all honesty, Niles, the entire county, including the judges, are in emergency mode, and it's difficult to make anything happen right now. Nonetheless, for the safety of the minor child, I'd try my best," he promised. "Also, keep in mind that once this storm blows over, we can revisit this idea about a fair situation for each parent and the minor child regarding hurricane threats and planned evacuations."

"That sounds good," Niles declared. "I do have one more question—"

"Yes?"

Niles's fingers became still for a moment. "If Riley was with me right now, could I evacuate with him?"

The line grew silent for a short period. In the background, birds in nearby trees continued to chirp, but neither Niles nor Mickey heard one peep that came from their beaks.

"Is Riley with you right now?" the attorney checked.

"No, he isn't," Niles answered as he locked eyes across the trailer with Mickey, who then glanced down and began fiddling with the gas containers.

"And Riley doesn't have a scheduled visit with you between now and when Ms. Franks plans to leave town tomorrow morning, correct?"

"That's true."

Suddenly, Niles began to wish that he hadn't asked the question.

"Then let's not play around with hypothetical situations at the time being, Niles," he encouraged. "That's risky business."

"I understand," Niles agreed, wondering if his attorney was contemplating whether his client might try to find a way to get Riley. Niles figured that he better not tell him that the thought had crossed his mind a couple of times. "I just want to know for future reference," Niles clarified.

"Once our community returns to normal, make an appointment with my office," the lawyer suggested. "We can sit down and hash out the options. For now, do what you need to do to make sure you are safe."

After hanging up, Niles explained the conversation to Mickey, although he knew his friend had been eavesdropping and probably had a good idea of what was being said on the other end of the line. They talked back and forth as they began to unload the equipment they would need to cut a handful of limbs overhanging the driveway at the house in front of which they were parked.

"What are you thinking about doing?" Mickey pried, realizing that something was bubbling between his friend's ears.

The sun was hanging high in the sky, only beginning descent, and it was hard to believe that in a few short days, the weather would be so much different. This was the calm before the storm.

"Hear me out," Niles started. "Tomorrow night is my normal visitation with Riley, right?"

The two of them began walking up the driveway, Niles carrying a ladder and rope, Mickey holding the chainsaw and pruning shears.

"Yeah," Mickey acknowledged, his brow furrowed. He was well aware that Riley always came over on Wednesdays. That's why he made sure to keep those nights free so he could hang out with the little fellow—wander beneath the canopy of trees, play video games, and munch on goodies—those sorts of things.

"But Eden is leaving tomorrow morning, so I won't get to see the little guy tomorrow," Niles explained.

"Right," Mickey said simply, understanding that part of the equation but unsure where this was headed.

Both of them stopped simultaneously as if they'd discussed the exact spot where they would place the supplies and set up camp for the job.

"So, I am going to ask Eden if Riley can stay the night tonight," Niles mentioned, raising his eyebrows.

"Wait," Mickey responded, suddenly feeling like the responsible friend. "Is there more to this plan?" he asked. "I heard what you said to your lawyer."

A sideways grin began to grow across Niles's face. "George Billings basically told me that Eden has the right to evacuate with Riley because he is with her now and will be with her through the time she plans to evacuate." He paused for a brief moment but not long enough to give Mickey a chance to interrupt his train of thought. "But if Riley is with me this evening, and we decide to evacuate tonight, then I would have the right to take my son with me," Niles articulated.

17

Eden's phone dinged, immediately displaying a response from Kirk. *I hope you'll decide to stay in New Bern*, the message read.

I want to stay, she texted back, *but my ex is putting me in a sticky situation.*

What do you mean? the next message asked.

Eden explained the dilemma of how Niles would have plausible grounds of evacuating with Riley if she chose not to herself.

That sucks, Kirk texted back. *He sounds like a wuss and a jerk.*

Eden hoped that Kirk would understand if she decided to leave. Honestly, she didn't know what was best. She wasn't so naïve that she didn't realize the chance that the storm could end up being devastating. Her parents were evacuating for a reason, and so was Niles. Her ex was a lot of things, but a chicken wasn't one of them. A nice benefit of being in a relationship with him over the years was the sense of safety he provided. In his presence, she always felt protected. One time the two of them had been in Atlantic Beach during the summer months, and two men approached them outside of a bar on the boardwalk. She and Niles were simply walking toward the beach, minding their own business, but these two bozos stepped between them, cutting off the path that led to sand and saltwater.

"Do you have a sister?" one of the guys asked Eden, slurring his words as he nearly fumbled the beer bottle in his hand.

The man who had spoken was wearing a tank top, and his muscles resembled small boulders. He was tall, too, Eden recognized as she found herself peering up at him. She and Niles had been holding hands, and she remembered Niles suddenly letting go, then using that hand to push her gently behind him, where she could still see around his shoulder.

"No, she doesn't," Niles responded on her behalf.

The other fellow, a little taller and bigger than Niles, chimed in. "You let him do the talking for you?" he barked, glaring at Eden, stumbling as he laughed.

"Like my husband said, I don't have a sister," Eden clamored.

"Look, she does talk," the first guy pointed out to the other. "I'm pretty sure I dated your sister," he added. "She was sexy, looked just like you," he complimented disrespectfully.

Niles spoke again. "Guys, we're just trying to take a walk on the beach; we don't want any trouble."

"The beach is closed," guy number two announced, picking up his beer from the boardwalk railing and clanking it against his buddy's brown bottle.

"Maybe the two of us will take your girl for a walk on the beach," guy number one suggested, laughing.

"I'm not that man," Niles uttered as calm as the water on the other side of the two drunk guys.

It was one of those nights where the air at the beach was as quiet as it ever was, and the ocean was as calm as the river. Eden could even remember hearing tiny little waves slap softly against the sand in the distance as the situation began to escalate.

"What man?" one of them growled.

"The one you can push around," Niles explained.

"I didn't push you, bud, but if you're feeling frisky, I can," he threatened.

Niles ignored the comment. "My wife and I are going to step past the two of you so we can have a walk on the beach; we'd appreciate it if you'd willingly let us through."

"Niles, let's just go the other way," Eden suggested, knowing there were several paths on the boardwalk that led down to the beach.

"I think you better listen to your better half," the second guy suggested.

Niles took a stride toward the beach, hoping the two guys would move aside, but they didn't. They closed the gap, and guy number one reached out his hand, placing it flat on Niles's chest. Eden remembered Niles pressing his left hand into her sternum, moving her back an arm's length. Then, she heard the crunching sound guy number one's wrist made when her husband twisted it forcefully, causing the grown man to flip awkwardly onto the tattered boards beneath their feet. With his left foot, she watched Niles pin the man to the boardwalk while still holding onto his broken wrist. "May we please pass," Niles requested, again speaking passively.

The bigger fellow seemed surprised by what Niles had done to his buddy but didn't appear intimidated. In fact, he became enraged and suddenly swung his beer bottle at Niles's face. Close enough to hear the whiz of the glass bottle as it circled through the air, Eden stood frozen as she watched her husband duck, pressing his foot into the other man's chest. At the same moment, she heard the gasping sounds coming from the mouth of the one on the ground. A split second later, the sole of Niles's right shoe pushed through the kneecap of the second man, and once again, the sound of crunching caused Eden's body to cringe. Instantly, guy number two crumpled over and joined his friend in obvious pain. Both were lying on the left side of the boardwalk, squirming.

"Enjoy your visit to the hospital, fellows," Niles said as he grasped Eden's left hand, pulling her to his right side and leading her toward the beach as he watched carefully to make sure the guys didn't try anything else. He didn't think they would, but they were drunk, so he didn't put it past them.

That was the first time Eden saw Niles fight in public. She watched plenty of his matches ringside yet had never been quite that close to the action. She knew he was quick and had observed him bloody up opponents one-on-one, but her jaw literally fell as he dropped two significantly bigger men to the ground in a matter of seconds.

These days, Niles had more of a temper. She wasn't sure if it was because of getting kicked out of the military, the accident, the divorce, or maybe a mixture of all three. He certainly wasn't as calm and predictable as he had once been. She often wondered what had happened during boot camp. What pushed the gentlest man she knew over the edge? He would never tell her the full story. She just knew that once again, this time during the middle of his training, he had sent two men to the hospital. Those in command might have been impressed if the victims hadn't been seasoned officers. Apparently, the military frowned on a soldier striking a superior, for obvious reasons, of course.

As Eden's mind wandered, her cell phone rang again.

"Hey, Mom," she answered.

"Hey, darling."

"How is Riley?" Eden asked.

"He's down for a nap," she explained.

These days taking naps were hit and miss for Riley. She guessed he'd grown out of them for the most part, but at other times, during growth spurts or if he hadn't slept well the night before, she figured his body still appreciated the extra rest.

"That's good," Eden replied. "Have you heard about the mandatory evacuation?" she asked.

"Yes, and that's why I am calling," her mom explained. "Your father and I think that you and Riley definitely need to leave town with us tomorrow."

Eden knew what she needed to say, probably even what she and Riley needed to do. "I think we'll plan to do that," she agreed.

Her mother let out a sigh of relief. "I do think that's best, sweetie," she confirmed. "I would be worried sick about you if you stayed here by yourself through this monster of a storm."

"We'll have to discuss all of the details later, though, I'm slammed at work."

"That sounds good," her mom declared but then asked a question that Eden was hoping would be left unasked. "Have you and Niles discussed this?"

"Niles knows," Eden huffed, wanting to leave it at that.

"Honey, is he okay with Riley going with us?"

"I've already explained this to you, Mom; it's not up to him."

"I know it's a decision that the two of you have to make together."

"The decision has been made, Mom," Eden urged. Why did her mother have to be such a peacemaker?

"Let him know he can go with us if he'd like. Your Aunt Becky would be fine with him staying in the guest house since all of us end up sleeping in the empty bedrooms in the main house anyway."

Aunt Becky's house was big enough for ten people to live in without being crowded. Eden loved going there as a child, and playing hide and seek with her cousins was one of her favorite pastimes. The game could go on for hours as they split up in teams and scoured through the place.

"Mom, Niles is a big boy; he can take care of himself." Eden wondered if the same offer would be extended to Kirk, although she hadn't even mentioned him to her mother.

"I just thought Niles might like to be near his son," she mentioned. "There's no telling how long we'll be out of town. They're saying that the roads in and out of here are going to flood like never before. It could be two weeks until we get back if we even have a house to come back to, that is."

"Niles already has plans to head to the mountains. Plus, I doubt Aunt Becky would agree to my ex-husband staying in her guest house."

"Darling, I've already asked her, and she's fine with it."

"Mom, you did not?"

"You know how I like to plan for every possible scenario, sweetie."

Eden's mind began to wander. "You haven't spoken to Niles about this, have you?"

"Certainly not, dear. I wouldn't do such a thing without your permission."

"Good, because he's not going with us," she declared. "I don't want him there."

"You just need to make sure that what you want is also what's best for Riley," her mom brought up.

Eden knew that if she kept deliberating with her mother, this phone call could go on for hours. Most conversations with her mom had to be ended by the other party, or else there was no end. Disagreements even more so; her mom would debate anyone until the individual agreed or walked away from the discussion. What was more annoying was that Eden would get mad, but the tone of her mother's voice would never waver nor would her facial expressions show any signs of disgust. The woman should have been a lawyer.

Nonetheless, Eden was able to transition back to work once she rushed her mother off the phone by telling her that she heard her boss coming down the hallway. It was the truth, and he did stop at her door and lean in.

"Do you have the file on the Purifoy case?" he requested. Standing in the doorway, her boss's gray head of hair wasn't far from touching the top of the frame. His slender body was covered with a pair of expensive dress slacks and a button-down long-sleeved shirt, impeccably accented with a yellow bowtie. The latter was part of his signature look. Each outfit he wore was professionally tailored, and Eden knew this because the invoices always ended up on her desk.

As he waited, she rummaged through one of the stacks of files piled high on her desk. "It's right here," she finally confirmed, plucking it from the others before standing to hand it over.

"Perfect," he said as he stepped in to meet her halfway. "You look a little stressed out today," he mentioned.

"I think we all are," she declared.

"You're right about that," he acknowledged, his brows rising to the ceiling. "I think I might give everyone the next three days off," he uttered, chuckling.

Knowing that he was being facetious, Eden smirked. During a short office brief this morning, he'd already made the announcement that the office would close at the end of the workday and wouldn't reopen until Monday at the earliest. Of course, he'd added that he'd expect everyone to remain attentive to their email and cell phones as he knew that urgent matters would continue to arise.

"I think we can all thank Florence for a little break," Eden mentioned.

He shook his head and laughed. "I'm pretty sure that my wife has been conspiring with Florence these past several days. In less than a few hours this morning, she managed to book a round trip flight to Seattle, secure front-row seats at the opera, and purchase tickets for a visit to the Space Needle as well as make reservations for the restaurant at the top," he shared. "We fly out in the morning and return Sunday evening."

"Sounds like fun," Eden responded. She'd never been to the state of Washington. Honestly, since giving birth, she had barely traveled anywhere outside of Eastern North Carolina except for one trip to her Aunt Becky's.

"Are you staying or going?"

That was the big question, Eden realized. If she heard it once, she heard it a hundred times in the past few days—in text messages from friends, strangers at the grocery store, and of course, Grandyma and Niles. "Riley and I are planning to leave with my parents," was the story she was sticking with for the time being.

Eden had been keeping a close eye on the weather app, trying to figure out with the rest of the world what this storm might do. Hundreds of models predicted the future path of the beast, including the well-known European model to less known ones produced by forecasters across the globe.

"I hope your ex is planning to leave, too. That treehouse of his is likely to end up downstream in the Neuse River."

Eden couldn't help but giggle. "I think he's planning to evacuate to the mountains." She didn't want her boss, or anyone, thinking that she kept tabs on Niles although she didn't have to since her friends so often did that for her. Such was one of the downfalls of living in a small town. Somewhere in the back of her mind she was curious to find out who the cute blonde at the bar was last night, the one who seemed to have an interest in Niles.

On the subject of bars, when her boss walked out, she glanced at her phone upon returning to her desk and discovered two new messages from Kirk. The first said, *I hope that calling your ex a wuss and a jerk didn't offend you.* As she read the message, Eden realized that she hadn't responded. Initially, her mind became caught up in the memory of the beach fight, then she ended up on the phone with her mom, and after that, her boss came in looking for the file.

To the first message, Eden responded, *No, it's okay. He can be a jerk.*

Kirk's second message said, *I understand if you decide to evacuate.* Finding the gesture sweet, Eden grinned as she read the rest of the text. *In case you do leave, you should come to watch my band's show tonight so we can spend more time together!*

Eden began to type. *I have Riley all night, so I doubt I can make the show. Sorry,* she apologized.

A moment later, a new text popped onto the screen. *Good, I'm glad the name-calling didn't bother you. I have a thought: Maybe you could let your ex have the little man tonight, appease him since he's upset about not getting to take the kid with him? Might be a win-win,* he suggested.

18

Prior to lunchtime, Reese had finished packing everything she could aside from the necessities she would use tonight and tomorrow morning—items like her pillow, cell phone charger, toothbrush, and other toiletries. People often forgot those things on one end of the trip or the other. She hated it when she left behind belongings, especially at a hotel since they so often went missing indefinitely. However, on trips where she was wearing a badge and a gun, things didn't seem to disappear from her room if she accidentally left something behind. Funny how that worked, she thought.

Reese enjoyed a peaceful lunch by herself at one of the local cafes. She briefly contemplated driving to her favorite restaurant in downtown Chattanooga but then thought better of it. The captain might not be thrilled to learn that she'd driven the Hummer into the next city before time to leave town, and she definitely didn't want to end up on his bad side. So, she made a quick phone call requesting permission to drive the unit's vehicle to lunch. She also asked about running errands and meeting the guys at the range for target practice. Otherwise, she would have had to ask someone to pick her up.

"I don't think you'll be shooting at anyone while rescuing and helping people post hurricane, but I guess it never hurts to get in a few extra rounds," the captain speculated. "Just don't let those guys talk you into staying out too late tonight if you all decide to celebrate with drinks after you wear out Brown at the range."

As Reese processed the comment, she felt a sense of relief that the two of them weren't having this discussion face-to-face. Otherwise, Captain Lawson would have surely noticed the shade of red that overtook her cheeks as the eyes above them nearly blasted out of their sockets.

"You know about that?" she investigated.

"I know about everything that happens in my police station," he confirmed.

The way the captain inserted the word 'my' before everything that had anything to do with the police station always made her chuckle inside. "Everything?" she asked, wondering if he would divulge more information.

"I know that you all send the rookies out to the doughnut shop on their first day, and not a single one of you have ever brought me a custard-filled doughnut."

Reese held her hand over her mouth and laughed into it, but she neither denied nor confirmed the allegation. "What else do you know?" she inquired. Asking for more information was part of her job, so it came naturally, but the captain knew that, and she realized that she wasn't fooling him.

"I know that Brown is the name of one of my detectives," he said pausing for a long moment before going on, doing so only because he knew that a question mark would temporarily form on Kirby's forehead. "I also know that brown is the color of part of the fence behind my station."

Reese nearly snorted into the receiver. "I've noticed that," she admitted after gaining control of her insides.

"I bet you have."

"Why are you telling me these things?"

"Because I want you to know that I know everything that goes on with my detectives," he reminded her. "Everything."

"Yes, sir," she acknowledged.

"Your daddy was one heck of a police officer, Kirby. I know that. He's why you ended up with the day off today rather than starting this whole trip process tomorrow morning as I'd originally planned," he divulged. "After what happened yesterday, you deserved a late night and a few too many glasses of wine, but as I previously advised, don't do it again tonight."

"Yes, sir," she responded once again, wondering if he had detectives following his detectives.

"Keep my Humvee and my search and rescue boat safe," he instructed.

"Yes, sir," seemed to be the appropriate reply one last time.

Now, a few hours after that phone conversation, Reese was smiling ear to ear just thinking about it as she cruised toward the local bookstore. There were a few new books on the shelves that she was looking forward to buying and taking on the trip. One was a thriller by Jeff Gunhus, and another was a trendy romance novel by Riley Costello. Dominguez's wife had told her about the latter and explained that readers could literally shop the characters' clothes. Something about that sounded very appealing to her, maybe because she had to dress sort of plain for work every day. She doubted that once she made it to Wilmington, she would have much time to read, if any. Still, during the next couple of days, there should be plenty of downtime in Hickory, and she planned to use the opportunity to catch up on reading something other than case files.

Once inside the local bookshop, she scanned the shelves for the titles on her mind and then read each synopsis on a handful of other novels. She loved how the owner knew interesting details regarding each book in her shop, as well as a tidbit about the authors. The woman, with long and frizzy gray hair, a shawl draped over her shoulders, and glasses hanging on the tip of her nose by a thread, recommended a fantasy book titled *Orewall* by Nicoline Evans. "She's an up and coming author," the lady mentioned, handing her a copy to look at. "This is book one in her *Namate Series*. I think you'll like it." During past visits, Reese talked with the owner about her eclectic style of reading. The next novel that the friendly woman recommended was the first in *The Light Series* by Jacqueline Brown. "Brown has a unique writing style," she relayed as she plucked the book from a shelf and handed it to Reese. The moment Reese heard the author's name, she knew she had to purchase this title if for no other reason than because of the name Brown which seemed to be the theme of the day.

Reese ended up spending more time in the bookstore than usual. She even sat at a small table by the front window and drank a cup of coffee while she read the first chapter of the book by Costello. On most days, when she visited, she was in and out, either in a hurry to get home and make dinner or do something else. Today, she took in the smell that only the pages of printed books could offer a world gone digital. Coupled with the aroma of coffee, she couldn't help but close her eyes and imagine that this would be the smell heaven would have to offer. She also thoroughly enjoyed watching people come in and out of the quaint shop. The owner would extend a sweet hello to every new patron and then offer to assist each one. Some she knew by name when they walked through the wooden front door, and Reese quickly figured out that the woman knew every customer by name by the time the bell jingled on their way out. This made Reese smile, especially because the woman had said, "Hello, Reese," when she walked in today. This lady cared about her business in the same way Reese cared about helping make society a better place. She sure as heck hadn't placed her left hand on the Bible for the salary. There was no amount of money worth putting her life in harm's way every single day. Most people would take a bullet for someone they loved, but she was willing to take one for someone she didn't even know. This thought made her think of her father, but she didn't want to sit at the table and drop tears onto the pages of her brand new book. So, she placed the bookmark, which the little old lady had given her, into the spot where she left off, said goodbye, and listened as the bell jingled on the way out.

About ten minutes later, Reese steered the Hummer into the bank parking lot and found an area large enough for the vehicle and the boat trailer. Once inside, she waited patiently between the rope lines for the next available teller. As usual, when she came into a bank with a firearm on her hip, some people stared. Most of them figured out she was an officer within a matter of moments. The badge next to the gun kind of gave it away. When she wore a jacket during the cold months, no one other than the bank employees who knew her had any idea she was carrying a weapon. Anytime her holster was exposed, Reese made sure her elbow was touching the barrel of the pistol, and her eyes were always a little more active, too. She'd found that most people felt safer when an officer was in the bank, especially the ones who worked there.

When the teller called her up, Reese requested cash, which her paperwork suggested she carry on the trip to the Carolinas. The report reminded her that credit card machines and ATMs might not be in working order once she arrived in Wilmington. Apparently, the locals rushed to the machines when a hurricane moves inland. Thankfully, the captain had supplied five hundred dollars in cash in the envelope. "If you have to use the cash in lieu of the card, make sure you obtain receipts," he reminded her. At first, five hundred seemed like a lot, but then he mentioned how paying for gas in a Humvee could add up real quick. Of course, she'd also need food, beverages, and possibly other random items. "You might want to take some personal cash, too, just in case you come across something you want to buy or in case the station's cash supply runs out," he recommended.

The teller handed Reese the money, and she slid it into the pocket opposite of her firearm before walking back out the glass door through which she'd entered. Her next stop was the grocery store where she picked up snacks and drinks that would last her about a week. After that, she went back home, took a short nap, then headed to the range to meet the other detectives. She was the first to arrive and decided to wait in the parking lot so that Brown wouldn't think she'd been inside practicing all afternoon. A few minutes later, Johnson's Charger pulled into the lot, and he and Reese opened their doors at the same time.

"Nice ride, Kirby," he said across the roof of his car as she climbed down.

As the two stood in front of the Humvee talking—the front end almost as tall as Reese—Brown and Dominguez drove up simultaneously.

The first comment out of Brown's mouth was: "Want to bet that vehicle on this shooting competition you're about to lose?"

"You wish," Reese responded. "I have nothing to lose in this game," she reminded him. Brown and Dominguez had bet tonight's 'going away' dinner for Reese on the friendly challenge. If Brown won, Dominguez had to pay for everyone else's meals, and if she won, Brown had to pay. This boded exceptionally well for her and Johnson because either way, they scored a free supper.

"You have your dignity to lose," Brown teased.

Reese lifted her head up and down. "True."

Dominguez entered the conversation. "Let's get this started, I'm hungry," he revealed, locking eyes with Brown as a smirk shot across his face.

Inside the range, all four of them huddled around two shooting lanes as Johnson fed a target on the line for each shooter. Even though no one was firing shots at the moment, the sawdust like smell of fired bullets lingered in the air as usual.

"How do you want to do this, Brown?" Dominguez asked. "One shot?" he proposed. "Or five, ten, fifteen rounds?"

Brown chuckled as he stared at the target then glanced at Kirby. "With only one shot, she might get lucky," he considered. "Let's go with five because I'm hungry, too," he decided with a smile.

"Five rounds it is," Johnson stated, taking charge. "Since Brown got to pick the number of shots, Kirby, you get to choose the distance."

"Twenty-five yards is fine," she answered nonchalantly.

"Fair enough," Johnson responded. "I get to pick the point system."

"What do you mean?" Brown questioned. "There's a point system on the target. That's what we always go by."

The two standard hanging targets wore silhouettes of a human torso and head. An oblong circle stretched from the base of the neck to the waistline region. In the very middle, an 'x' marked the bullseye inside the smallest area, which was painted red and worth the most points. Outside of that circle, there was a light gray circle, and from there, the next three rings, each growing larger, bore the numbers nine, eight, and seven, respectively. These circles represented the traditional way to score a target in the pistol range.

"Brown, when we have a special shooting competition between detectives, we do things a little differently here," Johnson explained. "You see that framed target on the wall?" he asked, pointing at a piece that hung in an area where every person who entered the range had to walk past.

"Yeah, I've seen it plenty of times."

"Do you know the meaning of it?"

He stared at it for a moment. Dominguez snickered.

"I've heard an officer lost a badge over that target."

"Do you know why?"

"Rumor has it that it's because he scored a zero on every shot," he said.

On the target in question, there were holes in random places, yet none were anywhere close to the silhouette of the person let alone piercing the oblong circle.

"Do you see the phrase on the placard below the target?"

Brown stepped closer. He'd read it before, but he didn't remember it word for word. "Everything is not always as it seems," he said, reading it aloud.

Johnson explained. "There are five x's on the target, not counting the one inside the bullseye. Do you see them?"

Brown took another step toward the framed target. "Nope, I don't see a single x."

"That's because they're all shot straight through," Dominguez pointed out.

"In this range, that's the true test of an expert marksman," Johnson explained.

"Are you saying you want me and Kirby to shoot those five x's on our targets?"

"Bingo," Johnson responded. "You get one shot at each x, and whoever hits the most wins," he stated.

Brown laughed. "I might not hit them all, but I'll hit more than she will."

Johnson turned to Kirby. "Are you good with that?"

"Your range, your rules," Reese replied. That's how things had been since day one, and she wasn't going to challenge it now.

"Ladies first," Brown offered, opening his palm in the direction of the stalls. "You can even pick which lane you want."

"Losers first," Kirby said, and Johnson and Dominguez both snickered in the background.

"I'll go first," Brown chirped. "Put all the pressure on you."

With noticeable confidence, he stepped up to the line, drew his weapon, and aimed at the target. The x's were all much smaller than the one in the bullseye, so tiny that he could barely see them. One was in the upper right-hand corner where the tally block was located. Three were in the top left-hand corner where the scoring range was identified, and the fifth was in the middle of a word in a random sentence that labeled the target.

Carefully, he aimed at the top right first then slowly squeezed the trigger. "Dang it," he said when his shot missed the x by about an inch.

"Not bad," Dominguez called out.

Brown didn't respond; he simply adjusted his stance, steadied his grip, and fired the next round.

"Ooh," Dominguez reveled this time as everyone watched the hole that the bullet pierced through.

Johnson peered toward the target. "I think you may have hit that one."

The next three shots felt good. Brown knew for sure he'd hit two of the x's, and if the second shot was on target, that meant he'd nailed three out of five. There was absolutely no way that Kirby would be able to match that. For all he knew, she might be a sharpshooter, but she wasn't an expert.

"I can smell my steak dinner already," Brown shared with confidence as he watched Johnson reel in the line.

Johnson studied the target for a moment then called out the score. "I'll give you three since your shot took off the bottom portion of that second x you went for."

Brown expected Kirby to challenge the ruling, but she didn't say a word. She simply stepped into the next stall, pulled her pistol from its holster, and fired off five shots within a matter of fifteen seconds.

Out of respect, Dominguez watched intently, paying careful attention to every single detail just as he had the first time he saw his partner shoot. Like that day, Kirby's hands had remained as steady as a mountain, and her entire body was as relaxed as a hammock. As each round fired, Dominguez didn't even look at the target, not then and not now. Her body language told him everything he needed to know—she had hit every single spot she wanted.

Faint waves of burned oil were sending curls of smoke out of the bore of Reese's firearm as she lowered the gun. Scattered on the concrete floor, all five bullet casings had released a cloudy substance similar to what was emitting from the barrel.

Brown held his breath as Johnson quietly pulled in the line, took off the clips, and walked toward the wall where the framed target was displayed. Everyone followed like baby ducks then watched their lead detective hold the new target up to the glass.

"If I hadn't been standing right there, I wouldn't believe what I'm seeing," Brown uttered. "Every single hole matches exactly with the one in the framed target," he articulated in shock.

As the three men stood in awe, Kirby snuck out the front door, and none of them even noticed it until the hinges squawked.

"I'm not trying to ruin this romantic moment we're having fellows," Dominguez said, drooping an arm over each man's neck. "But that right there," he said, turning to look at Brown, "is exactly what it seems."

Johnson let out a little chuckle. "I told you not to bet against Kirby," he reminded the rookie.

"Let's go spend your money at Kirby's favorite restaurant," Dominguez added.

"You guys set me up," Brown clamored.

"You set yourself up, loser," Dominguez teased.

"Do you want to know the real story behind this framed target?" Johnson asked Brown.

With air in his cheeks, he shook his head north and south. "Sure do," he said, blowing out a breath.

"A man gave up his badge over this target."

19

When Niles and Mickey finished cutting down tree limbs at their first job after lunch, they hurried to the next. Then the next, and another, and the chain just kept rotating. Niles had lost count of how many projects they tackled today. He knew that the list on the dashboard was full of marked off names, and that was a good thing. The sun seemed to be sinking as fast as they were moving, and when it began to touch the tree line, Niles was both excited and nervous. The most bizarre thing happened around mid-afternoon. He gave Eden a call and took a shot in the dark that she might allow Riley to spend the evening with him since he would miss out on his Wednesday visit.

"I'll be working until dark, maybe after, but it would be nice to take Riley out for dessert or something special like that," he said politely after apologizing for getting upset earlier.

"Sure," Eden agreed without hesitation.

That was the moment when Niles nearly fainted. Thankfully, he hadn't because he was standing in the middle of a dilapidated shed where loose boards with rusty nails were scattered all around his dusty shoes. The entire structure was so weak that he and Mickey pushed the whole thing over with much less than a hurricane-force wind. The owners weren't worried about the fact that the storm would likely knock over the old shed, but instead, they were concerned that the heavy winds would fling boards through windows and who knows where else.

"Really?" he replied without thinking, wondering if he heard right. He was almost positive that Eden had said *Sure*.

"Yeah, that will be fine."

Niles immediately wondered if Grandyma had talked some sense into Eden. He appreciated how that woman hadn't treated him any differently since the day he and her daughter split up. Even the morning when they sat at opposite benches during the custody case, she gave him a big bear hug and told him she still loved him. Nowadays, she often made mention of how she thought Riley should spend more time with his father. She had even been known to let Niles come over to the house for lunch on weekdays when she was watching her grandson. He was pretty sure that Eden didn't know about those visits.

"Is it okay if I plan to pick him up around eight o'clock and have him back home by ten?" Niles knew that ten was past Riley's regular bedtime. Still, he was hoping that Eden would make an exception based on the circumstances. Plus, he was likely to sleep in the car when they left town, so the little tyke would have an opportunity to catch up on any missed sleep.

"That will be fine; you can pick him up whenever," Eden offered. "If you and Mickey finish early, you can get him any time after six. By then, he and I will be home. I can feed him, or you can take him out for dinner."

Standing in the rubble, Niles wondered what happened to the woman he had been talking to earlier today. The person on the other end of this conversation reminded him of the Eden he loved so dearly. She was talking gently and being easygoing about every detail, even offering things he hadn't requested.

"Let me talk to my business partner," Niles mentioned. "Maybe we could swing by and get him in between jobs, and he could help us at a couple of houses."

Niles was hoping that this request wasn't pushing the limits of her newfound kindness.

Eden chuckled. "Niles, just say Mickey," she suggested. "He's Mickey to me not your business partner."

Niles laughed along with her, maybe the first genuine laugh they'd shared since the divorce, and he wondered what she was smoking. Must be the good stuff, he thought.

"I'll talk to Mickey," he said.

As Mickey tossed boards into the trailer from which they unloaded their supplies in order to make a couple of runs to the dump with the rotted wood, he cocked his head sideways at the mention of his name.

"Just let me know," she uttered as sweet as southern tea.

"I'll have to make sure we can work out the logistics because we have to run home and grab my vehicle so that I'll have a car seat," Niles explained. "Then I would be able to pick up Riley and meet Mickey at the next job." He wanted to make sure Eden understood that he wasn't planning to let Riley ride in Mickey's truck.

"Sounds good, Niles. Like I said, just let me know."

Niles was shocked that Eden hadn't taken a jab at him about the car seat. In all fairness, they'd both been sticklers about car seats ever since the accident. There was absolutely no way that Niles was going to let Riley ride in the truck; it didn't have a back seat. Mickey had asked once, but Niles had shot it down, explaining why, and his friend never mentioned the idea again.

"I will," Niles concurred, grinning from ear to ear as if he just won the lottery.

"Why don't you just keep Riley overnight," Eden randomly suggested. "Since we're not sure when we'll all make it back from this evacuation, that will give the two of you some time together."

Niles was pretty sure he was going to faint this time. "O—kay. I think that's a great idea," he agreed with a puzzled expression on his face.

"Perfect. Let's plan on that," Eden clarified. "I need to get back to work now, so we'll see you a little later."

The rest of the afternoon, Niles was as chipper as could be. The torn down shed project was the biggest that they tackled, but somehow they'd been able to get it done in less than two hours. Between jobs, he and Mickey discussed how they could make it back to the treehouse to get Niles's car and then meet at the next house on the list. They had a couple of jobs in the Bridgeton area, so it would work out almost perfectly.

After mowing a yard—which Niles found to be quite relaxing in the midst of the physical work they'd been doing the past two days—he decided to give Grandyma a call. He had a few miles of free time as they headed to clear out a garage that the owner was afraid would flood due to the proximity of the river.

"Hey, Son-In-Law," Grandyma greeted.

She never stopped calling him her son-in-law, and, of course, he still called her Grandyma. He wasn't sure which of those names got on Eden's nerves more, but he was pretty sure that she hated the name Uncle Mickey the most.

"How are you today?" Niles checked.

"I am fabulous, my dear," she informed him. "Eden tells me that you and Mickey are planning to evacuate from this monster of a storm. I'm so glad to hear that, honey. No one needs to be here when that hurricane rips through little ole' New Bern. It's going to wipe our quaint town off the map," she predicted.

Niles couldn't help but grin at the expense of her perspective. On another note, he knew he hadn't told Eden that Mickey was evacuating with him, but based on Grandyma's comment, it was apparent that his ex-wife made the assumption.

"I'm glad you all are planning to evacuate, too," he acknowledged. "I know I sure have been praying that Eden would decide to leave."

The purpose of Niles's phone call was twofold. He knew that Grandyma would tell on Eden if she wasn't planning to evacuate. The woman couldn't keep a secret nor tell a lie. If Grandyma revealed that Eden was staying, he decided that he was leaving with Riley early tomorrow morning and taking his chances with the law. On the way out of town, he would probably call his lawyer; given the situation, he felt it would be simpler to ask forgiveness rather than permission.

"Darling, I can't believe she ever considered staying," Grandyma confirmed. "I've been all over her like white on rice this week, trying to make sure she makes the best decision for herself and that the two of you make the right call for Riley. She did let you have a say about whom he was going to evacuate with, didn't she?" Grandyma probed.

Niles figured he better leave well enough alone. If he let on to the news that Eden hadn't given two cents about the idea of Riley evacuating with him, Grandyma was sure to call her daughter and give her an earful. Then, Eden might change her mind about letting Riley stay the night.

"Somewhat," he alluded. "Eden's letting me have him tonight, so I'm very thankful Riley and I will get to spend time together before you all leave. I figured I probably owe you a thank you for that," he added.

Thanking her was the other reason he'd decided to make the phone call. However, if he was honest, it was secondary to discovering whether Eden was really planning to head to Kentucky with her parents.

"Sweetheart, I didn't have a thing to do with that decision, but I sure am glad you'll see the little fellow before you all leave town tomorrow for different destinations. You and Riley need that time together," she forecasted.

Just as Mickey was parking the truck along the ditch bank, which separated the road from the house where they would be clearing the garage, Niles finished the conversation with Grandyma. He was trying to figure out how to get her off the phone when Riley asked for help with a puzzle, so it had been her idea to say bye. Niles was excited because he even got to say hello to his son, and when Riley uttered the phrase, "I love you, Daddy," it melted his heart just like it always did. No matter how many times his little boy spoke those three words, they were just as special as every time that came before. It was rare for Niles to talk to his son on the phone since Eden thought it was a bad idea for Riley to talk to his dad when he was at her house. "It's going to confuse him, Niles, if he talks to you while he's with me. He's going to be upset, too, because he will want to be with you and with me at the same time. I think it's just better if we respect each other's time with Riley and don't talk on the phone when he's at our respective houses."

Niles hadn't agreed with the perspective, but what was he supposed to do about it? He couldn't make her answer the phone if he called. If she answered, he couldn't force her to hand the phone to Riley. She could hang up on him; she'd done that before. There was always the option to call George Billings and complain, but that wouldn't help. He would just add it to the list of things that could possibly be tacked onto the custody papers if they went through the whole going-to-court process all over again. It was a mess, an absolute mess. No one should ever get married if they weren't entirely sure they could keep their vows. Of course, in his case, the accident changed things. He and Eden had all intentions of living a long and happy life together, but her addiction to prescription medication altered everything. There wasn't a day that went by that he hadn't wished he could go back and have the family that he had prior to the accident. Even now, he found himself wishing that he and Eden had found a way to work things out. The idea of meeting someone new seemed foreign. It also seemed impossible that he would meet someone who could live up to the standards that he had for a spouse. He would want someone like Eden used to be: A person who was easy to get along with, compassionate, and dedicated to making the most out of every situation. Who he wanted to avoid was someone like who she'd become. The medicine had messed with her mind, and he'd learned the hard way that living life with an individual who was difficult, selfish, and down and out was painstaking. Regardless of whether he liked it or not, he would have to deal with Eden until Riley was eighteen. Since she was his son's mother, he would most likely interact with her to some degree for the rest of his life. If he somehow married someone who wasn't an absolute pleasure to spend life with, he would end up with two difficult women to put up with, and that scared the heck out of him. Therefore, he hadn't talked to that cute blonde at the bar last night or any other woman that he found attractive. Maybe one day, he would date just for fun like Mickey, the professional ladies' man, but he wasn't there yet.

When he and Mickey finished clearing out the garage, Niles called Eden to let her know that he could swing by to get Riley in about thirty minutes. The guys made the quick stop at the treehouse for Niles to grab his car, then he and Mickey headed in separate directions on Highway 17. Niles crossed over the drawbridge, taking in the pristine view of the Neuse and Trent Rivers, which would most likely be raging wild within the next few days. He ventured through downtown New Bern on East Front Street, passing by Union Point Park and Persimmon's Restaurant before reaching a small stretch of road where the river paralleled so close to the street that he could literally toss a rock over the roof of his car and land it in the water. A small seawall was there and a sidewalk also ran alongside the road and the river. Tomorrow and Thursday, many locals, who either chose to stay or wait until the last moment to flee, would wander down to this area and watch as the water began to rise ahead of the storm. First, it would climb the wall, then it would lapse onto the sidewalk where, before long, it would cover the area entirely. During most hurricanes, the river crawled across the grass and eventually took over the street on which Niles was driving at this very moment. Florence was expected to bring unprecedented levels of water. As Niles thought about that, he peered out the driver's side window at the large historic homes and wondered if the river would reach them and possibly even flood them. If that happened, the river would literally be over the top of his car. It was hard to fathom such a reality.

Riley was standing at his mom's front door wearing a smile and a backpack when Niles pulled into the short driveway. Niles shut the driver's side door and met his son on the sidewalk as the little fellow ran and jumped into his arms.

"Daddy," he greeted with the enthusiasm that only a child offers. He went on to fling his arms around his father's neck and hold them there as Eden stepped out of the doorway.

"He's excited about helping you work," she called out.

Niles smiled. "Daddy's excited about having your help," he exclaimed, feeling Riley's ear pressed against his own. "I even brought your toolset."

During the stop at the house, Niles quickly climbed the ladder to grab his son's play tools, which the little guy had been carrying around with him in the woods for years. He would inspect everything, bang on trees, and continuously pretend to fix the boards and netting that surrounded the treehouse.

"Really!" Riley sounded, jerking his head back so that he could see his dad's face.

"Really," Niles responded, his eyes widening in response to watching his son's do the same.

"You guys have fun," Eden wished.

"Thanks for letting him go," Niles said over his shoulder as they made the short trek back down the sidewalk.

"We will!" Riley shouted as he peered over his father's shoulder and waved back at his mother.

Part of Niles wanted to hang around for a few minutes and be friendly since Eden still seemed to be in such a chipper mood, but then he thought better of it. He was afraid that he'd accidentally say something that would set her off, and she might decide to rescind the offer to let Riley spend the night. So, with his son strapped into the booster seat, Niles drove away, staring in the rearview mirror at Eden until his eyes could no longer make out the outline of her nearly perfect body. He hadn't been able to help but notice how pretty she looked wearing a pair of simple black dress slacks and a burgundy top. Her hair was a little curlier than usual, and for some reason, he had a hard time not staring at her pearly white teeth. They'd always been white, it wasn't like she had bleached them or anything, but Niles rarely saw them these days because she didn't seem to smile when he was around. As he and Riley passed by the old Maola Milk plant, Niles fought to let go of thoughts that led to places where he didn't know if his mind should go. Clenching the steering wheel, his thumb once again reminded him that he no longer wore a ring on his finger.

20

Eden stood in the doorway until the taillights on Niles's vehicle faded into the distance. She was happy with the way things worked out for Riley to spend the night with his dad. Not that she particularly wanted her five-year-old son around the dangerous equipment Niles and Mickey would be working with this evening, but, hopefully, the little fellow would return tomorrow morning without any scrapes, bruises, or other issues.

When Kirk came up with the idea to let her ex have the kiddo for the evening, Eden considered calling Niles and making that offer. However, she hadn't wanted it to come across as if she was pawning Riley off on him. Sure, he would have most likely taken the bait, but then he would have probably begun to ask questions. She didn't want to deal with those. She also didn't want Niles knowing that she was glad he'd called and asked if their son could spend the evening with him so that she could now have the freedom to go with Kirk to his concert. One of the downsides of having full custody of her son was a lack of freedom. It wasn't that she didn't enjoy spending time with Riley, but being a single mom was hard. A kid at his age seemed to require constant attention. Even though he could now tie his own shoes and brush his own hair, he always needed her for something.

Thinking about the evening ahead, Eden pranced toward the bathroom, where she slipped out of her work clothes and climbed into a hot shower. Kirk would be at the house in about an hour to pick her up, and the two of them were planning to have dinner out before he would need to begin setup at the bar. When he asked where she wanted to eat, the first restaurant that came to mind was Morgan's Tavern. It was in the downtown area near the location where his band would play later tonight, so it would be convenient. The atmosphere within the restaurant itself had always felt romantic to Eden. In the evenings, the lighting was dim, and candles were flickering on the tabletops. Not to mention, the food was delicious.

As both the mirror and Eden's mind began to steam up, she realized how stoked she was about the idea of being behind-the-scenes with the cutest drummer she ever laid eyes on. She imagined herself sitting in the front row as Kirk moved to the rhythm of the music while pounding the drum set with sticks gripped in the same hands that had so delicately touched her last night. Maybe afterward, he'd autograph them and toss them in her direction. As that thought traveled through Eden's mind, she couldn't help but giggle at her own silliness while lathering her body with a soap she'd picked up at the local farmers market last week. It was called Plain Jane, but she didn't feel so plain this evening. She felt rejuvenated and ready to let go again.

When Kirk arrived, Eden slipped her arms around him and gave him a short yet sensual kiss. While showering, she decided to take that initiative rather than let the situation feel awkward as both of them wondered how to greet one another after knowing each other for only a little over twenty-four hours but having shared intimate moments together.

"You smell superb," Kirk cajoled.

Eden blushed. "Thank you," she replied in an accepting but somewhat subdued tone. As she took a step back, she glanced at his outfit: A pair of dark-colored skinny jeans, a tight black shirt with a thin gray vest draped over and matching boots. He looked the part of the rocker that he was, but at the same time, his wardrobe was fitting for a dinner out at a nice restaurant.

"In one word, how would you define your day?" he inquired as he stepped into the foyer area of Eden's house.

"Busy," she answered. "I was honestly shocked to get out of the office before dark."

"How about your day?"

"Quite the opposite of yours," he recollected. "It appears that hurricanes fail to drive business to the music shop."

Eden laughed along with her new friend. "I guess buying a guitar isn't really a necessity when preparing for a big storm."

Squinting an eye, Kirk nodded his head side to side in a quick, repeated motion, reminding her of a bobblehead doll. "I can't fathom why," he teased. "However, hurricanes, craft beer, and good music typically bring out quite the crowd, so we're expecting a packed house at the gig tonight."

"Are you nervous?" Eden asked, plucking her clutch from the kitchen counter so that they could head out. She usually carried a purse, but tonight she didn't want to lug around the normal bulky one. A mother was required to have one of everything in her everyday pocketbook, but when Riley was with his dad, it was nice to lighten the load and go with the sleek look.

"Your presence may provoke such a feeling," Kirk replied with a grin, holding open the door as Eden walked out after thinking far enough ahead to flip on the porch light.

"You probably won't even notice me," she teased as they walked along the sidewalk toward his vehicle.

As the conversation carried on, he proceeded to open the passenger side door for his date.

"Of course I will," he exclaimed. "I have reserved a front row seat for you."

Eden's eyebrows rose. "Really? There are tickets for the event?"

"Technically, there aren't tickets, but there is going to be a cover charge at the door," Kirk answered with a smile as he began backing the car out of the short driveway.

"Does the band get part of that?"

He shook his head. "With this bar, we split it right down the middle."

"That's cool," she said, figuring his band would probably come out pretty good tonight.

There was a short wait at the restaurant, but as Eden and Kirk sat side by side on a wooden bench in the long hallway that led to the server's station, they enjoyed a conversation about favorite foods. Eden discovered that Kirk loved meatloaf—both the food and the singer—and she told him that the meal of her choosing was pretty much any chicken and pasta dish. Thankfully, Morgan's Tavern served both, and when they sat down to order, neither surprised the other. They continued on with the topic of favorites, going from candy bars to colors to words. The word Kirk most liked to use was *shenanigans*, and Eden had a difficult time deciding but went with *plethora*.

"I hope we encounter a plethora of shenanigans this evening," Kirk announced, topping the comment with a laugh as he and Eden headed back to the car after finishing dinner.

Once they made it to the bar, Kirk drove around back by creeping the vehicle down a small road that looked more like an alleyway before opening up into a tight parking lot. It took him a minute or so to maneuver the vehicle into an empty space. Even though Eden lived in New Bern her whole life, she had never been back there. The sight was far from surreal, just a view of the rear side of two and three-story brick buildings. Most were decorated with fire escapes and windows, one with an attached bird feeder and a few with trays of potted flowers. Nothing exciting.

After meeting the owner of the bar, Eden helped Kirk unload his drum set one piece at a time. She could tell that he was hesitant to accept her assistance, and she wasn't sure if it was because she was a woman or if he was afraid she would damage something. Regardless, she told him that she'd much rather carry things than stand around with nothing to do, and she promised to be careful with each item. It surprised her when she noticed the number of drumsticks he tucked into a leather carrying case; there were at least a dozen, and most of them were unique. One set was made out of some type of purple plastic material, another looked like thick pieces of pine straw wound together, and the ones that stood out the most had a marshmallow looking ball attached at the end.

"Do you use all of these?" Eden inquired.

"Not simultaneously," Kirk bantered, trying not to smirk but ultimately giving in when laughter pushed violently at the seams of his lips.

"Ha, ha, smartypants," she replied, pulling out one of the purple ones and playfully threatening to whack him with it for teasing her.

"I most definitely utilize every set, but some more frequently than others," he explained. "It all depends on the desired sound for each beat within a song."

"Don't all of the wooden ones create the same sound?"

"Not at all," he guaranteed. "It depends on the type of wood used to create the stick, the thickness, the shape, the length, and a plethora of other factors that are backed by scientific data."

Eden chuckled. "I like what you just did there, smoothly working my word into our conversation," she pointed out. "Which ones are your favorite?"

"These," he said, plucking a set of dark maple sticks from the bag.

"They're pretty," she complimented as she studied the wood grain.

"They are, but they also resonate an amazing sound."

"I bet. I can't wait to watch you work some magic with them tonight," she mentioned, pounding them on a set of air drums and earning a laugh from the drummer himself while her hair flung around like a mop.

As Eden and Kirk were discussing drumsticks, two other members of the band pulled into the parking lot. Shortly after their arrival, the lead singer showed up fashionably late. From there, the four band members worked in unison like machines on an assembly line. At this point, Eden mainly stayed out of the way, but Kirk or one of the other guys asked for help here and there. The lead singer's girlfriend came with him, but she seemed to be in a world of her own. She was dressed in all black, sported pink hair and long black fingernails, and was about as thin as one of Kirk's drumsticks. She said hello when introduced to Eden, but other than that, she didn't say much to anyone. As the guys set up speakers, ran wire, and tested the microphones, she could be found either outside the back door smoking a cigarette or sitting at the bar sipping on a beer. Prior to today, Eden had to admit that she had no idea how much work went into setting up for a band to play, and this was just at a local venue. It was hard to fathom the preparation that would be required for a famous person like Meatloaf at an amphitheater or coliseum.

21

Reese had waited outside of the range for the guys, and once they finally emerged—Brown with his head lowered and tail between his legs—she invited them to ride in the Hummer. Pulling rank, Johnson claimed shotgun while Dominguez and pouty face climbed into the back. As the four of them cruised toward Wally's Restaurant, a few jokes regarding the results of the competition were tossed about. However, by the time they unbuckled and reached for the door handles, everyone was having a good time. Riding in the department's Humvee had proven to be equivalent to a joyride in a limousine. The vehicle stood out like a sore thumb, and the team reveled at how nearly every person they passed on the street, whether in a car or walking, stared as if the President was hidden behind the tinted windows.

Wally's was a staple in the area, a place Reese had frequented with her parents for years on top of years. The sign out front proudly informed customers and passersby that the family restaurant had been in business since 1937. Her dad appreciated a good buffet, and she could vividly remember the excitement on his face when coming here and how he would brag about getting his money's worth. When police officers met at this establishment, they'd often have a competition to see who could consume the most food, which reminded Reese of those silly hot dog eating contests that aired on television. Much like those events, the officers who looked like a sure bet to win didn't always come through. Smiling, Dominguez brought up the idea today, but Brown instantly shook his head side to side as violently as a dog trying to shake off water after a bath.

"No more competitions for me," he laughed as they walked toward a table.

"You might actually have a chance at winning this one," Dominguez spouted over his shoulder.

Brown glanced down at his stomach and frowned.

When the team slid into a red vinyl booth, Johnson chimed in. "You two would beat the socks off Kirby and me."

"Even without having an eating contest, we'll make sure you get your money's worth, Brown," Reese teased, thinking about her dad when she made the jab.

The four of them devoured as much American comfort food as possible, then Reese drove the guys back to their vehicles and watched each wobble out like a stuffed turkey. It was literally a laughing matter, and that's when she realized she would miss their company while in North Carolina. Other than her mother, these three people were the closest thing she had to a family. Johnson was a father figure in a way, and Dominguez and Brown were like the two brothers she never had when growing up. Even so, she was missing that person in her life to whom she could genuinely open up, someone to share real emotions with and cry in front of when needing to let something out.

Police officers weren't known for shedding tears in the presence of one another, with the exception of attending a comrade's funeral. Thankfully, those were few and typically far between. Reese expected that most unloaded on their significant others at home, and she knew one thing for sure, people in her line of work had plenty to sob about. Most had witnessed scenes that no human being should. They marked off crime sites where blood crept around carpet fibers like volcanic lava oozing through a patch of woods. Reese hated to admit that she had become numb to the sight of blood, much like a nurse might. What haunted her dreams at night were thoughts of the lives beyond the bodies—kids who were robbed of a parent, adults who would never spend another moment with those whom they loved so dearly. If she had a dollar for every time she uttered the word "Why?" she could donate more money to victims' charities. A string of evidence almost always led to the answers to that one-word question, but rarely did the motive make any logical sense whatsoever.

These were the types of conversations she dreamed of having with her dad. Although he had been a highly decorated police officer, she knew he would have let her cry on his shoulder. Typically, a mom would be the parent with whom a child would share her emotions, but in Reese's life, her dad had always been that person. She and her mom had a healthy relationship, but they weren't close like her and her dad. Even now, Reese didn't spend much time with her mother. Thankfully, nothing really stood between them except they just didn't have much in common. Her mom enjoyed indoor hobbies like cross stitching and cooking while she preferred to be outdoors fishing or hiking. Reese had friends, but not a best friend, not even someone to eat ice cream and watch a movie with after a breakup. She would love to find a person with whom she could share secrets and fears, someone who would cherish her even more because of the wounds life had etched into her soul.

22

When Niles and Riley made it to the job site where Mickey was mowing the grass by himself, Riley went racing toward his tall, sweaty friend. Almost everyone literally looked up to Mickey, but to kids, he resembled a giant bean pole. Before Niles let his son's little legs run free, he made sure Mickey shut off the riding mower since his helper was on the way.

"Uncle Mickey," he hollered as if the sound of the mower was still swallowing the air around them. A moment later, he leaped into the air like a basketball player soaring toward the rim. His arms found Mickey's familiar neck, and he hung there momentarily like a monkey on a tree branch.

Watching in the background, Niles grinned as he unloaded the hedge trimmers. He loved seeing his son happy.

"Want to help me mow the grass?" Mickey asked Riley.

"Mom says I shouldn't ride on the mower."

Mickey let his eyes swell as he scrunched his face, causing it to look a bit like Popeye's. "Well, not by yourself, of course," he agreed. "But with Uncle Mickey, you're as safe as money in the bank."

Riley giggled with enthusiasm.

Mickey knew that Eden probably didn't want the little fellow riding on a mower with anyone, but she was just a worrywart. Mickey grew up sitting in his dad's lap on the rider, and that was back when they didn't have safety features like the riders these days. He popped Riley onto his lap in one motion, cranked the engine, and continued down the strip he'd been cutting.

Niles overheard what his son said, but he ignored it. He'd driven Riley around on the mower plenty of times even though he was fully aware that Eden was against the idea. Of course, he always wrapped an arm around his narrow chest just like Mickey was doing now. His free hand was helping the two little hands that were guiding the steering wheel as the mower moved at a slower pace than usual.

When Mickey and Riley finished mowing the lawn, they met Niles back at the truck.

"Want to use the blower?" Niles asked his son.

His bright hazel eyes lit up like a lamp in a dark room. "Can I?"

"Of course," Mickey barked.

Niles strapped the backpack onto his son, and since it was a bit heavy even for an adult, he held onto it as the two of them danced around blowing off the concrete driveway. Riley reveled at the sight of freshly cut grass blades falling like confetti in whatever direction the blower sent them. This also intensified the smell of grass that lingered in the air, a scent that consumed Niles's clothing daily. When at the house earlier, he forgot to grab Riley a change of clothes and now found himself hoping the laundromat washing machine would rid the stench before he returned the outfit to Eden.

Mickey darted to the truck to grab his phone, and a moment later, he was snapping pictures of their little helper who currently resembled a miniature ghostbuster. He couldn't pass up capturing the images, and he figured he might even be allowed to show these to Eden.

"Blow away that hurricane that's heading this way," Mickey shouted down the drive as he played the role of a photographer.

Riley snickered while wondering if he could. Niles laughed at the comment then helped his son finish the task as Mickey hastily loaded and secured the equipment. They tackled a couple more jobs where Riley was able to help by using his play tool kit and then headed for home. Niles asked his son where he wanted to have dinner, and twenty minutes later, they ended up sitting on the deck of the treehouse eating pizza like he and Mickey did the night before. Upon arrival, Riley was mesmerized by the plywood covering the windows, and he was openly eager to help write messages with spray paint. Ironically, the owner of one of the downtown stores whose windows the guys boarded up urged them to take the leftover paint; he said he bought way too much and doubted he would use it again. His generosity saved Niles and Mickey a trip to the store, and the man had given them so many cans that they used the paint on other boarded up windows throughout the day and still had plenty. Most of the homeowners didn't want messages written on their windows, but the businesses seemed to think it was fun, which almost seemed backward, Niles and Mickey thought, since companies were traditionally known for being professional. However, something about hurricanes brought out people's adolescent sides.

"You can paint whatever graffiti you want up there," Mickey explained to Riley. He started to promise the little fellow that he wouldn't end up in handcuffs like his Uncle Mickey once had for creating community art, but then he decided better. He knew Eden wouldn't like to hear that story again, at least not from the mouth of her five-year-old son.

Riley watched intently as Mickey shook a can of red spray paint—the little ball inside clinking around like the one in a pinball machine—before pointing the nozzle at the bare plywood. *Get The Flo Out Of Here* was the first message he wrote. Niles, glaring back and forth between Mickey and the phrase, shrugged his shoulders and lifted his open palms. Without saying a word, his body language asked, *Really?* Mickey shot back a look that said, *He's only five; he'll take it at face value.* Once the silent conversation ended, Niles wrote *Flo Away* then handed over the metal can to his son.

"What should I write, Daddy?" Riley asked several times.

"Anything you want," Niles explained.

"Write a message to the hurricane," Mickey suggested.

"Hurricanes can't read," the little fellow articulated.

Niles and Mickey both burst into laughter, and the sounds of fun times echoed in the darkened woods around them.

"Write that," Niles offered, finding it funny.

It had made Riley feel good when his dad and Mickey laughed at his comment, so he figured that writing *Hurricanes Can't Read* was as good of a message as any. However, since hurricanes couldn't read and Riley hadn't yet learned how to write sentences, Niles had to help him spell out the words. When they finished, he jumped up and down as if he'd won the spelling bee. Then, he looked at his pointer finger and laughed. "Look, I have paint on my finger," he showed them.

"That's evidence," Mickey said, stating the same words a police officer slapped him in the face with after finding him near the scene of the graffiti crime.

"What kind of evidence?" Riley asked.

"That you're a painter," Niles mentioned before giving Mickey a chance to tell a story he didn't want his son to hear.

"Exactly," Mickey agreed, showing the tip of red on his finger to Riley.

"I want to see yours, Daddy!"

Niles held up his blue finger, and Riley giggled.

"Let's do some more," the little fellow suggested.

Mickey wrote *Hurricane, Hurricane, Go Away!* Riley, after

writing *Flo Stay Away* with his dad's help, decided that drawing pictures was more fun than writing words. He made a frowny face with a tongue sticking out and said it was a message to the hurricane. Then, he attempted to draw his ark in the choppy water, which Mickey said Hurricane Florence would bring to the river.

When the three of them finished covering the plywood with spray paint, Niles was so happy that his son had been able to experience this with him. He decided right then and there that they would make this a tradition every time a hurricane threatened the area, even if it was a weak one. Then, he remembered his dad taking him to Atlantic Beach, which was less than thirty miles east, and letting him watch the roaring waves slap against the pier, warning residents that a storm was brewing.

"Mickey, let's drive down to the beach and let Riley see the waves," Niles suggested.

Mickey shrugged his shoulders. "I'm game," he announced without hesitating.

Highway 17 led the guys out of Bridgeton before connecting with Highway 70 just over the high rise bridge. The route took them through Havelock and Morehead City, then they crossed another, much shorter, high rise that led into the town of Atlantic Beach. The trip only took around thirty-five minutes, and it helped that there weren't many vehicles on their side of the road heading toward the beach. Traffic heading west, however, was heavier than normal as people were beginning to evacuate ahead of the storm. Tourists typically left first. The local residents would soon follow once businesses started to close, and their homes were secured. Although leaving a house behind in the hands of an unpredictable hurricane was always nerve-racking.

Niles and Mickey had spent countless summer days surfing in the Atlantic Ocean on the other side of the island they were on now. During daytime hours when at the top of the bridge, motorists could actually see across the entire stretch of land and make out a glimpse of the vast ocean. On some occasions, the water was calm, other days, it was rough, but most of the time, it was somewhere in between. Tonight, the sea would be turbulent Niles knew as they turned left at the only major stoplight on the narrow island. A few minutes later, they began walking on the tattered boards that made up the Oceanana Fishing Pier, which had been constructed in 1959 and had since seen its fair share of storms rip through the area. Many of the piers that once graced the same seashore had been wiped away by hurricanes and never built back. Now, this pier touted that it was the only one still standing in Atlantic Beach. Thus, it held the heavyweight title after winning many matches with dangerous opponents like Diana, Bertha, and Fran; however, it wasn't as though insurance companies were knocking on the door of a place like this for business.

Hurricane Florence was hundreds of miles away, but as soon as the guys stepped foot onto the pier, they could feel the entire structure swaying from the force of the waves pushing against the wooden beams that had been driven deep into the sand many years ago. Thankfully, Riley didn't seem alarmed by the movement beneath their feet, so Niles, holding his son's hand firmly, kept walking as if the rocking was typical. Given the current weather situation, it was, in fact, expected. On any given day, the pier didn't move that much.

This evening, as the night's sky frowned over the ocean, pole lights lit the path where fishermen were casting lines, and people from all over came to watch the waves. Niles fished here plenty of times. One of the beauties of pier fishing was that a saltwater fishing license wasn't required to cast a line here. However, each person did have to pay a fee to fish, but, thankfully, not to walk to the end of the pier, hang out, or watch the sunset which tourists and locals alike enjoyed. Niles and Mickey caught dinner here on many occasions. They would take home their catch and slap them on the charcoal grill then sit and eat on the treehouse deck much like they did tonight. There was something utterly satisfying about a human being providing his own dinner. For that reason, Niles showed Riley how to fish at an early age. He also took him hunting and even allowed him to shoot a 22 caliber rifle. He taught his son that there were only a few reasons to ever kill an animal: For food, self-defense of himself or another, or to put one out of its misery. Riley learned the latter lesson the hard way one cold day this past December when a turkey struggled up their long driveway after apparently being struck by a car on the road. The poor animal was beyond help, and Niles explained that they would be doing him a favor. Riley was hesitant but understood, and Niles could remember feeling the same way as a young boy when he and his father came across a fawn under similar circumstances.

Although they weren't here to fish tonight, Riley, for his age, was quite proficient with a rod and reel. He also knew how to clean his catch even though Niles never allowed him to handle a sharp knife. That would come later in life, he explained on numerous occasions. Niles could remember the first knife his dad had given him. The two of them were on the way home from a middle school basketball game, and the car needed more gas to drink. His father eased the vehicle into a country store with a single fuel pump out front, and when they went inside to pay, Niles spotted a display case full of knives next to the register. "Pick one out, Son," he recalled his dad saying proudly. This offer surprised Niles for two reasons: His father rarely bought anything, and up until that point in his life, he hadn't been allowed to use a knife other than to butter toast. He vividly remembered choosing a black knife lined in silver, the words *The Hunter* inscribed on the casing. To this day, he still kept that special gift nearby. He actually used it today to cut through the strands of a thick piece of rope that he and Mickey used to stabilize a maple tree that might or might not make it through the storm.

The further the three of them walked out onto the pier that stretched one thousand feet into the ocean, the more wobbly it became. About halfway, Riley made a comment about what he called the swinging feeling.

"It's kind of like the walkway around the treehouse," Mickey pointed out. "It's made to move when you walk on it."

Niles wasn't sure if that was the stark truth, but it made sense to a five-year-old, and he didn't see any need to question the accuracy of the statement. He was impressed at how quickly Mickey formulated a solid analogy to ease any fears that were possibly bubbling inside Riley's mind. Equating that word to Mickey's comparison made him think of Eden again. She probably wouldn't like the idea of Riley being on what she would call a rickety structure thirty or so feet above a roaring ocean. Nonetheless, they stopped periodically to watch the waves form, rise from the surface, develop a white cap, and slam into the pylons below. From above, it was hard to tell how tall the swells were, but Niles guessed about six to eight feet. He heard others on the pier say anything from three feet to fifteen feet. The latter, he knew, was way off. When the hurricane actually landed, it could produce such extreme waves, but if the waves were that high at the moment, they would all be running toward the other end of the pier. Even now, the occasional wave would cast a thin coat of sea spray up onto the dock especially when they reached the end where the waves were the fiercest.

Riley was loving every moment of this adventure. He leaned against the rail, peered over, and guessed the height of nearly every wave that smashed into the wooden structure. Niles never let go of his son the entire time they were on the pier. Even though he wasn't as cautious as Eden, he knew that this wasn't a playground. Kids loved to climb and hang, and it would only take him letting go and looking away for one moment for his son to end up in the raging sea below. There was no doubt that he would dive in and do everything in his power to rescue him, but this particular feat wasn't on his bucket list.

After spending a good fifteen minutes watching the waves, feeling the wind, and checking out the fish that others reeled onto the dock, Niles and Riley walked back to the pier house through which they'd entered. Niles let his son pick out ice cream from the freezer, and he grabbed something for him and Mickey, too. Then they joined Mickey once again and enjoyed their ice cream while the storm continued to move in their direction.

On the ride home, Niles found himself seriously contemplating the idea of staying on Highway 70 and heading straight for the mountains. By the time tomorrow morning came, Eden would have no idea where they were. Sure, she would send out a search party that consisted of family and friends, and eventually, the police, but they wouldn't find him and Riley anywhere in town. It wouldn't take long for local authorities to issue an Amber Alert. Then everyone within North Carolina and the surrounding states would be on the lookout for them. The make and model of Niles's car, along with his license plate number, would be revealed to the world, and someone would surely discover them within a few days. Yet, that would buy him the time needed to be one hundred percent sure his son was evacuated from Hurricane Florence.

For some reason, Niles had been experiencing a sickening gut feeling about the whole situation and what could possibly happen if Riley remained in New Bern. The rivers were expected to rise higher than ever, causing more significant flooding than Hurricane Hazel brought in 1954. Earlier today, an elderly customer had shared firsthand memories about that storm with Niles and Mickey. He vividly recalled being trapped in a building in downtown New Bern where he said he literally stepped out of a second story window into a boat. He thought for sure he was going to die. The historic hurricane had come ashore as a category four, and what was insane was that the winds from Florence could possibly blow stronger.

Lives would be lost, Niles knew that, but not Riley's. He would do everything in his power to keep his son out of harm's way.

23

Eden woke up the next morning in an unfamiliar bed with a man who was quickly becoming more familiar to her by the minute. Kirk's black hair stood out on the white pillowcase below his sleeping body. He looked peaceful and handsome, and the longer Eden stared at him, the more the events that led her here began to rush back into her mind.

Once the band finished setting up at the bar yesterday evening, she sat down with Kirk and his friends to drink a beer. As a crowd began to fill the establishment like mosquitoes swarming around a pond, the guys crept away from their drinks. Before she knew it, every light in the bar shut off simultaneously. A collective "Ooh" immediately echoed across the room, and Eden imagined that everyone was wondering why the electricity went out before the storm arrived. Then, in unison, a blast of music appeared to flip the breaker for the house lighting, and a streak of wild colors began to dance from the can looking lights above the stage. Eden felt her heart skip a beat even though Kirk, prior to walking to his drum kit, had given her a soft kiss and a warning. He said the lights were going to shut off and his bass drum would sound like an explosion the exact moment the electricity came back to life. Even so, she loved the rush of adrenaline the opening piece of the performance had sent zigzagging through her body. It gave a great first impression for the band, similar to the one Kirk himself made on her at the grocery store.

Eden sat at the end of the bar closest to the stage, as Kirk had promised when he made the quip about the front row ticket. She was close enough to him to feel the swishes of air being created by the rhythmic movements of his constantly flailing arms. He warned her that by the end of the show, he would be "Sweating like a nun in the North Carolina sun," which was a phrase she had never heard. Nonetheless, it made her laugh out loud. It also made sense as she imagined a Catholic woman wearing all of that black fabric during the summer months in this part of the state.

"Maybe I can sweet talk you into taking a shower with me after the concert," was the last thing Kirk said, with a wink, after the nun comment but before walking to the set.

Eden wasn't sure if she was quite ready to take a shower with a man she only recently met, but for some reason, the comment made her smile and, at the same time, feel good on the inside, maybe because of the tone of voice he projected. It sounded like one of those lines where a person was attempting to be funny, but if she were to agree with the idea, he would be perfectly okay with carrying on with it. Either way, she didn't let it keep her from focusing on the concert. She would be lying if she said that while watching Kirk work the drumsticks like a magician works a wand, she hadn't found herself thinking about climbing into a steamy shower with the man. He was beyond sexy—the hair, the tight jeans, his way with words, his musical talent. Whether or not she would admit it or actually go through with it, every woman Eden had ever known imagined, at some point in her life, taking a shower with a musician. It was on the unwritten bucket list, the one a lady would only discuss with girlfriends and never with a significant other.

The music that Kirk's band covered mainly fell into the rock genre, and she recognized songs belonging to Aerosmith, Pink Floyd, Coldplay, and others she'd heard throughout the years. They also performed original music, and while she had a difficult time making out some of the lyrics, it sounded nearly as good as the titles she knew. At first, she hadn't even noticed that a microphone was set up above Kirk's drum set, but when he began to sing backup, she quickly realized that his voice was fantastic, adding another talent to his list. The way he would glance at her while he sang the sweet parts of a few of the slower songs made her blush. No one else probably noticed, but in her mind, every eyeball was staring directly at the visual conversation being held between her and the sexy drummer. Thankfully, Kirk hadn't spoken into the mic: "This song goes out to the lovely lady at the bar with the blue dress and the dazzling hazel eyes." After the concert, though, he uttered those very words which made her blush again.

The performance came to a close in the reverse fashion of the way it had begun, with the lights shutting off momentarily as the music came to an abrupt stop. Then, the band members made their way to the bar for fresh drinks while Eden's ears kept ringing. It took the guys longer to return from the set than it had to get to the instruments initially because people from the audience were flocking to them like geese to a loaf of bread. Eden didn't notice any of the groupies asking for autographs. Still, they were certainly in awe of the band members, and she was pretty sure that more than a handful of the women, who'd been dancing with their beers held up like lighters at an outdoor show, would be more than happy to hop into the shower with Kirk.

When Kirk returned to her side as sweaty as predicted— although he had quickly changed shirts and used a towel to remove as much moisture as possible from his skin—she made sure not to make a comment about his female fans. Of course, many of them stared hard when his tight black t-shirt came off as he walked off stage. He hadn't tossed it into the crowd, and so far, none of them charged the stage to grab it as a souvenir. The last thing Eden wanted him to think was that she was jealous of those women. Okay, she was a little jealous, especially of the ones who put their hands on him, but she assumed it came with the territory. This made her want to put her own hands on him even more, both at the moment and later tonight when they were alone. As she rubbed his back at the bar while he chugged a bottle of water, she shot a couple of the more aggressive women a look that said, *I'll be the one taking a shower with the drummer tonight.* She could tell that some of them were openly irritated to find out that someone had been waiting on him at the bar. Thankfully, Kirk planted a kiss on her lips as soon as he walked up, and she had to admit that it made her feel like a million dollars. It also seemed to keep the other ladies at bay, unlike what was going on around the lead singer who had a couple of women hanging on him. His girlfriend didn't seem to care one bit; she just kept drinking and disappearing every once in a while for a smoke break. When she would come back, he always made the person who'd taken her seat get up, so Eden guessed that was what mattered most to her. Their interactions, or lack thereof, baffled her.

Following a post concert drink, Kirk asked Eden if she wanted to head out. He mentioned that some of the band members would stick around for a while, but said he would rather enjoy some alone time with her. Of course, she was fine with this idea and ended up helping him load his drum set.

"One day, when you're famous, you'll have someone to do this part for you," Eden teased.

"I must be more famous tonight than I was at my last concert," he professed.

Eden furrowed her brow. "How so?"

"Because I have a beautiful woman helping me load my equipment," he acknowledged, staring at her as she carried one of the stands that had held a large golden cymbal.

The comment caused a smile to play on her face.

When the two of them said goodnight to the other members of the band, Eden made sure to tell each one that it was a privilege to meet him. Kirk then asked if she wanted to go to his place.

"Sure," she agreed.

Because he had picked her up, she had somewhat made the assumption that they would end up back at her house, but it didn't really matter. After the shower comment, she had oddly enough found herself wondering if he brought a set of clothes to change into. Of course, she later discovered the replacement t-shirt, which had already begun to absorb sweat from the internal temperature his body was emitting. Still, she had no idea if he kept another outfit in his vehicle or if he brought one along, knowing that they would most likely spend time together after the concert.

The outdoor temperature was brisk but felt somewhat refreshing after being cooped up in a tight spot with at least as many people as the fire marshal would allow. Eden brought along a lightweight beige cardigan to throw across her shoulders if needed, and she did just that as they walked in and out of the bar carrying pieces of the drum set. While indoors, the spaghetti strap dress proved to be a perfect choice; otherwise, she might be sweating along with Kirk right now.

"Did you enjoy the show?" he asked as his vehicle coasted down the same narrow drive through which they entered hours ago. This time, the headlights pointed the way past a few random trash cans to the main street.

"It was amazing," Eden shared. "You were amazing," she exclaimed as an image of him, sitting on the small rotating stool surrounded by cymbals and what he told her were called toms or tom-toms or something like that, popped into her mind.

Kirk grinned as he turned onto the blacktop and peered ahead at the stoplight at the end of the block. "You're very gracious to utter such compliments."

"They're true," she insisted. "I think I expected you guys to be like one of those local bands who practice in a garage every once in a while and end up basically being decent background noise at a bar. But, I was way off; y'all are very talented."

"Thanks," he said appreciatively, reaching his hand across a cluster of unused napkins in the center console so that he could take ahold of hers. "Benny's vocals are off the charts, so that helps the rest of us sound even better," he added with a wink.

Eden let Kirk slide his fingers between hers as she took in the warmth of his skin. The backside of her hand ended up flat on her bare leg just beyond the hem of her dress with his hand resting on top. The tips of his fingers and fingernails were touching the legs she'd shaved in the shower just before he picked her up this evening.

"Benny does have a nice voice," she agreed, realizing she forgot the lead singer's name until Kirk just mentioned it. Visualizing them on stage again reminded her of something, and she suddenly felt the urge to punch her drummer friend in the shoulder. "And you . . . you didn't tell me that you can sing," she blurted out.

"Ouch," Kirk said with a smirk, pretending to grimace from the surprise whack. He puckered his lips a little and put a frown on his face. "Anyone can sing."

"Yeah, in the shower," Eden pointed out. "By the way, what was the deal with the shower comment you made before going on stage?"

She wanted to put him on the spot, see how he would respond in the hot seat, which at the moment was the driver's seat. Wearing a neutral look on her face, she peered across the car and waited for an answer.

"After a gig, the first thing I want to do is make a beeline to the nearest shower," he revealed, keeping his eyes on the road. However, he was pretty sure he could feel Eden's eyes staring a hole through his temple. "Asking you to join me sounded like fun at the moment," he inserted. "But no pressure, I'm perfectly happy hanging out with you with or without clothes on," he added, squeezing her hand gently.

Eden bit her lip tenderly, but on the side of her mouth where he couldn't see it, and she turned her face and could see herself in the window as clearly as if it were a mirror. "That's good to know," she replied.

"To which component of that sentence is your response directed?" Kirk questioned with a slight snicker.

"Well, I am glad to discover that you have good hygiene," she said, lightening the mood a tad. "It's also pleasant to know that you are fine with me keeping my clothes on if I choose to reject your shower offer."

"If?" he wondered aloud, glancing at her from the corner of his right eye.

Eden always enjoyed the playful banter that she and Niles shared even after they were married, and taking a shower together was a normal routine. The two of them sure could steam up the glass door. There were so many nights when her fingers had traced sketches of tender artwork in the condensation, and there were others when she found herself grabbing the washcloth rack to brace herself. She missed those nights, and she missed the regular exchange of flirty words, which was probably why she was engaging in this conversation topic with Kirk.

"If I had a bathing suit in my purse, I might hop in the shower with you," Eden answered, half-serious.

"Do you?" he inquired.

"I left the purse that doubles as a suitcase at home," she reminded him. "Only brought this clutch," she said, holding it up with her free hand.

"You know, a bra and underwear are basically the same things," he pointed out.

"True," she agreed, "but a shower kind of gets those things wet, and in addition to not having a swimsuit in the purse I don't have, there's not a bra and underwear in there either," she teased.

Kirk nodded his head as he made another turn. "I'll take a raincheck," he tantalized. "If you change your mind, though, I have a pair of boxers and a t-shirt you can wear," he added with a wink.

"Good to know," Eden responded with a snicker. "Even if I don't take a shower with you, will you sing for me while you're in the shower?" she requested.

"Of course," he said. "You can have your very own after-the-show private concert."

"Do I get to make requests?"

"Do I look like a jukebox?" he asked, furrowing his brow.

"A sexy one," she answered, this time being the one who squeezed his hand.

"I'm not certain that I've ever observed a sexy jukebox, but, nonetheless, I will take your words as a compliment."

"What if I said you kind of look and sound like a young Jon Bon Jovi?"

"If I had chops like Jon Bon Jovi, Benny would be the backup singer," he laughed with sincerity.

"Well, I think both of you are very talented, and I really enjoyed the show that you put on. I could see your band on the big stage, for sure."

"Thanks. I'm glad you were able to come," he mentioned, "and by the way, we do practice in a garage."

Eden laughed all over herself as she remembered making the garage comment earlier in the conversation, then she and Kirk continued to talk about the concert as he drove them to his apartment. He never let a lull fill the air and usually had something interesting to talk about. As his eyes darted between her and the road, he explained what he thought his band had done well this evening and what they needed to work on the next time they practiced in the garage. She chuckled again as he made that garage comment after using words like decibels and vocal range and other things she didn't fully understand.

Kirk's apartment was undeniably a bachelor's pad with clothes strewn here and there, paperwork tossed around in random places, and eclectic pieces of furniture scattered throughout. Once inside, he gave her a quick tour and decided that he would remove the drum set from his vehicle tomorrow. Then, he led her into his bedroom where he mentioned she could sit or lie on the bed and call out songs for him to sing while showering in the adjacent bathroom. He left the door wide open, and even though Eden couldn't see the shower, the thought of him undressing in the next room kind of turned her on. She heard the soft flopping sound his t-shirt made when it hit the ground and then the metal clank of him undoing his belt. Suddenly, he appeared in the empty doorway with his pants unzipped and said, "Last chance."

Five seconds later, Eden was off the bed and in his arms. She kissed him passionately as they fell against the door and into the wall. Then, she removed her own dress as he led his pants down his skinny legs. Wearing only underwear, their bodies became flush again until Eden stepped into the shower and pulled him in.

The next morning, wearing a baggy AC/DC t-shirt and a pair of matching boxers, Eden remembered precisely how she ended up in Kirk's bed. Continuing to think about last night, an absolutely unforgettable night, she rolled over. She reached to a nightstand cluttered with junk mail, an empty cup, and candy wrappers. As she and her drummer boy had talked from pillow to pillow until they could no longer keep their eyes open, she was pretty sure she'd set her phone somewhere amid all the mess. When she finally unearthed it, she checked the screen to see if Niles messaged or called her. In her haste to see Kirk yesterday evening, she realized that neither she nor her ex had mentioned a specific time or place to make the Riley exchange. The clock on her phone told her that it was almost eight o'clock, and she knew her mom would soon be hounding her about leaving for Kentucky at a set time. Her dad wanted to leave at ten o'clock after checking a few houses in different phases of construction to make sure each had been properly secured by his crew. The thing was, though, Eden hadn't packed a single bag. Now, she didn't even know if she could get Riley and be ready in time, nor did she know if she wanted to. Lying here next to Kirk made her want to hunker down in New Bern, and when he opened his eyes and slipped his hand around her thin waist, she desired to stay even more. Then, Eden made her final decision when, in a sleepy, yet seductive voice, he asked, "Are you leaving me today?"

24

Although she could have slept in today, Reese woke up around the normal time for a regular workday. Before crawling beneath the covers on her comfy bed one last night before voluntarily heading toward the path of Hurricane Florence, she had even made sure not to set the alarm but to no avail. The plan was for her to spend the next couple of nights on a cheap motel mattress. Once she eventually made it to Wilmington, she would likely end up in an emergency management center on a cot as hard as a piece of foam board. In such places, it was difficult to sleep no matter what. There were typically dozens of strangers packed into a relatively small room where some would snore; others would have bladder issues; and then there would be those who would want to stay up all night telling their life story to anyone who would listen. In a sense, it was college dorm life all over again. Ultimately, everyone would end up with too little sleep and too much caffeine.

Thankfully, Reese finished packing almost everything prior to bedtime. This morning, after treating herself to a long, warm, soothing bath, she grabbed items purposefully left out until the last minute: phone charger, pillow, and a bag containing toiletry items such as her toothbrush, makeup, and hair products. She also made sure not to forget the shadow box, which she planned to keep beside whatever bed she ended up in during the coming days. The only thing she almost forgot was vitamins unless she realized something else an hour down the road, which was when such things often dawned on a traveler. Her health had always been superb, so she didn't have any medications to remember, and she prayed that didn't change anytime soon.

Once her personal items were tucked securely into the Humvee, she switched on the GPS—linked to the laptop computer mounted in the center console area—and an unfamiliar voice suggested the scheduled destination would be reached in a little under five hours. As Reese eased the vehicle out of the neighborhood and made it to the highway, she kept one ear on the police radio. She soon discovered that an Amber Alert had been issued in the state of North Carolina. Knowing that she was heading in that direction, she made a mental note to keep an eye out for the vehicle described as well as the young boy who had been taken by a man.

Thinking of the photos that used to appear on milk cartons, Reese shook her head in disgust as she passed by another mile marker. Both the police and most civilians took every alert seriously, and the new system saved thousands of children's lives in recent years. The chance that she would cross paths with this vehicle or these people were slim to none, but she had been trained not to let the odds derail the mission. Since she wasn't technically working, Reese didn't have anything else to distract her focus. However, she was planning to listen to an audiobook while driving through the mountains. Whether on-duty or not, she always carried a firearm, and if she wasn't working, it was typically concealed. While driving now, her pistol was tucked into a body-strap purse that she would simply slip on over her head upon stopping for food or gas. When working undercover, she often wore the same appendage. It held multiple mags, cuffs, and mace, and allowed her to wear anything from a skirt to yoga pants to the navy blue sweat pants she was rocking today along with a form-fitting long-sleeved t-shirt. This particular strap kept her from having to wear a belt to carry a firearm. She also had a couple pairs of holster shorts, which were basically like the spandex undershorts that athletes wore under their pants or shorts. Only the ones she wore had built-in pockets for carrying a pistol in a variety of areas around the waist or thighs. She usually positioned her firearm at the 4:30 setting on her back. It was easy to access and pull and felt relatively comfortable when sitting or standing.

Reese figured her biggest distraction of the day would be the uneasiness of towing the search and rescue boat along winding roads, which included steep ascents and descents. The downhill part was the most frightening because that's where she would have to apply the brakes to slow down the massive SUV along with the trailer and boat it was hauling. As an officer, she responded to plenty of accidents in the mountains where a boat trailer fishtailed and caused quite a scene. One of the last things she wanted was for the East Ridge Police Department's special operations vehicle and equipment to end up on the front page of newspapers. If she survived such a crash, she might as well turn in her badge and begin looking for a new job.

The confident side of Reese's brain reminded her she'd driven through mountains her entire life and this wasn't any different than the pickup truck and boat trailer her dad taught her how to maneuver in similar terrain. Throughout the years, they'd gone on fishing excursions from places like Knoxville all the way to Asheville. A good night's sleep was a plus, and the coffee occupying her right hand was helping to keep her alert as she passed by *See Ruby Falls* roadside signs and eventually kept her eyes out for falling rocks. She never saw a rockslide happen in person. However, she came across a few on trips and also took part in investigations that involved incidents caused by them. On another positive note, the forecast today called for sun, no rain, and nothing else that came as a red flag to Reese.

25

Niles woke up with his son lying safely beside him. Instinctively, he reached his left arm across the little guy's waist and held onto him like a teddy bear. Riley's chest was rising and falling in a slow rhythmic movement, and Niles watched his son's shirt move steadily to the beat as he felt the effect on the underbelly of his arm. He looked so peaceful resting there with his eyelids collapsed, and little fingers stretched across Banana. Absorbing the moment reminded Niles of the time his son asked him if he cuddled with his stuffed animals when he was away at his mom's house. The question made Niles cry on the inside that day and many others. He felt confident that Riley was asking for two reasons: One, the little fellow wanted to make sure his snuggling partners were taken care of when he wasn't there, and two, he felt like his dad needed something to cuddle with in his absence. Niles and Eden argued a handful of times about Riley not having his own room and sleeping in his dad's bed.

"It's not healthy for his maturity," she would state. "He needs to gain independence."

Niles would fight back with facts like, "Families used to live in one room houses; do you think their children had any trouble growing up to become healthy adults?"

"Families don't live like that anymore," she would argue.

"Yeah, and look at how wonderful the independent children in our society are turning out," Niles would spat.

The debate never changed things on either side of the equation. Niles talked to plenty of parents who wished they hadn't pushed their children to be so independent, especially at young, impressionable ages. Being fair, he also spoke to moms and dads who agreed with Eden's perspective. However, he never pointed out to either camp that the deliberation was a personal one. Another point he often made was that when Riley was in bed with him, he knew his son was safe. How many kids had been kidnapped from bedrooms, and the parents had no idea what had happened until they went in to wake their child the next morning? He realized child abduction was a rare occurrence. Still, he also knew that he didn't have to fall asleep worrying about it happening in his home. A kidnapper would have to pry his pistol and his child from his arms for that to transpire.

As Niles peered at the little boy who had become his whole life's purpose, he knew if Grandyma hadn't assured him that his ex and son were planning to head to Kentucky with them, he and Riley would now be in a motel bed in the mountains rather than in the treehouse. Last night, he was pretty sure he would have kept traveling west toward Interstate 40 rather than turning north when he made it back to the high rise bridge in New Bern. Now, it was morning, and Riley would be going back to his mother's house soon.

Niles was having a hard time taking in the reality that he might not see his son for a week or more, depending on the severity of the storm. These were the things that made tearing a family apart so difficult. Families who could all pack up in one vehicle and evacuate together had no idea how good they had it. The kids would have both their mother and father with them for the trip, and the parents would be able to enjoy the presence of their children. He hoped that such families didn't take for granted what they had, but he doubted any of them could understand what divorced parents and kids went through. It was one of those life situations you literally need to be a part of to begin to comprehend the complexities involved. He absolutely hated hearing people talk negatively about any individual or family who had been pulled apart. The divorce itself was more punishment than such people deserved, and typically only one person in the relationship made a choice for all of the others. Of course, it usually took two people to end up in a situation where the divorce was the best answer, and he still questioned whether this was the case for him, Eden, and Riley. He also learned that you can't always believe everything you hear about the other spouse. Typically, there was truth on each side of the story, but neither was one hundred percent accurate. That's why he chose to do his level best not to talk badly about his son's mother, especially in front of Riley. Nothing good could come from it, and any parent who was caught up in such nonsense should quit immediately. They weren't only damaging the ex's reputation like they were probably begrudgingly hoping to accomplish, but they were also contaminating their child's relationship with both parents by driving a deeper wedge where divorce had already left a permanent crease in their heart.

On chilly nights, Niles and Riley often slept in sweatpants and long sleeve t-shirts. The lack of insulation in the treehouse walls made keeping the heat inside and the cold outside difficult. The heater worked well enough, but Niles liked for them to have a layer of clothes on under the sheet and blanket. Riley had a habit of kicking his socks off in the middle of the night, so Niles often found himself waking up to make sure the covers were pulled over his son.

He thought about waking Riley but then figured there wasn't any reason, and he probably needed as much sleep as possible. At the moment, Niles had no idea what time he would need to return his son to his mother. Thinking of the exchange that way made it sound like the little fellow was a package, which made Niles ponder the stork myth, which, in turn, made him snicker silently as the sheet he pulled up to Riley's chest continued to rise and fall. This little guy was one of the best two packages he ever received, and as he lay there watching him sleep, he sure wished the other package was lying right beside him. Thinking of Eden, too, he wondered why she hadn't mentioned a time to take Riley back or for her to pick him up. Usually, she was on top of things like that. *Oh well*, he decided he wasn't in any rush, so he figured he would wait until he heard from her. With that thought on his mind, Niles realized he hadn't picked up his phone since waking up. He grabbed it from the small nightstand next to the bed and took note that there weren't any messages or missed calls from Eden. There was one text from a customer asking about stabilizing a wooden fence to withstand hurricane-force winds and a missed call from a number he didn't recognize. Once he held the phone to his ear and listened to the voicemail from that caller, he realized the message was from a neighbor of a customer requesting help with hurricane preparation. Although he and Mickey hadn't set any appointments today, they discussed doing a few jobs this morning. Mickey really wanted to leave right after lunch so that they could get settled into the motel this evening in time to go out and enjoy the nightlife. The trip to Hickory would take about four and a half hours of driving time. Mickey would want to veer off at every gas station on the route to buy snacks and candy, so that would add thirty minutes if Niles could limit him to a couple of stops. They would probably need to exit at least once for gas and a restroom break.

Last night, after they made it back to the treehouse, they sat on the deck beneath the stars and tossed around ideas for the name of the business.

"What about Grasshoppers," Riley offered with a smile, completely enamored by the thought of helping come up with a name.

Both Mickey and Niles instantly loved the suggestion. The one Mickey had previously mentioned, Cricket Crunchers, which made Niles cringe and laugh simultaneously, proved to be the seed that led to Riley's epiphany. Everything about the name was perfect. The obvious correlation was that the name Grasshoppers included the word grass. The little creatures also spent most of their time in the grass, like Niles and Mickey. Then, there was an even deeper meaning brought on by the thought of the guys constantly hopping from one yard to another mowing lawns.

"Our logo could have a grasshopper mowing grass," Mickey suggested as they brainstormed the idea further.

"Grasshoppers don't mow grass, silly," Riley chuckled. "They're too little."

Niles laughed so hard that he spit out the gulp of water he just poured into his mouth. Mickey nearly fell out of the seat beneath him, and Riley enjoyed watching both of them respond to his comment in such a way.

"It would just be pretend," Niles explained.

"Like cartoons?" Riley queried.

"Exactly," Mickey answered.

Riley's eyes suddenly grew as big as the moon hovering above the treetops. "It could be a cartoon grasshopper mowing," he suggested.

Both Mickey's and Niles's eyes widened as they peered at one another over the little genius sitting between them.

"That's an amazing idea," Niles applauded, rubbing his son's hair as though he was scrubbing it in the bathtub like he'd done many times throughout the past five years.

"We might need to hire you as our business manager," Mickey added.

Lying in bed this morning, still gazing at his son, Niles was so proud to be his dad. The little fellow loved throwing around name and logo ideas for the business last night. With that in mind, Niles wondered what Riley would be when he grew up, and at that moment, one word popped into his mind—happy. Regardless of whether he chose to be a policeman, a doctor, or a landscaper like his dad, Niles hoped Riley would love his life. He prayed that he would meet an amazing woman, have a couple of kids, and never ever get divorced. If there was one thing he could plan for his son, that would be it.

As if knowing his dad was watching him, Riley's hazel eyes fluttered to life. Last night, when his eyelids grew heavy as they were all sitting on the deck talking, the little guy made him smile when he, as usual, uttered sleepily, "I want to go to bed now." Looking up from his pillow this morning with his arms still wrapped around Banana, Riley grinned. Niles loved his son's bedtime routines. He could vividly remember how happy Riley was every time he woke up since birth, and he cherished it both then and now. *You will be happy*, Niles whispered inside his head.

A few minutes later, the two of them were eating Cheerios with Mickey, whose hair was an absolute mess. So much so that Riley laughed out loud at the first glimpse of Uncle Mickey when he stepped out of his bedroom with groggy eyes. During breakfast is when Niles received a text from Eden. The message read: *Can you bring Riley home as soon as possible?* Niles frowned as he read the words a second time as if Eden forgetting to get her son before leaving for Kentucky had been a possibility.

Before climbing out of the treehouse, Niles and Riley brushed their teeth and gathered a few belongings. Mickey rode along with them, brushing his hair in the car, but Niles wasn't sure if his friend had brushed his teeth. He didn't ask, and he didn't get close enough to find out. Niles hated this drive, even more today than any other day. He despised the idea of not seeing his son for an extended period. As they crossed over the bridge toward New Bern, the idea of heading west rather than taking the exit ramp to downtown played across his mind one last time. This was his final opportunity to know without a shadow of a doubt that his son would not be harmed by Hurricane Florence.

26

Eden absolutely dreaded giving Kirk a goodbye kiss this morning when he dropped her off, but the kiss itself was long and amazing. Even though she wanted to stay with him, she knew she couldn't ask Niles to drop off Riley at a strange man's house. That certainly would not go over well. While lying in bed with her musician, she had ignored her mom's messages and phone calls for as long as possible but then reached out to her after she arrived home.

"Mom, I'm going to have to alter my plans for the hurricane evacuation," she started.

"Darling, what do you mean? Why?"

Eden could sense the confusion in her mother's voice. "Work," she said simply. Blaming the change on her job was the simplest solution, plus there was some truth to it. "My boss needs me to take care of a few emergency situations that have arisen at the last moment." Technically, the email he sent late last night stated that Eden didn't have to come into the office. She could handle the issues via phone and email while evacuating with her family to Kentucky.

"How long will it take?" her mother inquired.

"I'm not sure," Eden explained, leaving herself wiggle room, knowing her mother would formulate a backup plan.

"I know your father is going to be ready to leave as soon as he gets home from work, but I might be able to talk him into waiting until lunchtime, honey."

"It's okay mom, you two go ahead and leave," she insisted. "I've come up with an alternate plan."

"What kind of plan, dear? You're not thinking about riding out this storm, are you? Please tell me you're not."

The worry in her mother's tone resonated with Eden. Honestly, she had no idea where she and Riley would be when Hurricane Florence swept through New Bern. The storm wasn't even here yet, and her mind was swirling a million miles per hour. "Riley and I will drive separately," she divulged.

"It doesn't make much sense to drive two vehicles all the way to Kentucky," her mother pointed out.

"I understand that, Mom, but this will allow me to stay behind and take care of my responsibilities at work, and after the storm passes, I'll be able to return home whenever I'm needed at the office," she stated. "This will also give you and Dad the freedom to visit with Aunt Becky longer if you'd like." She knew that was a valid point since once the storm passed through, she would have to return to New Bern for work within a reasonable timeframe. Plus, her mother was always talking about how she wished she could spend more time with her sister, especially since they weren't spring chickens anymore.

"I guess that would be convenient, but I don't like the thought of you and Riley driving alone all that way."

"We'll be fine, Mom," she insisted.

For a moment, Eden thought the line was going to fall silent, but not with her mom on the other end, she was quickly reminded.

"Let us take Riley with us," she offered. "Then you can focus on your work and get it done quicker, and once you make the drive to Aunt Becky's, you'll only have to take care of yourself."

The line grew quiet for a moment. Eden hadn't even thought of that idea. If Riley evacuated with her parents, she could stay here with Kirk, and both dilemmas would be solved. Her decision not to leave wouldn't give Niles leverage in a future custody case, and she would get to spend time with Kirk. In fact, she would have *alone* time with him since Little Man would be away. Although the thought of not seeing her son for a period of time longer than the weekends he spent at his dad's house nearly made her cry into the speaker.

"I know your daddy would be fine with Riley tagging along with us," her mother assured once the silence became too much.

27

In between listening to scenes from the novel *Necessary Lies* by Diane Chamberlain, Reese took phone calls from her mother, Dominguez, and Captain Lawson. Road trips were so much fun because it gave her an opportunity to relax and think about things that didn't matter in the grand scheme of life. For instance, she had been trying to decide whether she preferred a male or female voice when listening to audiobooks. The narrator of the story playing through the speakers as she guided the Hummer carefully along mountainous roads was a woman, and Reese quite enjoyed her tone. The book was set in the 1960s in a rural North Carolina town. The location was why Reese selected the novel in the first place. As the dialect of a southern lady painted images of life on a tobacco farm in a different era, she imagined what it would have been like back then. Those were the days when her dad grew up, and some of the stories he told reminded her of the book. She imagined how it would feel to wear handmade dresses or overalls, and she was nearly certain that she would have preferred the latter of the fashion options. It was difficult to fathom having to walk barefoot into town on dusty roads or plant, tend to, and pick crops in a wide-open field with the summer heat bearing down. Food wasn't easy to come by in those days, and she recalled her dad sharing stories about splitting a sandwich three ways with his brothers on more than one occasion.

"Did you ever have to split a dinner with your siblings?" Reese asked Dominguez when they were on the phone.

"We grew up about as poor as a family could be without being homeless," he reminded her.

During their time as partners, they talked a lot about their respective childhoods and what led each of them to become police officers and eventually detectives. Dominguez personally witnessed so much crime in his community that he wanted to do something to help put a stop to it. He later came to the realization that ending violence was for superheroes. Nonetheless, he wanted to put a dent in the number of 911 calls.

"So, you did?"

"Of course," he said. "We would share a chicken leg, a piece of corn on the cob, and a biscuit. I think my dad had stolen the meal from one of the local restaurants," he laughed.

Reese shook her head sideways and smirked a little.

Her first conversation today had been with the captain who checked in after the morning meeting. It sure was nice to be able to miss out on that daily ritual, she'd thought to herself while driving mostly in the right lane. For some reason, motorists didn't seem as intimidated by a police Humvee pulling a boat, and she discovered this over and over as she watched vehicles speed by in the left lane. After sharing this insight with the captain, he chuckled.

"Did you grow up on a farm?" she asked her boss near the end of their phone call.

"What does this have to do with your trip to North Carolina, Kirby?" he examined all businesslike as if talking about something personal was against official police rules.

"Nothing," she divulged.

"Yes, I did grow up on a farm. Picked tobacco. It's just as tough of a job as being in the military crawling through swamps in a foreign country or chasing America's most wanted with a team of FBI agents."

Reese raised an eyebrow. She knew about the captain's last two resume lines but not that he grew up on a tobacco farm similar to the one in the currently paused novel. Apparently, she touched on a talking point because he spent five minutes talking about farm life and why he respected and appreciated farmers nearly as much as those who placed themselves in harm's way for the sake of others. The final thing the captain mentioned was to be on the lookout for the vehicle described in the Amber Alert. Of course, she went on to explain that she heard the announcement and was paying close attention to updates regarding the case. While closing in on the North Carolina border, she learned that the man and boy might be traveling west and possibly began driving yesterday evening or this morning, which meant they could have very well made it to any of the areas she would be driving through or stopping at today. They could have even made it into middle Tennessee by now, she realized, but that wasn't going to deter her from watching for red flags.

When Reese chatted with her mother, the conversation was a bit lighter. The baker on the other end of the line discussed in grave detail a molten chocolate cake that was currently rising in her convection oven. She mentioned something about needing to turn off the fan, which went over Reese's head. Then she went on to explain that a group of six women from her bridge club would be joining her for tea and brunch. In turn, Reese filled her in on the minor details of the trip, including a driver who had shared his middle finger for no reason, but probably because she was a police officer. On a happier note, a little boy in a car seat waved at her with great enthusiasm and made her morning even more than the cup of coffee now sitting empty in the cupholder. She smiled and returned the gesture, and just as she had with every vehicle that passed by today, Reese looked closely at every person. The people in that particular car, however, didn't come close to fitting the description on the Amber Alert.

Listening to the audiobook once again, Reese began to consider searching for an exit where she could find a second round of coffee and a clean restroom. When she pulled off the interstate twenty miles later, she eased the vehicle and boat into a gas station. In that area, she noticed a swarm of utility trucks that had apparently stopped for similar reasons. While driving today, she spotted these large vehicles by the dozens, all headed east like her to help with the damage that would be caused by the hurricane.

28

As twilight began to soften the colors of the sky, Niles guided the car into the parking lot of a familiar motel where he and Mickey lodged on previous trips to Hickory. While a subtle combination of pinks and blues painted a magnificent scene overhead, the place where they would wait out the hurricane wasn't much of a sight. However, it worked perfectly for the budget, or lack thereof, of two bachelors in their early twenties who recently started a small business. During the trip west, the guys spoke the words Grasshoppers Lawn Care a dozen or more times. There had been three pit stops at gas stations for the smaller bladder in the car, and while there, Mickey loaded up on sugary treats just as Niles predicted. While eating sour candy and destroying rock songs lyrics, they had kicked around other Grasshopper-related name ideas such as Grasshoppers Landscaping, Grasshoppers Lawn Maintenance, Grasshoppers Mowing, Grasshoppers Lawn Service, and simply Grasshoppers. Always thinking about their line of work was an occupational hazard, and Niles couldn't help but notice that the motel could use their services. However, they weren't here to work. Mickey echoed that sentiment and then pointed out that there would be plenty of cleanup jobs waiting for them back at home once

Hurricane Florence floundered out. For that reason, they ignored their phones during the trip and focused on having fun.

The grassy areas around the dated establishment were ankle high with sprouts of weeds pretending to be wildflowers, and the bushes looked like green balls of fire shooting flames haphazardly. The entrance to each room was a black door on the exterior of a red brick building. Like ivy, rusted stairways climbed all three floors to outdoor walkways, which stretched the length of the motel on every level.

After checking in at the front desk where a woman smacking gum and watching soap opera reruns handed over a key—a literal brass key—to their room, the guys plucked three bags from the trunk of the car and began to climb the stairs to the top floor.

"I'm so glad we didn't get stuck on the first floor," Mickey announced, shouldering his luggage with ease and feeling comfortable with the climb in a pair of mesh shorts and a t-shirt. "I hate being at ground level at any hotel, but at this place, it seems even worse."

Niles snickered. "Well, once you told the attendant that you'd rather sleep in the car than on the bottom floor, I think she realized how much of a chicken you are, and she felt bad for you."

"This chicken can kick your butt," Mickey declared, suddenly swinging his left leg toward Niles's rear end causing Niles to dance while attempting to balance a bag weighing down either shoulder.

"You missed," Niles pointed out as he began to climb another floor. "What is it about the ground level that freaks you out so much?"

"I'm not scared of being down there," Mickey stated, glancing over the railing and standing there for a moment to watch his spit drop to the blacktop. "It's just annoying. Vehicles drive in and out of the parking lot at all hours, shining lights in the windows; people slam car doors and walk by your room, talking loudly and acting dumb. It's just weird," he said. "Plus, if it floods, you're screwed."

"Uh, Mickey, we drove almost the entire way across the state to avoid the flooding, remember?" Niles reminded him. "We probably won't even get rain from Hurricane Florence here."

"Dude, I grew up in this area. Hickory is a mixture of plains and mountains. Water can move in mysterious ways in this foothills region."

Mickey pushed the key into the doorknob, and a moment later, the hinges squealed as the guys stepped into the dingy room, letting a burst of light into an otherwise dark square.

Niles sniffed as he entered. "This room smells like it's been flooded a time or two," he proclaimed.

Mickey snickered. "That's your feet, bro," he teased.

"By the way, Hickory is known for furniture, not flooding."

"Apparently someone forgot to tell the owners of this motel that," Mickey laughed as his eyes surveyed the room's decor.

The furniture looked like it was straight out of a 1970s sitcom. The ceilings were low, which seemed to make the random stained splotches appear more prominent. Thankfully the bedding looked clean, and when Niles put down the bags, he noted that the linens smelled relatively fresh.

Each of the guys wandered around the room, independently checking out the random things most people investigate within five minutes of being in a rented space: light switches, lamps, television, microwave, mini-fridge, closet, and bathroom.

"Check this out, there's a Jacuzzi tub in here," Niles's voice echoed from the bathroom. Mickey poked his head in and then rolled his eyes. "Just kidding," Niles added with a laugh.

The small bathtub was stained more than the ceiling, but Niles guessed that such was to be expected.

"Jerk," Mickey titled his friend as he took in the view of the sink and the toilet. "It's all good, though, we won't be spending much time in this place anyway. There's no sense unloading a bunch of cash on a room we're only going to sleep in; when the lights are out, we won't be able to see any of this stuff."

Mickey was an on-the-go type of person, no matter where he was. From past experiences on out-of-town trips, Niles knew that his friend always preferred to be doing something, whether it was checking out a new bar, rock climbing, or zip lining.

"As long as bugs aren't crawling on me, I'll be fine," Niles responded. "But, you know what's weird. When we camp out, there are insects everywhere, and it doesn't seem to bother us one bit."

The two of them did a lot of camping over the years. It all started in their backyards when they were kids, and now they liked to visit random places and pitch a tent for a night or a weekend while basically living off the grid. It fit their lifestyle.

"True, but you remember that time when the roach crawled into your ear?"

Niles saw this story coming from a mile away. If Mickey told it once, he told it a hundred times.

"How could I forget?"

"Dude, that was freaking crazy. You woke up screaming like a baby."

Niles drew a questionable look with his face. "I was only ten, and I thought I had a major ear infection."

"You had a roach infestation," Mickey exclaimed. He used that line before, but it never got old. "It was crazy how your parents looked into your ear with a flashlight that night and couldn't see anything."

"I think they gave me some Tylenol and sent us back out to the tent."

"Yeah, your dad said to 'Suck it up, buttercup.'"

"How long did it take to find out there was a bug living in your ear?"

Niles couldn't help but chuckle now although, at the time, it had been painful and embarrassing. "I believe I went to the doctor a day or two later, and through that tiny microscopic looking thingy they use, he happened to catch a glimpse of a tiny leg somewhere deep in my ear canal."

"You're lucky that you didn't end up with hearing damage?"

Niles squinted his eyes and tilted his head like quizzical dogs often do. "Huh?" he said, then couldn't help but laugh again.

"Let's go get some grub," Mickey randomly suggested, changing the subject without even meaning to. "I'm already tired of being in this place," he announced.

Niles shrugged his shoulders in agreement. A moment later, he and Mickey grabbed a few personal items, and then Niles pulled Banana from the small suitcase and laid him on one of the pillows.

29

Pacing from one room to another like a dog in a cage, Eden was freaking out. After waking up in a heavenly mood, the day had not gone at all as expected. So far, she spent much more time than she wanted on the phone. There were numerous conversations with her attorney, a judge, and even the police. An Amber Alert had been issued first thing this morning, and ever since then, the day became a whirlwind. She was providing paperwork to authorities all over the place and responding to questions she'd never heard before. What made the situation even more strenuous was that her support system wasn't here to help her work through this dilemma. Her parents were on the road to Kentucky; her friends evacuated to places all over the country; and most of her coworkers, including the boss, did the same. A terrible headache set in early in the day, and she was afraid it was going to become a migraine if she wasn't careful. Although there was only so much she could do about that, she didn't have time to sleep it off like she usually would. If her count was accurate, so far today, she'd taken eight ibuprofen, at least two of her nerve pills, and prescription migraine medication. Trying to drink plenty of fluids and eat a little here and there had been challenging, and honestly, she didn't have an appetite.

On top of that, there hadn't been time to make a meal or even grab fast food. The protein bars she nibbled on would have to do. She made multiple trips to the office, went back and forth to her house several times, and had driven all over the county on a wild goose chase. As if the hurricane hadn't caused enough of a stir, now this, she thought as tears zigzagged down the paling skin on her aching face. Of course, Niles wasn't answering his phone, and she had a good idea why. No one seemed to know where he was and whether he'd left town. There had been a time when she always knew where Niles was; when they were married, he was the type of husband who told her everything. If he was going to a friend's house, he would give her a heads up. If he was taking Riley Cameron to the park, he would check in with her first. She hated not being able to get up with him.

Kirk was with her now and had been helping, but he just didn't fully understand the situation at hand. How could he, though, she contemplated; this man didn't have kids of his own. Before a person has their own children, they just don't quite realize the responsibility of being a parent. She knew she hadn't, although, in her adult years, she hadn't known life without being a parent. As a mom, she now knew that she would do anything for her child. The Amber Alert reminded her of that and had instantly brought out her mother bear mentality. She would defend Riley with whatever means necessary. She would hurt someone, anyone if the situation required it. Killing a human being under such circumstances would become as natural as it was for a wild animal. These thoughts circled through her mind like they had been doing all day, and she wondered if the medicine was making her feel even crazier than she should. Her vision was splotchy, and she was seeing auras. She wanted to take something else to help dull the pain, but she knew that wasn't in her best interest at the time being. She needed to focus, and it hadn't helped that Kirk just kept saying, "What can I do to help?" She didn't know how else to answer him. She already said, "Find Riley," "Get me alcohol," "Leave me alone," "Just hold me," and some of those statements she uttered more than once. She even cried on his shoulder a time or two. Right now, though, she needed space. She needed to be alone. That was the reason she requested his presence in the first place, to have someone help keep away all of the distractions. She also needed him to drive her around and make sure she didn't stop until this was over.

As Kirk guided the car down a city street near her home, she scoured a small patch of woods with her 'mom' vision. She searched for his vehicle in every parking lot, each driveway they passed, and on every road as traffic was moving heavily due to the storm. This part of the process wasn't her job, but as a mom, how could she not look? How could she sit at her desk or on the couch and wait for a phone call? That seemed impossible. She wanted to help find him. She wanted to restore life to normal, to go back to worrying about the hurricane and the evacuation.

30

As darkness was completing its goal of taking over the evening sky, Reese eased the Hummer and trailer into the motel parking lot. Upon arriving in Hickory this afternoon, she went straight to the police station rather than checking into the room where she would be waiting on the storm to make its move. When she shook hands with the officer who her captain had been in communication with about the hurricane supplies, she could instantly tell that the man was a kind human being. He went on and on about how he wished he could help firsthand with the efforts in Eastern North Carolina. Reese made sure to remind him that both he and the department were helping mightily by providing water, toiletries, and other supplies that would directly benefit victims in the aftermath of Florence. It took three officers fifteen minutes to load everything into the Humvee. As Reese forged her own parking spot in the motel parking lot, she noticed again that she couldn't see out of the back window. When she thought about how the added weight would cause the vehicle to get even lower gas mileage, she snickered. That must be where the department planned to spend the budget for this trip because it certainly wasn't being spent on this motel, she knew. Keeping an eye out for the Amber Alert vehicle, she found herself scanning the parking lot, which endured cracks making it appear as though an earthquake had shaken the area a time or two. She didn't see anything that fit the description of the getaway car, but she did notice how the grass needed a haircut, and the stairways that guests climbed to reach rooms on the upper floors appeared as though they could cave in at any moment. On paper, The Hickory Valley Motel sounded much cuter than in real life. She imagined that if Captain Lawson's assistant had researched the place online, the photos must not have highlighted the asphalt, railings, or the woman in the front office who looked like she'd recently woken from a catnap.

When Reese checked in, she couldn't help but stare at the bronze key for a moment. *Really?* That was the only word that came to mind. On a positive note, she could attach it to her keyring, making it easy to keep up with. This way, she would be less likely to lock it in the room accidentally like the plastic card keys and then have to feel dumb asking for a replacement.

Upon entering her room, she checked out the amenities or lack thereof but delighted when she bent down and smelled the fresh linens. There wasn't a cookie on the pillow, but she wasn't planning to use the motel's pillows anyway. A moment later, she moved it and tossed her own on the bed and then set her dad's shadow box on the dated nightstand beneath a lamp that could pass for an antique.

Taking in the place made her appreciate the decision to wander around town and stop for dinner prior to heading to the motel. However, if she had known about the yellowing walls and funky smell, she would have opted for dessert and read a few chapters in one of her new books while sipping on a beverage rather than coming here.

Sitting on the edge of the bed, she decided to pick up the local attractions book. The lady at the front desk mentioned that the motel was within walking distance of downtown, so she searched for a decent bar where she could have a couple of drinks to pass the time. Knowing there wouldn't be any reason for driving the department's vehicle for the rest of the evening, she figured she was now on personal time and could legally consume alcoholic beverages. After reading the reviews of a couple of places, she took a shower and pulled on a pair of comfy jeans and a maroon V-neck top. Wearing the same tennis shoes she slid on at home this morning, she turned the lock with the newest key on her keyring and began walking toward the Olde Hickory Tap Room. The guide promised that the popular establishment wasn't far. Still, as the brisk air wafted against her face, blowing her short hair back toward the motel, she was glad that she'd snatched a lightweight pullover from her suitcase. It kept her arms warm as she waltzed down the sidewalk before reaching a beautiful commons area, which separated two rows of attached buildings in what she assumed must be the hub of downtown. There were parking spots scattered around the bricked pedestrian walkways, and she could imagine this place brimming with an eclectic group of people on the weekends. A Wednesday evening in September proved to be a bit slower paced. However, cars still dotted the area, and a handful of people were sprinkled about the walkways, quaint grassy areas, and beneath the modernly-designed verandas. Two couples were walking dogs; a woman around Reese's age was jogging; a few people were sitting under the canopies; and others appeared to be heading into or out of the restaurants, bars, and shops. Reese assumed that many of the stores had probably locked their doors at five o'clock.

Again, she found herself scanning the rows of parking for the Amber Alert vehicle. One drew a red flag, but once she inconspicuously stepped closer, she realized the color didn't quite match, and neither did a couple of the other details from the report. She watched people, too, although she doubted this would be a place where someone would bring an abducted child. On the other hand, the motel where she was staying would be a more suitable hideout for a night or two. Pressing on, she made a mental note to glance over the lot upon her return. The areas she would walk back through later this evening to get from the bar to her room were relatively well lit. Still, she didn't like not having her firearm while in an unfamiliar place. However, like any other citizen, she wasn't permitted to carry a gun when consuming alcohol. The badge didn't allow that, but, of course, right next to the bronze key, a tube of pepper spray was her best friend.

31

"We're here to party, drink beer, meet hot young ladies, and have fun," Mickey reminded Niles as they sat in a high-back booth inside the Olde Hickory Tap Room.

Nearly everything inside the establishment was made from wood: the bar, walls, booths, tables, and floor. The only things that weren't made of wood seemed to be the green seat cushions, the golden light fixtures, and the beer.

"I am having fun," Niles promised even though at the moment, his mind was on Riley's whereabouts rather than impressing women. Mickey, on the other hand, had already received a compliment regarding his bow tie, which accented a button-up shirt and a pair of dress slacks. Niles preferred to wear comfy gym clothes like the ones he'd worn all day, but he let the guy sitting across from him convince him to change into a pair of jeans and a polo shirt. "However, the birthdate on my driver's license states that I'm not supposed to drink alcohol, but as long as our waitress doesn't catch on to the fact that we're sharing yours, I'll continue to drink beer with you," he laughed, knowing that the volume of the music coming from the surround sound speakers wouldn't allow anyone to overhear their conversation.

A few minutes ago, the server removed their emptied dinner

plates, and now Mickey was waiting on his fourth beer of the evening. Ordering enough for Niles had been something he'd done since he turned twenty-one earlier in the year.

"I can't wait for you to turn twenty-one so that we can legally drink together," he snickered. "I still can't believe that you didn't let me get you a fake I.D."

"Dude, I have a five-year-old son; I can't get busted with a fake I.D.," Niles reminded his friend as bottles were being passed around like business cards at a Chamber of Commerce function. "Eden's lawyer would eat me alive."

"I know, I know. But it's crazy that you were able to join the military and are legally responsible for a five-year-old but can't lawfully drink booze. What's wrong with our country?"

"A lot of things," Niles answered, leaning toward Mickey as he spoke. "However, the reason a lot of people our age have kids is because they drank too much alcohol," he revealed, although such wasn't true in his case. When he and Eden started having sex, they hadn't recognized the risk, only the reward. Even so, he wouldn't trade his baby boy for all the freedom from responsibility this world had to offer a single man with no children.

"True," Mickey agreed, and then his eyes lit up like a sparkler on the fourth of July. "Speaking of sex and alcohol," he began as he reached into his pocket. "I had these made for us," he revealed, sliding two black and gold square wrappers across the table at his buddy.

Like a paper football, the packages slid quickly across the slick wooden surface, and Niles caught them just before they could fall into his lap.

"Why are you showing me your condoms?" he queried.

"The wrappers are custom made," Mickey shared. "There is a whole box of each in my suitcase at the motel," he added with a grin that matched his wild, frizzy hair.

Mildly embarrassed by the thought of patrons at nearby tables noticing the items Mickey plucked from his pockets, Niles's face reddened a shade. "What the heck?" he snarled as he studied the packaging closer.

"Is that sweet or what?" Mickey shrieked. "Think of all the fun we can have with these things," he announced. "I mean, even before they're opened. Girls are gonna think these are hilarious."

Although Niles wasn't fond of this idea, he couldn't help but snicker. Before he could come up with a legitimate response, Mickey began to explain what Niles was figuring out with his own two eyes.

"They're rubbers with our names and phone numbers printed directly on the packaging. Well, your name and phone number are on your set, and my name and phone number are on mine," he said proudly.

"I didn't even know that such a thing existed," Niles proclaimed.

"Bro, you can order anything online," Mickey declared.

Suddenly, a voice hovering above the table interrupted the conversation. Before looking up, Niles found himself clumsily attempting to cover the condoms with a napkin.

"I brought your beer," the waitress announced with a well-painted smile, placing a glass filled with golden liquid in front of Mickey.

Mickey glanced up with a grin, winked, and said, "Thank you, sweet girl."

Niles could see their server from the corner of his eye but rather than look at her or Mickey, he gazed at a wood knot interrupting the flow of grains in the table. As he waited for her to walk away, he began to realize that this was the same sensation he felt as a student in high school when trying to hide a love letter from the teacher.

"Happy to serve you, my friend," she responded cheerfully with a smile that Mickey thought was a little wider than what she had been sharing with customers at the other tables. Then she turned to Niles, and he could sense her eyes beaming right through him. "And you don't have to hide your rubbers; I've seen a few of those in my days."

As she walked toward the next table with a grin on her lips, Niles's face completed the process of reaching another tier of redness.

"She's so hot," Mickey declared. "And I think she likes me."

"You think every woman likes you, Mickey," Niles reminded his friend as his face slowly began to thaw out. "Plus, she's probably forty years old."

Mickey jerked his head back, and his hair followed. "You think she's that old?"

Niles furrowed his brow. "At least."

"Who cares," Mickey answered, taking a swig of his fresh drink. "She's smokin'," he uttered. "But, I can't talk her into partying with us tonight since she's working late." He'd already asked.

Niles shook his head and snickered. "Bummer," he responded, pushing the napkin that was covering the condoms toward the center of the table. "Why did you order these with my name and number on it?"

"Because you need to get laid."

"This is stupid," Niles disputed. "What do you even do with them?" he inquired. "I mean, would you just leave one on the table for our waitress?"

"Try it," Mickey encouraged.

"Heck no, I'm not leaving a condom with my number on it for some woman who I don't even know."

"Why not?" he asked. "Are you afraid she might call?"

"Her boyfriend or husband might call," Niles exclaimed.

"That's when you just tell him that someone was playing a prank on you," Mickey suggested as though he'd thought out specific scenarios.

"Yeah, good luck with that. I'm not trying to get shot over some dumb condom."

"I'd recommend asking her if she is single first," Mickey suggested.

"Dude, these things aren't going to work, and I'm not going to use them."

"Suit yourself, but I am planning to give one to the blonde at the bar before we leave this place," he shared.

Niles glanced at the blonde, knowing exactly which one his friend was referring to; Mickey had been talking about her ever since she walked in the door and sat at the bar alone. Honestly, Niles was kind of surprised his buddy hadn't made his way over there yet, but he also knew that Mickey loved food and beer as much as he did women.

"You get dibs on the next cute lady who walks in the door," Mickey said the moment after noticing an attractive, petite woman with short black hair step in without anyone in tow.

"Sounds fabulous," Niles answered sarcastically. "But it's a weeknight, so your blonde might end up being the only single lady in this joint tonight."

"I think you're wrong about that," Mickey responded with a nod of his head.

Niles twisted his neck and set eyes on one of the most attractive women he had ever seen. As she confidently made her way to a barstool across from their booth, he forced himself to look away so that he wouldn't be caught staring. Mickey didn't seem to mind.

"You set me up for that one," Niles noted.

Between the bar and where the two of them were sitting, a single row of high-top tables ran parallel through the area, and only half of those were occupied. The gorgeous lady was now less than ten feet from their booth, and Niles could sense her presence.

"Sure did," Mickey agreed with a slick grin. "She needs a condom with your name on it," he howled.

"Not going to happen."

"I'll help you out," Mickey offered. Ten seconds later, without permission, Niles watched his confident friend plop down in the empty barstool next to the woman as if she had been saving it for him.

"I know you just walked in," Mickey said with a friendly expression covering his face, "but my policy is that a woman should never have to buy her own beer."

"Really?" she inquired, and without skipping a beat, she asked: "Did you buy a beer for that overweight female sitting alone at the end of the bar?"

Mickey glanced in the direction in which the woman's eyes shifted at the mention of the other person.

"I bought her water," Mickey replied without hesitation, somehow keeping a straight face. "I figured she didn't need the extra calories."

The petite woman's black eyebrows rose toward the jagged part in the middle of her hair. "You have a way with women, huh?"

"The truth is my buddy is too shy to walk over here, introduce himself, and buy you a beer, so I figured I'd do it for him," Mickey revealed.

With a poker face, she stared at Mickey for a moment then glanced over her shoulder at Niles, who was fidgeting with his fingers. "You guys have much luck playing good cop, bad cop?" she asked, surprising Mickey by knowing who he was referring to when he mentioned his friend.

"How did you know which guy I was talking about?" he asked with a smirk, assuming that she must have thought at least one of them was cute.

"In my line of work, I notice people," she stated bluntly.

"Did you notice how cute he is?"

Mickey was pretty sure that his comment elicited the slightest of smiles from the black-haired lady.

"I noticed he's shorter than the average man."

"That's not nice," Mickey said, standing up for his friend.

"It's not nice that you didn't buy the fluffy woman a beer either, but you didn't." She paused for a moment. "And if you really sent her water, then that's just plain mean."

"You were the one who said she was overweight," Mickey growled.

"And you're tall," she noted. "I'm just pointing out facts; I'm not insulting anyone."

"Neither am I."

"You've insulted me," she accused.

"How do you figure?" Mickey asked, somewhat taken aback.

"By assuming that I need a man to buy me a beer."

"I'm not assuming anything," Mickey shot back.

"You come across as a man who gets paid to talk," she declared. "How do most women that you hit on get you to shut up?" she inquired.

"Some of them kiss me," Mickey said with a serious face. "Others slap me," he admitted with a mischievous grin. "But you don't need to do either," he acknowledged. "I'm genuinely trying to help out my friend, and I thought I'd come say hey, try to make you laugh, and tell you what a great guy he is," he explained. "On second thought, though, I doubt you would be good enough for him." The bartender danced over, and Mickey asked her to add whatever the lady was drinking to his tab. "Here's the good thing," Mickey started, backing away from the woman he was sitting next to who shocked him by ordering a beer. "I'm going to leave you alone now and go try a different pick-up line on the cute blonde at the opposite end of the bar from the overweight chick you pointed out. You don't have to worry about my friend coming over here to bother you because . . . well, his wife left him over a year ago, and I'm not sure he has talked to a chick other than his mother ever since. As for the beer, you can drink it if you like, or if you want to buy your own beer, you can send it down to the chunky girl. You can even tell her it's from me if you want payback for the apparent insult."

Oblivious to what had been said, Niles watched Mickey abruptly stand up from the barstool, turn in his direction long enough to wink, then head toward the blonde. The entire time that his friend sat next to the cute girl with the short black hair, Niles wished he was a bird sitting on Mickey's shoulder. He figured that Mickey was talking about him, and he even caught a glimpse of her eyes when she'd turned and looked in his direction. Of course, at that very moment, Niles shifted his head just as quickly as he moved his hands earlier to cover the condoms.

Sitting alone, Niles wondered if Mickey thought he would actually go up to the bar and talk to the woman. The way Mickey winked at him made him believe that she might be interested, but he found himself hoping that she wasn't. In fact, he was pretty sure that she wasn't. Otherwise, Mickey would have come back over to tell him rather than going to talk to the woman who was now laughing at his friend's jokes. On the other hand, Niles hadn't noticed the girl with the black hair laugh a single time; she spent more time staring straight ahead as Mickey talked rather than looking back at him. Niles was pretty sure that his sidekick had just struck out for him. Was that worse than striking out for yourself?

Growing bored, Niles thought about paying for his meal and walking out of the place alone, but instead, he took another swig of the beer Mickey left behind. His mind shifted to Riley, and he found himself hoping that he made the best decision this morning. He knew it was the right one, but in life, he learned that the right choices weren't always the best ones. A moment later, he felt his whole world turn upside down when the petite woman wearing a pair of blue jeans, a burgundy shirt, and black tennis shoes sat down across from him. For a moment, neither of them spoke a word as he stared directly into a set of the most unique green eyes he'd ever seen.

"Thanks for the beer," she finally greeted, lifting the bottle slightly with her left hand, which had been holding onto it since she joined him.

"I didn't buy you that beer," Niles admitted. He didn't want to be rude, but he didn't want her to get the wrong impression either. Mickey was here to pick up women, but he wasn't. She sure was cute, though.

"If you guys are playing good cop, bad cop, you're horrible at it," she declared.

"I'm not playing anything," he answered simply.

The woman pointed the neck of her beer bottle toward Mickey. "Then it seems your friend over there is playing on your behalf," she reported, setting her beverage on the table and clasping her hands as she leaned toward Niles. "He gave me a sob story about how your wife left you over a year ago and said that you haven't been interested in women since."

"He really told you that?" Niles queried, glancing from her intertwined fingers to those green eyes that were now a little closer to him.

"Nope, that's my pick-up line," she answered sarcastically, sharing a quaint smirk for the first time since sitting in the seat that Niles would rather his best friend be occupying. "Yes, that's exactly what he told me, and I decided to come over here and find out if he was lying."

"How would you know?"

"Let's just say that I have good instincts," she divulged.

"What are your instincts telling you?"

Niles suddenly felt like they were playing a game of cat and mouse.

"Based on first impressions—of you, not him—I now believe he was telling the truth."

"What if he lied?"

"I figured I could walk away from you as quickly as I was able to get him to walk away from me."

"So, you fell for his challenge?" Niles quizzed, knowing whatever seed Mickey planted in her mind sparked enough interest to lure her to the table where he was sitting alone. Now, Niles realized exactly why Mickey hadn't come back. "Did you come over here to see if you could restart my heart?" he inquired, half-jokingly.

"I'm not a paramedic," she acknowledged. "But I figured that if you weren't a lady's man like your friend, then maybe you and I could have a real adult conversation. It would sure beat sitting at the bar and having guys like him hit on me while I attempt to have a couple of drinks in peace."

Niles let out a chuckle. "Mickey thinks he's a lady's man," he revealed with raised eyebrows.

"So, his name is Mickey, like the mouse?"

Niles laughed again. It wasn't the first time he heard that line in reference to his best friend's name, but the way she put it was funnier than usual. Maybe because she hadn't laughed or smiled or showed any emotion along with the comment. "He didn't tell you his name?"

"Nope, he wasn't interested in me, and I could tell that from the beginning."

"Really?"

"Yep, it's that sixth sense that I have," she disclosed as she picked up her beer again. "It's in my DNA."

"Did he tell you my name?"

With her lips on the rim of the bottle, she slowly nodded her head and then pulled the beer away without taking a swig. "He didn't."

"I'm Niles," he revealed, almost sure that this was the first time he'd shared his name with an attractive woman since becoming single. It was still odd to think of himself as single, and as these thoughts flashed through his mind, he felt his thumb touch the bottom of his bare ring finger.

"It's a privilege to meet you, Niles," she said easily with a genuine smile playing across her face. Then, she reached her right hand across the table and said, "My name is Reese."

32

Reese gazed at Niles as their hands touched for the first time and then slowly fell apart above the rectangular wooden tabletop where thousands of other people had shared a meal throughout the years. When her father taught her how to shake hands, his instructions were to look directly into the person's eyes, speak clearly, and grasp firmly. Competing with the beat of the music and lyrics that she could barely decipher, Reese made sure to talk loudly, too. This man's aqua green eyes were as inviting as any ocean she'd ever visited, yet as lonely as a discarded shell half-buried in the sand. She was almost certain that beneath the layer of skin he revealed to the world, there were deep emotional scars that only time had the chance of healing. From the information his friend divulged, she assumed the pain had something to do with whatever transpired between him and his ex-wife.

It wasn't normal for Reese to approach a man in a bar, especially one with chin-length hair. However, his stringy, dirty blond hair was tucked neatly behind his ears, and the lower portion was clean cut. He appeared a little rough around the edges, she gauged but predicted he was about as harmless as a turtle, or maybe a snapping turtle. As long as someone didn't invade his bubble, he probably minded his own business. Come to think of it, Reese couldn't remember a single instance where she had been the one to make the first move. Although, technically, in this particular situation, the mouse started the whole thing, so this was more a reaction than an action.

"What's your story, Niles?" Reese inquired as she studied him almost as carefully as she would a person of interest in an interrogation room.

Niles furrowed his brow. "My story?" He wasn't sure what she wanted to know or why. Her voice was firm, confident.

"You know, your life's elevator pitch?"

His eyebrows forced another wrinkle to settle in on his forehead. "My elevator pitch?" he questioned.

"Yeah, your life described in thirty seconds as you're stuck riding in an elevator with a stranger?"

"I don't usually tell strangers my story," Niles sneered as he took in a whiff of a sizzling steak being delivered to a nearby table.

"I like you," Reese revealed, unable to miss the aroma of the steak, and even though she couldn't hear the hissing sound it was making, memory recalled it for her. "You really aren't the typical man, are you?"

"Who is the typical man?" he wondered aloud.

"Your buddy over there," she referenced, once again pointing the rim of the bottle in Mickey's direction.

At that moment, Niles and Reese allowed the conversation to halt as they observed the interaction at the bar between Mickey and the blonde. From the booth, they couldn't hear what was going on over there. Still, they could see the giggly expressions taking place as though the air around the two people they were watching had been sprayed with laughing gas. Every few seconds, Mickey was touching the woman on the arm, the low back, or some other body part, and she was returning the favor without fail.

"She's going home with him tonight," Reese predicted as the taste of a familiar beer slid across her tongue.

"I don't think so," Niles contested. "We don't live here," he added with a snicker.

Reese laughed across the table as she turned her attention back to the man in front of her. "Well, wherever he is going when he leaves here, she's going with him," she concluded. "Where are you guys from, anyway?"

"A little town over on the coast."

"Does it have a name?"

"We call it New Bern," Niles professed.

"You're funny," she declared, giving him a complimentary chuckle. "I believe the map calls it New Bern, too," she proclaimed, finding it ironic that these two guys were from one of the cities where the captain had considered sending her this week.

Niles shrugged. "Most people haven't heard of it."

"Well, it's becoming a lot more popular ever since Hurricane Florence started planning a trip to that area," she informed him.

"Technically, a good portion of the population is evacuating," Niles reported. "So, in a way, it's not all that popular right now," he suggested with a grin.

"Is the evacuation what brought you and your buddy to Hickory?"

Niles nodded his head. "It wasn't worth the risk to stay."

"That makes sense," she agreed, watching him closely as her hand circled the bottle she brought over. She'd never met a man who was so guarded, and she wondered what it would take to tear down his wall. "So, your name is Niles, you're from New Bern, and your ex broke your heart," she reeled off. "I think we're beginning to put your life's elevator pitch together."

Niles felt his lips shift as he thought about the three facts she just put on the proverbial table. "Once we leave this bar, I'll probably never see you again," he pointed out. "So, I'm not sure why you are interested in my life story, but for kicks, here it is: My name is Niles North. I was born in California, moved around to a few other places but spent most of my life in North Carolina. My dad was military, and he died serving this country. In high school, my girlfriend, who was also my soulmate and now my ex-wife, got pregnant. Now, my son, Riley, is my whole world. Mickey and I own a landscaping company, and we live in a treehouse," he revealed. "Oh, and I was also kicked out of the military before I could finish boot camp," he added for good measure.

It suddenly felt as though the music and the roar of nearby conversations faded entirely, and the drop of an ink pen could be heard from the other side of the bar. However, lips were still moving, and the speakers were still spreading sound waves. Niles purposefully shined a bright spotlight on his less than stellar life. Although he wasn't certain if Reese had been interested upon floating over to the table, he was pretty sure that within the next few minutes she would find an excuse to leave.

Reese's heart sank as she swallowed the truth that poured out of Niles's mouth as forcefully as any waterfall she'd ever swam beneath. She studied his eyes and his overall posture and watched him take a long swig from a beer that he hadn't wrapped his fingers around until now. As he glared back at her from across the table, his shoulders seemed to relax for the first time. The words he spoke were probably the truest words that any man had shared with her in her adult life, and she felt that there was only one way to respond.

"My name is Reese Kirby. I was born and raised in Chattanooga, Tennessee. My dad was a police officer, and I always wanted to be just like him. He was my best friend, but he was taken from me way too early when he was shot and killed by someone who didn't even know his name. I've never been married, and I don't have kids, but one day I'd love to have both." She paused for a moment to collect her thoughts, to hold back the sudden urge to cry in the middle of a noisy bar in the presence of a man who had been a complete stranger ten minutes ago. Taking a deep breath, she reached for her beer, took a long swig, and then sat it on a random napkin in the middle of the table. The bottle didn't sit flush, however, and she barely got a secure grasp on it before nearly spilling brown liquid all over the tabletop. The sudden jolt caused the napkin to shift, and beneath where it had been set, she spotted two condom wrappers.

Niles froze as he realized the series of events that brought about this dilemma. Somehow, distracted by Mickey walking over to the bar to talk to Reese and then her unexpectedly ending up across the table from him, he completely forgot about the contraceptives. This time, the revelation automatically caused his face to reach the deepest shade of red on the color wheel, and there was no time nor need to attempt to cover the evidence. It was apparent that the woman sitting across from him had already seen the unmistakable shape of the packaging. At the moment, his gut feeling told him that she wouldn't have the same perspective about rubbers on the table as had the waitress.

With her free hand, Reese reached for the two black and gold packages. That's when Niles recognized he should have snatched them up even after her eyes locked onto the squares like a heat-seeking missile. Too late now, he realized.

"Really?" she asked, glancing up at him before shifting her focus back to the evidence. "Please tell me that these belong to the mouse," she pleaded as she began to study them closer. She wondered if Niles's life's elevator pitch had been a ploy; if this was a game that these two clowns played on many naïve girls. "Oh, wait, they say 'extra-large,' so they can't be his," she jabbed, then she flipped the wrappers and held them closer to her face. Against her fingertips, she could feel the squishy sensation and the rim of the condom through the foil. At this point, she had no idea how fast Niles's heart was beating inside his chest, but when she looked up, she couldn't help but notice the color of his cheeks. "This one has your name and phone number printed on it," she noticed. "Is this like your business card?" she inquired, sliding both packages in Niles's direction. Then, rising from the table, she chose not to make a scene but decided that this conversation was over.

As Reese left her half-empty beer bottle behind, Niles felt like a complete idiot. First, he dropped his head into his hands. Then, he began to jump up and follow her through the bar in hopes to explain but then realized that first, he better snatch the two packages that had already caused enough of a stir. The last thing he wanted was to receive harassing phone calls from the waitress or her significant other. He also took a moment to reach into his pocket and toss three $20 bills onto the table. He knew he was leaving more than enough to cover dinner, drinks, and a tip, but he didn't have even a few seconds to figure out the total in his mind. By the time he hurried for the door through which Reese exited, he wondered if he would be able to catch up to her. As he passed by the area where Mickey and the blonde had been sitting, he realized their bar stools were as empty as the shot glasses from which they had been chugging. They must have slipped out of the place while he and Reese were sharing their life stories, he figured.

When Niles made it outside, he didn't even notice that the air had become a bit cooler as the night sky settled in. Immediately, he began scanning the town commons area and eventually caught a glimpse of Reese in the distance. She was all but running to the far corner of the open space between the two rows of downtown buildings. Soon, she would make it to the sidewalk and be out of sight. At this point, he figured he had two options—either let her go or run after her. Neither seemed best, but as he tried to decide which route to take, he suddenly knew without a shadow of a doubt which was right.

Between him and Reese, there was a group of rough-looking bikers standing in the parking area across the way. When Reese moved past them, Niles could hear them hooting and hollering at her. As he began to move in that direction, he also noticed that she didn't respond to them, she just kept speed walking. Suddenly, he found himself wondering if she was scared and if she was in danger. Then, things appeared to quickly escalate when a few of the men began to follow Reese on foot while the other two hopped onto their motorcycles. Niles yelled out her name, but the roar of loud pipes overpowered his voice as he watched the two-wheeled vehicles rush down the street where she turned the corner and vanished from his sight. He had a good idea that these guys were up to no good. However, no one else in the area even seemed to realize that anything out of the ordinary was happening. He suddenly found himself wanting to search for Mickey because he doubted he could handle all of these bikers alone. Unfortunately, there wasn't time and being outnumbered sure as heck wasn't going to stop him from trying. It wouldn't be the first time he'd stuck up for a woman only to be jumped by a group of grown men and eventually beaten by sheer numbers.

It was then that Niles took off in a full sprint, covering as much ground as possible. Soon, he made it across the commons area and around the corner of the building where the sidewalk led past more downtown shops and eventually to his motel. He wondered if Reese parked in this direction or if she was walking back to her own home or hotel somewhere nearby. He hoped to find her safely locked in her car, where he figured the men would probably leave her alone. At that point, he could simply ease back into the darkness and, hopefully, forget about the last half hour of his life. Unfortunately, this wasn't the case. The two men on motorcycles whizzed past her in no time flat, parked their bikes a little ways ahead, and then began to walk back in her direction. He watched her pause as she realized what was happening, and then she turned and spotted the three men coming up behind her. They spread out like wide receivers on a football field, and at this point, she was surrounded by a circle of five aggressive men. When Niles was within thirty yards of the closest one, he slowed his stride, knowing that the element of surprise would work in his favor.

"Hey, baby," one of the guys called out.

As Niles walked at a steady pace, he began to feel out the competition. He was almost sure that the one who'd spoken first was the leader of the pack because he was a middle-aged man with a decent build and the most patches on his leather jacket. The one who looked the most nervous was a young guy who was fidgety, and Niles figured this might be that dude's first rodeo. A short, chubby old man with a gray beard wearing a mischievous grin on his face was closest to the rookie. The other two fellows, probably in their thirties, gave off the vibe as the fighters in the group. One was lanky and had even more tattoos than the rest; his arms and neck were covered like a tree with bark. The other had a few scars on his face and a black leather vest with no shirt underneath to showcase his muscular physique.

"Where you in a hurry to get to?" the grandpa in the group asked.

"Hop on the bike with me, and I'll take you wherever you need to go," the lanky fellow offered with a wry smile and eyes as dark as Halloween.

In the middle of five scary-looking men wearing leather, chains, and tattoos, Reese circled as if she was the sharp point on a protractor. Like Niles, she began to size them up. Knowing she didn't stand a chance to fight off all of them, she inconspicuously reached into her pocket. A moment later, her finger was resting on the nozzle of the pepper spray. She knew better than to hold it up and warn them. It would be best for the capsaicin chemical to be a complete surprise, but she didn't know if she could stun them enough to flee. It probably depended on how brave and quick the ones left standing were after she squirted a couple of them and took off running. Of course, she didn't have her badge or gun, and she figured they wouldn't believe or care if she told them she was a police officer. Guys like this didn't have much respect for authority anyway, and it might even work against her.

Just as Reese was about to extract the bottle from her pocket, she spotted Niles approaching and immediately knew that he would be a helpful distraction. When she called out his name, every single one of the men turned in his direction.

"Niles, call 911," she hollered, using the opportunity to pull out the pepper spray.

Closing in on the man closest to his path, Niles gritted his teeth at the realization that he just lost the element of surprise. He knew that Reese meant well, but two on five wasn't a fair fight, and, no offense, but his partner was a woman—a petite one at that.

"Welcome to the party," the muscular biker announced, clenching his fists while he cracked his neck with a slow-motion effect.

Unintimidated, Niles forced himself not to laugh.

"Hey, guys, we won't call the cops if y'all just let us walk where we were headed," Niles pleaded, pretending that he and Reese were on their way somewhere together.

"Brother, she was running," the old man nearest to Reese called out. "Probably from you," he heckled.

Reese spoke up. "I was in a hurry to get to the car while he paid for dinner," she lied. "He's my boyfriend, and his mom is in the hospital." Sometimes in a situation like this a fabricated story would help ease the tension.

"We'll take care of your girlfriend for you while you go check on your mommy," the tattooed guy stated, using a childlike voice.

Even though the dilemma Reese invented wasn't real, it pissed off Niles to no end that these guys seemed to have no mercy. That was the moment when he realized that he and Reese wouldn't be walking away from this situation. "I'm not that guy," Niles proclaimed.

Every one of them snickered. "What guy?" the leader of the group asked with an extra chuckle.

"The one who you can talk to like that," Niles exclaimed.

33

The moment the warning spilled from Niles's mouth, the skinny, tattoo-covered guy abruptly lurched within arm's reach of Reese. She decided that spraying him at such a close distance wasn't the best option. Then, every eye widened when she popped him square in the nose. Niles's mouth fell open an extra half-inch because he realized that the diminutive woman hadn't just punched the dude with her knuckles like a tomboy might, she shoved the palm of her hand into his nostrils, and blood began spewing like released water from the fire hydrant he just passed on the sidewalk. It was his turn now, Niles knew, as the gang of macho motorcycle men stood frozen like statues. He decided to make a grand entrance, knowing that most of them would hesitate if he could land a roundhouse kick on the leader's temple. A moment later, the man fell like a domino, and within five seconds of the first blow, it was suddenly two on three.

In her lifetime, Reese witnessed more than her fair share of fights but never had she seen a human being so quickly and effortlessly kick a man in the head the way Niles North had. As the older man approached her, she pointed the bottle of pepper spray directly at his eyes, and when he covered them like a frightened dog, she kicked him right between the legs. At the moment, it felt better than it would have if she had pressed the nozzle and heard him cry for a different reason.

"Good thing you won't be having any more kids anyway," she said as he collapsed to the ground like a broken slinky.

Now it was two on two, Reese realized, and she knew that she and Niles had the advantage. The young guy was the closest standing person to her, and he barely moved an inch since the moment she relocated the tattooed fellow's nose.

Niles felt a surge of adrenaline when he realized that he'd get to go one-on-one with the biggest bad boy of the gang. Even though the fellow appeared a little stunned by what had just happened to his friends, Niles could tell that he wasn't intimidated. He had enough scars on his face to remind himself that he won his share of fights. When he threw a nasty right hook, Niles dodged it with ease and rebounded as if his head was on a spring. In the foreground, Niles watched Reese spray the young guy with something, and he instantly fell to his knees on the pavement and began screaming and rolling around as though he was on fire. The dude Niles was fighting turned for a glance at the commotion. Since Niles knew the others could possibly recover and join the fight, he decided to end this one-on-one battle instantly. He sidestepped and drove his foot into the exterior of the man's kneecap. When his body collapsed in what was obviously an unfamiliar direction, Niles landed a punch square across his face. The moment before he began to fall, though, with his head turned toward Reese, she pointed the bottle at him and pressed the nozzle. The portion of the pepper spray that didn't land shot over his head and Niles found himself shifting his own face as quickly as possible to avoid the substance. Still, a trace amount beat the closing of his eyelids and began to burn instantaneously.

Reese's mouth gaped open for a nanosecond as Niles's eyes fluttered faster than a butterfly's wings. Then, she instinctively yanked off her pullover and carefully dabbed at the residue on his face and in his hair so that no more of it would enter his eyes, nostrils, or mouth.

"I'm so sorry," she cried out, grabbing both of his hands—holding her loose shirt between one of her hands and one of his—and tugging him in the direction of the motel as she spoke. "Don't touch your eyes," she instructed, squeezing his fingers. "The effects are only temporary," she educated, loud enough so that the guys wallowing around like drunken pigs could hear as well. She figured it would be best if their assailants didn't race off to the hospital where they would be hounded with questions which might point authorities toward her and Niles. She knew that the two of them were only defending themselves; however, she didn't want the captain breathing down her neck about this situation. Nonetheless, she decided against telling the bikers they'd most likely be dealing with the symptoms for thirty minutes and possibly longer if they didn't research the side effects.

Niles had never experienced pepper spray before, so he decided to listen to Reese's suggestion since she sounded like an expert on the substance. When she released one of his hands and with the other pulled him like a little girl on the playground racing off with her crush, he followed. Honestly, he had no other viable option.

"Come with me," she instructed.

With his eyes and face burning, and throat beginning to tighten, Niles ran hand-in-hand on the downtown sidewalk away from the city lights.

"I have first aid kits in my vehicle," Reese huffed as she fought to catch her breath in mid-stride. The running wasn't the issue, though, it was the running after the fighting, but adrenaline was still surging, so she knew she could run for miles if need be. Thankfully, that wasn't the case since the motel wasn't far. "You're obviously a fighter so use your mind to overcome the psychological effects of the spray," she explained to Niles.

Niles instantly understood her advice meant for him to ignore the anxiety he felt the moment the spray lit his eyes on fire, and then the frenzy that set in when he began having trouble breathing. The unknowns were what caused fear in situations like this. Questions immediately began to race into his mind. Would he be able to see again? Would he pass out? Running didn't seem to make sense, but he decided to trust Reese as he jogged blindly, only opening his eyes enough to see through foggy eyelashes every once in a while when he second-guessed his instincts. When fighting in a ring, he always envisioned himself knocking out his opponent. In this scenario, he knew he needed to visualize the two of them making it to her vehicle to clean his eyes.

"The fresh air against your face will be good for you," Reese added as the soles of their tennis shoes pounded the pavement. Thank God, she hadn't worn heels or even loafers.

She knew that running down the middle of the road would be easiest for Niles since, at the moment, he probably wouldn't be able to see even if he dared to open his eyes. She held his hand firmly and talked him through every obstacle in their path. When she spotted oncoming headlights, she lured him to the other side of the street, and, thankfully, there wasn't much traffic. They were forced onto the sidewalk at one point, and she had to instruct him when to hurdle a fallen branch. Then, they had to avoid a couple walking a dog before making a turn and finding asphalt again.

"How long is this going to burn?" he finally asked, coughing as he spoke.

"The worst sensation can last up to thirty minutes, but I think you'll be better before then," she explained as they rounded another corner. "Focus on your breathing as if we were running a marathon. Take slow and steady breaths."

"Where are we going?"

"To my motel," she indicated, thankful that the growl of motorcycle engines hadn't come to life and forced them to make any detours.

"I thought you said the first aid kit was in your vehicle."

Niles hadn't expected to run this far, and in all honesty, he was shocked that he hadn't fallen flat on his face. If Reese hadn't practiced this drill, she was a natural. Every time they needed to make a move, whether it was turning a corner or jumping over whatever was on the sidewalk, she first gave the instructions and then squeezed his hand the instant it was time to act accordingly.

"It is . . . at the motel," she explained.

Niles knew he wasn't thinking straight or acting straight or running straight, so he quit talking and tried to focus on his breathing like Reese suggested. He'd never jogged with a blindfold covering his eyes, but that's what this felt like. Plus, the mucus flinging from his nostrils like drool from the mouth of a Saint Bernard reminded him of running in twenty degree weather and being too cold to wipe the snot from your own face.

After what seemed like five minutes of sprinting, Niles and Reese made it to the motel parking lot where she led him to the Humvee.

Lifting his head to catch a glimpse of their surroundings through tiny slits of lubricated eyelashes, Niles was pretty sure that her motel was also his motel. He couldn't quite make out the make and model of the vehicle she was reaching into, but either he was delusional, or it had a bar of police lights across the top. It also appeared to be connected to a boat trailer. At the moment, though, his eyes and face were burning too badly to ask questions, plus his throat was so tight that he wasn't sure if he could even talk anymore.

As Reese led him toward the less than attractive building, Niles began to dread climbing the metal staircase in this condition. He figured that to anyone who could see him like this, he probably appeared drunk, which was kind of how he felt. As he was searching for the will to make it, he heard the jingling sound that only keys make, and then the call of rusty hinges followed.

"You're on the first floor," he proclaimed as they stepped into a room where a familiar odor slapped him in the face.

"I always stay on the ground level," Reese shared, kicking the door shut with the sole of her shoe.

Prior to entering, she carefully surveyed the parking lot and outlying areas to make sure no one was following them on foot. She knew she didn't even have to pay attention to the vehicles on the road; it wasn't like those guys were driving a Prius. Motorcycle engines were easy to pick out, and as she and Niles ran toward the motel, she was relieved not to hear the unmistakable roar. Most likely, the bikers were still picking each other up from where she and Niles left them spread out like fallen acorns from one of the trees hovering above the sidewalk.

"That's fantastic," Niles announced in a huff.

Reese tossed the first aid kit onto the bed and her pullover onto the floor at the end of the room, then she guided him straight into the bathroom where she twisted the nozzle above the bathtub faucet.

If the two of them entered this motel room under other circumstances, Niles would have thought things were about to get wild when she unbuttoned his shirt and told him to keep his eyes closed as she lifted it over his head.

"This will need to be washed," Reese explained as she pulled off the polo and threw it into the hallway where it landed on top of her pullover. "It might have residue on it which could cause more issues if not properly treated."

Quickly, she washed her own hands and then helped Niles lower himself onto all fours before sticking his head over the side of the tub.

"Keep your eyes closed," she advised again as she pushed his head beneath the water. First, she splashed his face thoroughly and then began to run her fingers through his silky blond hair. She couldn't remember how long it had been since she washed a man's hair, but this certainly wasn't how she would have chosen for it to happen this time around.

Water was streaming everywhere: Onto Reese's arms and down Niles's back, dripping onto the floor causing small puddles to begin to collect on the tile around their knees. Of course, that wasn't of any concern to Reese at the moment; she could clean up the mess later with one of the towels hanging on the metal wall rack that looked like it might fall at any moment.

"Are you wearing contact lenses?" she checked.

"No," he answered, water still gushing over his head.

"Good, because if you were, either you or I would have to reach into your eyes and pluck them out," she mentioned. "Which would probably be quite uncomfortable."

"Yeah," Niles huffed, speaking one-word answers when needed so that he wouldn't swallow the water wrapping around his face.

"You can open your eyes now," Reese confirmed. "I'm going to rinse them for you, so try your best not to let them shut."

It stung, but Niles forced both eyes to open wide, and Reese instantly began to splash water into them over and over. With every wave, the heavy burning sensation began to subdue little by little. Once she told him that she thought that part of the job was done, Niles lifted his head and let out a deep breath. His vision was still foggy, but all of a sudden, his attention turned to his throat, which felt like a boa constrictor was wrapping around it and squeezing him like a juicer.

After instructing Niles to wash his hands, Reese led him out of the bathroom and toward the bed, where she put her cold hands on his bare skin. One fell onto his shoulder, and the other pressed against his stomach as she guided him onto the bed like a patient in a nursing home.

"Lie here," she instructed, "and focus on your breathing." She reached into the first aid kit sitting at the edge of the bed. "Do you want a bag to breathe into?" she asked.

"No, thanks, I'm not that wimpy," he laughed, coughing again, his abdominal muscles tightening with the movement.

As Reese pulled a wipe from the kit and began to gently rub the contours on his face, she couldn't help but notice that his chest and abs looked as though an artist sculpted them perfectly from clay. When she'd been sitting across from him at the bar, she wouldn't have pegged him to be this fit and especially not to be such a great fighter. She knew better than to apply oils or lotions, which would only trap the irritant and possibly result in blisters, but she also understood that a cool fragrance-free cloth would feel refreshing at the moment and probably help calm his nerves.

Niles fought to keep his eyes open, but the combination of the lingering burning sensation along with the relaxing touch of a wipe tracing his skin caused them to flutter. They still felt better closed, but he found himself wanting to watch Reese as she moved above him. He was perplexed by her ability to not only fend off her attackers but to leave macho dudes lying on the ground in obvious pain. Sure, she used pepper spray, but she handled two of them without any assistance. Now, she switched into this delicate nurse mode, which made him grateful for her even though she was the reason why the gunk was all over him.

"Thank you for taking care of me," he offered genuinely. "But why did you spray me?" he inquired, knowing she hadn't done so purposefully but curious as to why she sprayed the guy he was fighting.

"I didn't mean to spray you," she explained, expressing her sorrow through the saddened demeanor on her face. "When the young guy started screaming, the buff dude fighting you turned, and I saw an opportunity to take him out quickly so that we could get away before the others had a chance to regain their strength. I just happened to press the nozzle the moment you knocked him out."

"You know I had him under control, right?"

"I was just trying to help," she pointed out. "Plus, the only spray that hit you was the splatter off his face and head," she clarified. "So, don't be a baby, you didn't succumb to a direct hit like those guys," she teased.

"Well then, I sure don't want to know what they're feeling like right now," he admitted.

"Their egos are probably starting to hurt as bad as the physical pain," she laughed, blotting his cheek gently as she spoke.

"Are you a cop?" he decided to ask, gazing up at her.

"Yes," she answered.

"Then why didn't you pull out your gun back there?"

"Because I didn't have one."

"How can you be a cop and not have a gun?"

"I have a gun; I just didn't have it on me."

"Why not?"

"Because I went out for drinks, and I'm not allowed to have my weapon if I'm under the influence."

"Ah, that makes sense," Niles said, letting his eyelids collapse as Reese dabbed them.

"Where did you learn to fight like that?" she asked.

"My dad, my sensei, and my MMA trainer taught me most of what I know."

"How come you didn't include that in your life story?" she inquired.

Niles smirked. "I wasn't trying to impress you," he revealed with a chuckle but then realized that stretching his cheeks caused the skin to burn.

"Well, you did, at least back there on the street," she admitted.

"You're quite the fighter yourself," Niles proclaimed. "Where did you learn how to move like that?" he asked. "I doubt they teach those moves at the police academy."

"They do a solid job teaching self-defense, but my dad taught me how to take care of myself from an early age." Tommy Waters was the first to find out the hard way.

"He did a fine job," Niles concluded.

"Thanks," she replied, glancing at the display on the nightstand, knowing her dad would be proud of her.

"Is that your dad?" Niles probed, studying the photograph and the badge.

"Yes, it is," she revealed proudly.

"Do you still live in Chattanooga?" he asked, noticing the city's name on the badge and recalling that was where she said she was from. "I assume you don't live here since you're staying in a motel."

"I live in Chattanooga, but I work for the East Ridge Police Department, which is nearby."

"What brought you to Hickory?"

"Hurricane Florence," she revealed.

Niles furrowed his brow but then realized that was painful, too. "You'll have to explain that one to me," he requested.

As Reese continued to care for a man she barely knew, she disclosed that she was heading to the Wilmington area but stopped in Hickory for supplies and to let the storm pass. She went on to tell Niles a little bit about her captain and the team of detectives she worked with daily.

"That's cool that you're a detective," Niles declared.

"It's a rewarding job."

"I don't think I've ever hung out with a detective before."

Reese chuckled. "I'm just a normal person."

"Normal people don't have badges," he claimed.

"True," she admitted. "You're not very normal yourself, you know," she professed.

"Maybe not, but nothing is exciting about hanging out with a landscaper," he pointed out with a quiet snicker, trying not to bring on any more pain.

"However, it is exciting to spend time with a landscaper who I just watched knock out a man with a single roundhouse kick."

Niles's lips spread out just a bit further. "I guess I've practiced that a time or two."

"He never saw it coming."

"I could have taken all five of them if you hadn't blown my cover," he proclaimed with a snicker.

"Really?" she questioned, eyebrows raised.

"Definitely," he lied. "Well, maybe," he added with a fresh smirk.

"I was pretty sure I couldn't take all five of them, which was why I tried to use you as a distraction," she admitted, laughing about it now. "I was planning on spraying a couple of them and hoping I could outrun the rest of the group since they were wearing boots."

"I see how it was."

"I really did want you to call 911," she confirmed. "By the way, how did you know those guys were following me?"

"I was trying to catch up with you to tell you that those condoms don't belong to me," he explained. "When I made it out of the bar, you were almost out of sight. Then, I noticed that those guys were heckling you, so I figured I'd try to help."

"Thanks," she offered. "I really appreciate it, and I hate to turn the conversation back to the contraceptives after what you did for me, but how can a condom with your name and phone number on it not belong to you?" she pried.

Niles slowly shook his stringy wet hair against the pillow holding up his head. "Mickey ordered those things for him and me, but I didn't know anything about them until right before he went to talk to you at the bar. I promise."

"I think I believe you," Reese forecasted.

"You can even call and ask him, he'll tell you the truth. Mickey is a smooth talker, but he's always honest even when it plays against him," Niles guaranteed, retrieving the condoms from his pocket. "Here's his number," he said.

Reese giggled at the sight of the black and gold squares. "That's okay," she responded. "I'd rather talk to you than him. Plus, he's busy right now with that bubbly blonde," she reminded Niles, then picked up one of the packages. "He might even be wishing he had one of these at the moment."

Niles let out a laugh, and it hurt; the feeling reminded him of a bad sunburn. "I'm sure he has a backup," he snickered.

"That's what took you so long to get out of the restaurant, huh?" she inquired. "You had to make sure to grab your protection—figured you might need it?" she investigated. "Are you positive you didn't know about these?" she probed one more time, poking his ribs with her pointer finger.

Niles flinched. "I guarantee you I didn't know about them," he assured. "But I didn't want to leave them on the table for that promiscuous waitress."

"That would have been quite the tip," Reese declared.

Niles smiled in his own way. "I also needed to pay for the meal and our drinks."

"I guess that means that you paid for my drink after all," she teased, wearing a big grin. "Thanks."

"I guess so. It's a good thing I did because when I was hustling out of the restaurant, I noticed that Mickey had disappeared."

"I told you," Reese reminded him.

"He's probably in our room, which is at this same motel," Niles revealed.

"Seriously?"

"Yep, but we're on the third floor because Mickey is afraid of the first level."

Reese laughed. "How come?"

Niles explained then pulled his phone from his pocket for the first time since leaving the restaurant. Glancing at the screen, he found a message from Mickey: *Janet and I are in the room. Text before you come back. Good luck with the cute black-haired chick!* Niles chuckled and decided to show the message to Reese.

Reese laughed all over herself as she read the words on the screen. "We should go up there and beat on the door," she suggested.

34

Although pounding on the door behind which Mickey and his new friend were doing who knows what would have been hysterical in a certain sense, Niles and Reese decided against it.

"It seems a little immature," she said on second thought. "Like something I would have done in high school."

"Knowing Mickey, he wouldn't come to the door anyway," Niles figured aloud. "Or he might open it in his birthday suit!"

Reese smirked, then a thought hit her about what would be best for Niles to do next in regards to the effects of the pepper spray. "I hate to suggest that you move from your comfy position on the bed, but you should probably take a shower to ensure any excess pepper spray on your skin is washed away," she advised. "Since your roomie is currently hogging your room, you're more than welcome to use my shower if you'd like." She glanced at his bare chest then away quickly. It was mind-blowing how the man she plopped down across from in the bar ended up in her room with no shirt, wet hair, and now she was offering him her shower. "I have a hoodie that might fit you until you have clearance to retrieve your own clothes," she teased, forcing herself to stand up from where she was sitting on the edge of the bed.

Reese was nearly certain that Niles wasn't the type of guy who would take advantage of a situation like this. She would be shocked if he walked out of the bathroom with a towel draped around his naked body and attempted to make a move on her. Otherwise, she would have never offered her shower to him.

"Are you sure?" he checked. "I can probably make Mickey let me in."

"It's fine," she assured. "As long as you keep your condoms in your pocket," she issued with a smirk, "I'll keep my gun in the holster."

A moment later, Reese walked across the room and grabbed the oversized sweatshirt she'd brought along in case she encountered cold nights while on this trip. "I wish I had a t-shirt to lend you, but I don't think you'd fit into any of mine," she said over her shoulder.

As she moved across the cramped room, Niles's eyes traveled carefully up her body. Even though he wasn't looking for someone these days, he couldn't help but notice the curves that Reese Kirby wore so well. He always found petite girls more attractive than those who typically adorned the covers of magazines, and he figured this bias likely had something to do with his own height. Eden was a couple of inches shorter than he was, so he always looked down to kiss her, and he'd never been able to imagine tilting his head upward to reach a woman's lips. But what he did know was that Eden Franks was the only person he had ever really kissed.

"The sweatshirt will be perfect," he insisted, fully believing that beggars can't be choosers.

While Niles let warm water trickle through his hair and down his body, Reese stripped the sheets and pillowcases off the bed and tossed them into one of the far corners of the room. She then stepped out the door and walked across the parking lot to ask the front desk attendant for another set of bedding. Thankfully, she'd been wise enough to remove her personal pillow from the bed prior to letting Niles lie down, although she doubted he had much residue in his hair or on his body. Still, it was always a good idea to be overly cautious in these cases.

The lady behind the desk, the same one who checked her in, acted as though it was an act of Congress to walk into the next room and retrieve clean linens for a guest.

"What happened?" were the words that spat out of her mouth as soon as Reese made the request.

"Nothing," Reese reported at first but then realized the woman was expecting some kind of answer as to why there was a need for new sheets before she'd spent a night at the motel. "I accidentally sprayed something on them, and now they have a funny smell."

The response on the attendant's face was a mixture of disgust and puzzlement. Thankfully, though, the reason seemed to suffice, and a couple of minutes later Reese trekked across the parking lot with folded sheets and pillowcases as she scanned the area for the Amber Alert vehicle. Earlier, when she and Niles ran into the parking lot as if it was the finish line for a race, she had completely forgotten about the missing child. Her focus had been on grabbing the first aid kit and getting him to the sink. As she walked at a steady pace now, she couldn't help but glance up at the third floor and wonder which door Mickey and the blonde girl were behind. She contemplated what type of guy he really was. The lady's man persona was distinct, but that didn't make him a bad person. If Niles was friends with him, she figured that the mouse must be a decent fellow.

When Reese reentered the room, she found Niles sitting on the edge of the exposed mattress wearing the same pair of jeans he'd worn into the bathroom, which made sense because he didn't have any other clothes to change into. The top half of his body was covered with her hoodie, and his wet hair was tied back. The sporty look suited him quite nicely, she couldn't help but recognize, and the sweatshirt fit as though it belonged to him. When the door squeaked open, she noticed his focus shift from tying his shoelaces to making sure it was her who was entering, and then he greeted her with a smirk. She guessed they were both still a little on edge.

"You look like you're about to run away," she said jokingly.

"I thought you had run away," he responded, holding his grin.

Reese snickered. "I took the sheets up front and got new ones."

Niles glanced over his shoulder at the bed. "I figured that might be the case," he formulated, nodding at the splotchy mattress.

"I also put your shirt into a bag," she revealed, pointing to a plastic one on the floor next to the doorframe.

"Thanks," he offered. "I appreciate everything you did for me," he uttered authentically.

"It was the least I could do," she explained. "I owe you, Niles North," she said in a serious tone, thanking God that he made the choice to follow her out of that restaurant. She'd like to think that she would have been able to wiggle her way out of the situation with the bikers, but if Niles hadn't shown up, who knows what would have happened.

"You don't owe me anything," he assured, standing to his feet and feeling like a new man compared to twenty minutes ago.

Reese reached into her purse on the nightstand then handed a card to Niles. "This is my business card," she shared. "If you ever need anything, feel free to reach out to me."

"Let me give you one of my cards, too," he suggested, reaching into his back pocket to grab his wallet. "It's not all that attractive. However, Mickey and I came up with a real business name this week—Grasshoppers—and we're planning to create a logo and eventually order nicer cards," he revealed as he handed her the card he'd been passing out all over Craven County.

"I'm just relieved that you didn't hand me the condom," she laughed.

With his hands tucked into his pockets, one still palming her card, Niles chuckled. "I'm going to burn those things."

"I don't blame you," she agreed. "And, by the way, I love the business name," she added with a smile.

"Thank you."

For a moment, there was a lull in the conversation as Niles wondered about the best way to excuse himself. He figured Reese was expecting him to leave. Otherwise, she wouldn't have handed him the card and said what she'd said. Of course, she probably realized that finding him tying his shoes meant he didn't want to make either of them feel uncomfortable by overstaying his welcome. Plus, it was getting late, and he figured she would probably like to get some shuteye.

"I think I'm going to head out now," he finally said.

"Okay. Did you hear from Mickey?" she wondered aloud.

"Not yet," he answered. "I might text him in a little while, but I think I'll just chill outside for a bit and take in the cool air."

Reese's eyes perked up at the comment. "Fresh air is one of the best things for a person exposed to pepper spray," she educated.

"That's good to know," Niles confirmed as he drifted toward the door.

"Would you mind if I join you outside?" Reese decided to ask. "I'm kind of riled up after all of the action," she unveiled.

"Me too," Niles agreed with a revealing huff. "I have a hard time sleeping the night after my matches, and what you and I just experienced is much more exhilarating." He paused for a moment, wondering if he should tell her that he wanted to be alone. However, for some reason, he couldn't tell her no; he enjoyed her company, and something about this woman made him want to know more about her. "You're more than welcome to join me if you'd like."

Niles twisted the knob, and Reese followed him out the door, locking it behind them just as she had when she walked out earlier. Once again, she inconspicuously listened for the roar of motorcycles. That would probably be on her mind until she left this place, maybe longer.

"I thought there might be some chairs out here," Niles said after studying the sidewalks and the area near the check-in office.

Reese looked around, too, but didn't see any options other than the metal staircases. "Me too," she acknowledged. "Which vehicle did you guys drive here?" she asked out of curiosity as each of them was scanning the parking lot.

"That one over there," Niles answered, pointing to the compact car he'd been driving since he turned sixteen. "It's not much, but it got us here."

Reese studied the vehicle. She actually saw it earlier when picking up the sheets. It wore a North Carolina license plate, which was true for about half of the cars in the lot, but other details jumped out at her. She couldn't help but notice the significant dent in the rear bumper and the rust that had all but taken over the hood.

"Does it belong to you or Mickey?" she asked.

"It's mine," he divulged, not sure why it mattered. "Mickey drives a truck," Niles announced, pulling his hands from his pockets for the first time since exiting the room.

"I figured it was yours because I see the car seat in the back for your little guy," she observed. "Where's he at?"

Niles wasn't quite sure how he should respond. "He's with his mom," he said hesitantly, feeling awkward about answering questions about his son and his ex-wife, especially from a detective.

"Did they evacuate, too?"

"They are," he said simply.

"Where to?"

"Kentucky."

"Did you want to bring him with you?" she inquired, recognizing an uneasiness in his tone.

"I thought about it," he said.

She walked closer to the aging vehicle and peered into the window. "You said he's five?"

Niles wondered why she was looking into his car and asking questions, but they were both walking by it as they talked and walked toward the staircase.

"Yeah, that's right."

Suddenly, Reese turned and grabbed Niles's left arm before he could even realize what she was doing. Startled, he flinched and nearly twisted her hand in self-defense. An instant later, he felt a slap on his forearm, and all of a sudden, the curve of a silver handcuff wound around his own wrist. Stunned, he wasn't quite sure what to think or say as he stared at her with panic in his eyes.

"Come with me," she instructed, pulling him toward the police Humvee on the far side of the parking lot. "I have a place where we can sit."

"Where?" he asked. "And why did you handcuff me?" he snarled.

Reese clasped the other handcuff onto her own wrist, and she used her off-hand to grab him by the arm and lead him to the backdoor of the vehicle.

"Are you going to put me in there?" he asked, half-joking.

"No," she smirkingly confessed. "I just realized I'd left the handcuff key in the vehicle." She reached in for it. "I only cuffed you to see if I could. I saw how fast you were in the fight earlier, and I couldn't help but wonder if I could move fast enough to catch you."

Niles let out a deep breath. "I thought you were about to arrest me," he uttered.

"Why would I arrest you," she asked. "Have you done something wrong?" she inquired, cocking her head as she waited for an answer.

"I almost did," he admitted, suddenly realizing that he could have ended up in handcuffs this week for a different reason.

Holding the key, Reese furrowed her brow. "What?"

"Have you heard about the Amber Alert for the little boy today?"

"Yes," she reported, furrowing her brow. "Why?"

"That could have easily been me," he admitted.

Reese glared at him. "What do you mean?"

With their wrists handcuffed together, Niles began explaining the idea that had been weighing on his mind this week. "I wanted to bring Riley with me because I was afraid that his mom wasn't going to evacuate with him," he shared for some reason. "Honestly, I still have this gut feeling that something isn't right."

"She wouldn't let you bring him?"

"No," he uttered with a snarl.

"I'm sure she'll do the right thing," Reese offered. "You did," she added.

"Yeah, but is it the best thing?"

"The other father who took his son against the custody agreement has police and everyone else searching for him," she reminded Niles. "You don't want to put yourself or your child in that situation."

"I did, though," Niles admitted. "I wanted to know Riley was safe."

"I understand that, but it's against the law."

"I still can't help but wonder if that man made a better decision."

Reese slid the key into the hole on her cuff and turned it then did the same to the cuff wrapped around Niles's forearm. "I'm not a parent, so I can't fathom how hard it would be to leave your child behind, not knowing," she conceded. "But I do know from experience—arresting parents under similar circumstances and having to testify against them in court—that taking your own child outside of the bounds of the custody agreement can result in long-term consequences."

"Thanks for reminding me of that," he said.

Reese wasn't sure if he was serious or being sarcastic. "I'm sorry that you had to make such a difficult decision," she declared.

"I felt like I had some wiggle room based on the custody agreement. Still, there's no doubt in my mind that the police would be looking for both that other guy and me right now if I had brought Riley along."

"Thank God that we're not," she reported. "I would have had to leave those cuffs on you even after you saved my life," she teased but was as serious as a heart attack.

"I guess I dodged a bullet," he laughed.

"Let's sit in the boat," she suggested. "That's where I was bringing you when I cuffed you. There are padded chairs that will feel much more comfortable than the metal stairs, and we'll still be out in the open air."

Reese hopped onto the trailer hitch using it as a step to get into the search and rescue boat, and Niles followed the path of least resistance. They walked to the rear of the vessel and plopped down on the thick vinyl cushions.

"This is definitely more comfortable than the stairs would have been," Niles agreed.

"I wonder if they've found the missing dad and boy," Reese mentioned.

"I don't think so," Niles shared. "He's actually a client of the firm my ex-wife works for, and she's been helping with the case all day."

"That's crazy," Reese replied.

"The sad thing is that if Mickey or I had been paying attention to our phones during our trip rather than jamming out to music and ignoring work calls, I could have turned around and spent more time with my son," he huffed. "Eden had to stay in New Bern long enough to provide documentation to the authorities, and she needed me to watch Riley," Niles announced sadly. "By the time I saw her messages, we were too far away, and she'd found someone else to keep an eye on him."

"Is that why you were in a bad mood when I met you?"

"I guess so," Niles admitted, gazing toward the stars hanging above the shadows cast by a line of mountains in the distance. He found himself wishing that he could be sitting beneath the night's sky with Riley. Still, he had to admit that he was enjoying Reese's company, especially since his best friend abandoned him for a woman he'd just met.

"I understand your disappointment."

"I just hope she leaves with him in the morning like she promised," he mentioned. "She was even out searching for the missing boy. Apparently, he has relatives that live in Craven County."

"I'm sure she will," Reese hoped. "The missing boy lives in Greenville. How far is that from where you live?"

"A little less than an hour," Niles answered. "Her firm has clients all over Eastern North Carolina," he explained.

"I've had my eyes out for the vehicle all day," Reese revealed.

"Really?"

"Definitely. It's one of the things I'm trained to do," she mentioned. "So, your son's name is Riley?" she asked.

"Yes."

"I love that name," Reese offered.

"Me too," Niles said with a slight grin.

"Your ex-wife's name is Eden?"

"Yes, detective," he snarled, chuckling a little, trying to let his shoulders relax.

"I've never met anyone named Eden."

"She's the only Eden I've ever met."

"Do you still love her?" Reese asked out of the blue.

Niles was taken aback by the audacity of the question but answered anyway since he already shared more with Reese Kirby than with anyone other than Mickey since his divorce. "I do," he admitted. "I imagine that I will always love her."

"That says a lot about your character."

"It says more about her," he professed.

Reese let the comment settle beneath the night's sky, and she found herself hoping that one day a man would love her the way this man loved his ex-wife.

"Why did she leave you?"

"How do you know she left me?"

"That's what Mickey said earlier, and you didn't deny it when we were talking at the bar."

The comment Reese made in the bar about Mickey telling her that his ex-wife had left him began to flood his mind again. He'd never told Mickey that Eden left him. As far as Niles knew, everyone in their hometown assumed that he had been the one who wanted the divorce, and he let them think that. He never spoke publicly about her addiction to pain pills either because he didn't want anyone to think less of Eden. He wanted her to recover, and he wanted their life back.

"I've never told anyone that Eden was the one who left me."

"Why do you not want people to know?"

Niles lowered his head and closed his eyes. "People are judgmental, and they look down on the person who made the decision to split up a home where a child is involved."

"And you want them to look down on you rather than your ex?"

"Yes, she's been through enough already."

"Can I ask what happened?"

Niles bit his lips together and nearly swallowed them. "Sure," he finally said, "but you might wish that you hadn't."

35

*G*azing into the night's sky with Reese Kirby, Niles North began
to tell a version of a story that he had never told anyone.

"A while back, Eden and I were traveling to Durham one
morning to take our son to Duke for an appointment with a
children's oncologist. We'd made the trip too many times already
but were hoping for positive results on this particular visit," he
declared. "No kid should ever have cancer, and no parent should
have to watch their child suffer. It's one of the most helpless
feelings in the world, and at that moment, neither Eden nor I
realized that we could feel even more helpless. We were running
late from the moment we left the house, and we had to stop for
gas about midway into the trip, so we were in a major hurry. While
at the convenience store, I pumped the fuel, and she hastily
managed bathroom breaks. We always worked well as a team, and
on that particular day, as our minivan pulled away from the pump,
she thought I had strapped in the child safety belts, and I thought
she had. It wasn't like it was a job specific to either one of us, and
we'd both been in and out of the rear sliding doors grabbing
snacks, stopping and starting the DVD player, and doing other
things. We made it back onto the highway, reached full speed, and
thought we might possibly make our destination on time." With

tears pooling in his lower eyelids, threatening to spill at any moment, Niles paused as he vividly recalled the scene. He found himself wishing he could go back to the very moment that he was talking about now. Since the accident, he imagined a second chance a thousand times, maybe more. As the images ran through his mind like stills on a movie screen, his tongue rolled around the inside rim of his lips before he spoke again. "I'm not sure why children's car seats don't have built-in alarms that ding when a child is in the seat but not buckled, but I sure do pray that someone invents one soon if they haven't already. In my opinion, they should be mandatory," Niles declared as the crisp air blew over the boat as it sat motionless on dry land. In the distance, crickets were chirping, and the leaves from nearby trees were waving casually.

Reese never thought of the concept but agreed wholeheartedly as she wondered where this story was going. Based on things Niles already shared, she had every reason to believe his ex-wife and son were still living, so, thankfully, it sounded like no one had died if there had been an accident. It also seemed like his ex was a relatively responsible adult and able to take care of their son. Of course, that didn't speak to what state his son Riley was in, but she found herself wondering if she was about to find out that something terrible had happened to him. The unmentioned reason behind the oncologist appointment also made her curious. However, rather than ask questions as trained to do in her line of work, she listened eagerly as Niles continued. "Riley was the one who told us about the buckles. As we were driving fifty-five miles per hour, the words 'Our seatbelts are unbuckled' flowed from his mouth as fluidly as any words ever had. As his voice trailed off, Eden and I both whipped our heads around. My gut told me to apply the brakes and get off the road as soon as possible, but before I could do anything, her motherly instincts kicked in full gear. She was out of her seatbelt and halfway in the middle row of our minivan before I could even tap the brake. As she began to reach for the buckles, I told her that I was going to pull over on the shoulder of the road. She said, 'Keep going, it's more dangerous to be stopped on the side of a busy highway than to be driving down it.' I could see a string of vehicles ahead of me and even more in my driver's side mirror, but the only thing present in my rearview mirror was Eden as she quickly worked on attaching the child restraints. As I tried to keep my focus on the road, I remember hearing buckles snap, but I wasn't sure if it was Riley's or Cameron's or both." Suddenly, a burst of silent tears dripped out of Niles's eyes as he fought to clench his lips, swallowing the sound of cries that he'd inhaled too many times. Without hesitation, Reese let her hand fall softly onto his arm and rest there as she wondered: *Who is Cameron?* "I should have just stopped," he disclosed, forcing the words through the tears that were falling toward the bottom of the boat. "If I had stopped, we wouldn't have gotten into an accident."

Niles paused and said absolutely nothing for at least a minute. He just stared blankly into the distance and worked his jaw back and forth.

Reese wasn't sure if she should break the silence, but she decided to anyway. She didn't know if the statement she was thinking was accurate, but she felt compelled to share it as she clenched his arm. "You don't know that," she uttered. "It could have been worse. Roadsides are extremely dangerous," she admitted, knowing the facts all too well. She personally investigated crash scenes and heard of countless others where vehicles had pulled over for one reason or another and ended up causing multiple fatalities.

Niles continued. "Riley and Cameron were our little boys; they were the cutest twins in the whole world. They did everything together from the moment they were born. They were best buddies and were supposed to grow up side by side, share memories, and be in pictures together until their hair turned gray. Then, suddenly, a pickup truck that had stopped on the side of the road pulled right out in front of us. It had mattresses piled so high in the truck bed that I couldn't see over them when our van rammed into the back of the vehicle at nearly full speed. The brake pedal below my foot may have helped slow us a little but not much. I later found out that the reason they stopped was to secure a bungee cord that was flapping in the wind. Somehow, when they decided to pull back onto the highway, they didn't see our van, and we slammed into their lowered tailgate. Out of the corner of my right eye, I watched in what seemed like slow motion as my wife's body flew from the middle row and crashed through the windshield of our minivan before literally slamming into the stack of mattresses. Every emergency worker who ended up at the scene said that if it wasn't for the mattresses, she wouldn't have lived. The airbag smashed into my face with far more force than any punch I've ever been dealt, but as soon as the vehicle came to a stop, I knew I had to get to my boys and my wife. I managed to unbuckle and forge past the airbag, but when I made it into the center console area of the van where I could see the boys' seats, I nearly fainted. I had blood dripping out of my nose and staining my white shirt, but that wasn't why I almost passed out. Riley was staring straight at me with his big hazel eyes, and he looked nearly frozen in shock, but Cameron's seat was empty," Niles explained in a soft voice as he sniffled. "He didn't make it. Our little boy, who was going to beat cancer, didn't make it."

Niles didn't speak a word for several minutes; he just sat there with his back against the thick cushion, sniffing every few seconds. Reese let her hand move up his arm to his shoulder and back down again, following this pattern as his body continued to tremble. What a horrific accident, she thought to herself over and over while thanking God she hadn't seen it in person yet knowing she would never forget the images Niles had relayed.

"What did you do then?" she finally asked.

"I did what I felt was best at the moment. I put myself between Riley and Cameron so that Riley couldn't see his little brother. I told Riley to close his eyes and pray. He was asking where Mommy was and why Cameron wasn't in his car seat, but I also heard him asking God to take care of all of us. He named us one by one over and over like he did when we would say our bedtime prayers every night. Once I knew without a shadow of a doubt that Cameron was gone, I unbuckled Riley, wrapped my arms around him, and went to check on Eden. I made sure to keep his face tucked into my chest because I was afraid of what we might discover when we found her body. I didn't want him to see her like that and the whole time I was praying that he hadn't seen his twin brother. God must have heard our prayers because when we made it to Eden, she was fully conscious, although I could tell that she suffered a severe concussion. I let Riley lie on the ground next to her until the paramedics arrived. Then, they wanted to check out each of us."

Niles stopped talking, closed his eyelids, and let the scene filter through his mind once again.

"I can't even begin to imagine how painful it is to lose a child," Reese uttered. "I'm so sorry."

"It's not your fault," Niles responded.

"It's not your fault either," she made sure to tell him just in case no one else ever had.

He shrugged his shoulders. "I blame myself every day," he admitted. "For the accident, for the divorce—all of it."

"Does Eden blame herself, too?" she couldn't help but wonder.

"Not like I do."

"That's good, but why not?"

"She suffered a minor head injury from hitting either the window, the mattresses, the pavement, or all of the above. The memory of the accident has never come back. She says she doesn't even remember leaving the gas station. However, the moments prior to the accident are basically the only thing from the past that she doesn't remember, which has been a blessing in disguise."

Reese stared into Niles's aqua eyes. "You told her that you were the one who forgot to buckle the children—"

"You're the first person I've ever told anything different," he admitted. For some reason, it felt good to finally tell the whole truth. He often wished he had someone to talk to about all of this, someone who didn't know him or Eden, someone whom he could tell everything and not feel judgment toward him or Eden.

"So everyone—your family, her family, and all of your friends— think it was your fault?"

"Yes," he said simply. "No one needs to live with that," he uttered. "And the oncologist agrees with me, but I don't believe him."

Reese furrowed her brow. "What do you mean?"

"When he found out why we didn't make the appointment that day, he called to share his condolences. Then, he took time out of his insane schedule to show up for the funeral. After almost everyone else had left the graveside, he pulled Eden and me aside." Niles paused for a moment and shed another tear for one of the most precious men he ever had the pleasure of meeting. "He told Eden and me that he had something to share with us that he couldn't have divulged in the office that day and he said that he would never speak this news aloud again." Niles recalled the words verbatim: "Cameron wasn't going to make it much longer," the doctor revealed. "The cancer was too aggressive, and the remainder of his life would have been miserable for him, for the two of you, and tough on Riley as well. I know you don't want to hear this but given the situation, I hope this revelation will provide some relief. God knew it was time to take your little boy home so that he wouldn't have to suffer," he said through tears that Niles never would have known about otherwise, tears that the doctor cried every single time one of his patients didn't beat cancer. He found himself hurting as if they were his children. "I have kids," the doctor added, "and if I were in your shoes, and you were in mine, I would have wanted to know why God let that accident happen."

"Why didn't you believe him?" Reese asked.

"Because he's an amazing man and he said exactly what I would have said if I was in his shoes, regardless of what the scans had shown."

"Did you ever see the actual results?"

"No, we didn't want to, it would have only made things more difficult," Niles admitted.

"So, I'm assuming that all of this took a hefty toll on yours and Eden's marriage," Reese stated.

"We tried to deal with it as best we could, but it's unbearable, and Eden was also dealing with back and neck pain from the impact which made things worse. She ended up on painkillers, antidepressants, and all kinds of other medication. To make a long story short, she became addicted to them and began to overmedicate," he explained. "Slowly, she became a different person, and one day out of the blue, she told me she wanted a divorce. I thought I could talk her out of it, but she never budged. We didn't go to counseling; we didn't talk to our pastor, nothing. We just split up, moved to separate homes, created a separation agreement, and watched the world we built together tear apart."

"You're a good man Niles North," Reese declared.

"Thanks for saying that, but I rarely feel like one."

"I bet your son thinks you're an amazing father," she said.

Niles began to think of all the times he and Riley had spent together since the divorce, and he knew he couldn't deny Reese's statement. He knew his little boy loved him as if he was the superhero in the movies they watched together. Riley was the reason he went to bed sober most nights and the purpose of his waking up every morning. Losing a child and a wife was enough to drive a man crazy, but Niles promised that he'd always be there for the son he was fortunate to still have.

A few minutes later, Niles began telling Reese stories about Riley. He showed her the photos Mickey had taken of his little boy with the leaf blower backpack strapped onto his shoulders. Then, as the two of them chuckled over the story about the messages the guys painted for the hurricane, the thunder of motorcycle engines suddenly interrupted their fun. Reese and Niles had been laughing so hard about the words written on the plywood that they hadn't heard the distant rumble. Now, they doubted they had time to make a run for the motel without being spotted.

Peering around the transom and over the gunwale, they saw a slew of single headlights coming up the road parallel to the motel.

"I don't want to fight those dudes again," Niles said, making sure to keep his head tucked low. "Especially now that there are even more of them."

There were at least fifteen headlights, maybe a greater number because they all blended together.

"I definitely don't need an altercation to happen in this motel parking lot," Reese divulged as she tried to think of the best option to avoid one. "Let's hide in the bottom of the boat until they pass," she suggested. "There's a tarp beneath these seats."

When they slid into the floorboard, Reese pulled a dark tarp from the storage area and draped it over her and Niles like a blanket. It was small and square, so the two of them were forced to tuck in real tight and hold each other close as the sound of barking motorcycles took over what had previously become a calm and peaceful night.

"They'll never see us under here," Niles whispered, inches from Reese's beautiful face.

The holler of the engines vibrated the hull as the parade of bikers cruised through the parking lot. Niles and Reese both knew precisely who they were looking for and that they were seeking revenge.

"Yeah, I'd say it's highly unlikely that they'll get off their bikes and look in a police boat," Reese murmured, her lips so close to his ear that he could feel her breath.

"What if they're staying at this motel," Niles suddenly considered.

He could barely see Reese's eyes, but he could tell they were expanding as rapidly as his own. "That would not be good," she claimed. "We might have to sleep in the boat."

Fortunately, within a couple of minutes, the growl of engines exploded when the motorcycles made it full circle through the parking lot before racing back up the road. Niles and Reese waited a bit longer to come out of hiding, and when they did, they again peered over the edge of the boat to make sure all was clear.

"I feel like we're on a stakeout," Reese joked.

The two spent the next hour in deep conversation. When she asked Niles why he'd been kicked out of the military, he figured he might as well tell the whole truth.

One of the officers in charge slapped a female recruit across the face for back-talking him. A moment later was the first time outside of a ring that Niles landed a roundhouse kick against a man's face. Several other highly ranked officers immediately came charging at Niles. By the time the fight was over, two of them ended up in the same hospital where he too lay on a gurney, black and blue, but as proud as could be. Apparently, though, the military frowned mightily on a peon in boot camp fighting his superiors regardless of the reason. In the end, Niles had been happy about how things turned out because it proved to be a blessing in disguise. He was able to go back home and spend time with his family, especially Cameron, who ended up leaving them way too soon.

When Niles finished telling the story about boot camp, Reese decided to reveal the sad truth about her father's death. It was a scene that often replayed in her mind but one that she seldom discussed. She had been standing next to him when he was shot and killed simply because he was wearing a police uniform. It was the last time he had taken her out in his patrol car; she was a senior in high school, and it was career day. Reese had been looking forward to the opportunity all year. Unfortunately, the two of them ended up in the wrong place at the wrong time. Ironically, they were enjoying a picnic lunch in the middle of his shift at one of the safest parks in town when a drive-by shooting occurred by gang members simply searching for a cop to gun down. As bullets sprayed around them like heavy raindrops, she remembered her father diving on top of her, and the next thing she noticed was blood oozing all around her. He saved her life that day but lost his own. From beneath her father's body, she had been able to hone in on the opened car window and the man who pulled the trigger of the gun sticking out of it. She vowed that she would never forget his evil-looking eyes. When she saw them again for the first time two days ago, it took every fiber of her being not to pull the trigger as he was standing over the woman he'd been beating. After Dominguez cuffed the perpetrator, she picked up his firearm. Then, she walked up to him, stared directly into his dark pupils, and said, "My dad forgives you, and God does, too." She'd paused for a moment, started to walk away, then turned back and added, "But I'm not sure if I ever will."

The man killed her father and best friend, and arresting him gave her more pride than anything she ever accomplished. Every police force in the area had been searching for that man for years. They knew exactly who he was and had stacks of evidence against him; they just hadn't ever found him until Reese ended up in the right spot at the right time.

When she finished telling Niles the story, it sure felt comforting to cry on his shoulder for a few minutes. Unlike him, she had been unable to hold in the moans that accompanied the pains of losing her father. Moments later, she found out that his father died in Iraq as a hero when he jumped on top of a grenade to save his platoon's life . . . Dominguez's platoon.

After pouring out their hearts, Niles and Reese were able to lighten the conversation a bit. They talked about how their lives led each of them to this very moment in time and nearly forgot they were sitting in the back of a boat in the middle of a parking lot with no water in sight. They discussed Hurricane Florence and what each of them thought it might or might not do, and most of all, they enjoyed one another's company. Niles and Reese somehow shelved away the tragic stories they shared with each other, and in a way that neither of them could quite pinpoint, they each felt like the heaviest of weights had been lifted off their shoulders.

36

The next morning, Niles jogged down the metal staircase with an extra pep in his step. Once at ground level, he met Reese at the door to her room but wasn't quite sure how to greet his new friend. Luckily, she took care of the quandary by giving him a one-armed hug from the side as she reached the key toward the doorknob and steadied her shoulder-strap purse. It made Niles feel comfortable to discover that Reese was wearing an outfit similar to his, khaki shorts and a nice-looking t-shirt. Of course, his shorts were a bit longer than hers, which he noticed closely when their hips became flush for a moment. He had to admit that even though he only wanted the two of them to be friends, it felt pleasing to be the recipient of an attractive woman's touch. Similar thoughts rushed through his mind last night when lying underneath the tarp with her. He would be a liar if he said he hadn't felt jitters coursing through his entire body from the instant they ran away from the fight holding hands. Of course, he felt a lot of other things, too, but that was the feeling that stood out the most, even more than the sting of the pepper spray.

"This key is the oddest thing," she declared as she tugged it back out of the rigid hole with a forceful yank.

Niles couldn't help but notice that Reese smelled a lot like the sweatshirt she let him wear. *Buttercream* was the word Mickey used to describe the scent when Niles walked into their motel room late last night wearing police gear.

"I'm not sure if the motel has made any upgrades since the eighties," Niles laughed as they stepped around potholes in the cracked asphalt, making their way toward the Humvee on a sunny morning. Reese's pullover was draped over his shoulder. When he mentioned that he made sure to bring it so he wouldn't forget to give it back to her plus he thought they could take it along on their excursion in case either of them became cool, she agreed that such was a good idea. It actually worked out quite well because she had forgotten to grab anything with sleeves.

"I'm so pumped about riding in the Hummer," he announced as Reese pressed the button on the key fob to unlock the doors.

Last night, after nearly falling asleep together in the boat, Niles made mention that he always wanted to ride in a vehicle like the one Reese was driving. That's when she invited him to explore Hickory with her today. Their first stop was going to be breakfast at a local joint that supposedly served the best pancakes in town.

"How did you sleep last night?" Reese asked with a smirk as they climbed into the vehicle.

The question reminded Niles of one of the final conversations he and Reese shared in the boat well after the motorcycles cruised through the parking lot. Niles looked at his phone and found a message from Mickey that read: *Where in the heck are you? I know you're not still with that black-haired girl this late at night. The blonde is here with me in the room, but I thought you'd be back by now.*

"I slept well, thank you," he confirmed, then divulged the information for which he knew Reese was fishing. "You were right, though; she did stay the night, but thankfully, Mickey has his own bed."

"I told you she would," Reese declared, clenching the steering wheel before shifting the vehicle into drive. "They didn't keep you up all night, did they?"

"No, but Mickey asked fifty questions about the fight and went on and on about how badly he wished he had been there to help us kick some butt," Niles revealed, laughing.

"Did you tell him those guys were light work?"

"I made us sound like ninjas," Niles said with a wink.

Reese reached across the center console and gave him a fist bump. "That's right," she agreed with a smirk. "Were they still in bed when you left this morning?"

After waking, Niles had taken a shower first thing and figured that by the time he was dressed and ready, Mickey and his new lady friend would be stirring. When he walked out the door, however, the two of them were still cuddled beneath covers with their hair spilling all over the pillows. Niles made sure to place Banana—who had been his cuddle buddy last night—face down on the bed so that Riley's little monkey wouldn't witness any shenanigans that might scar his innocence.

"Mickey woke up enough for me to point to the car keys I left on the nightstand, then he rolled back over into the cocoon."

"Losers," Reese called them.

Since the moment Niles climbed into the Hummer, he had been studying every feature inside the vehicle. A high-tech laptop was nestled on a swivel between the driver's and passenger's seats, and there were all kinds of nifty gadgets on the dashboard. As Reese drove them toward the restaurant, she showed him which switches turned on the blue lights and the siren, and even let him try them out. Niles talked about how he felt like a kid in a candy store and told her that he would never be able to tell Riley about riding in this vehicle.

"He loves police cars, fire engines, and ambulances," Niles explained. "Even more than most kids," he added.

"Letting kids check out my car is one of the perks of my job," Reese shared.

"I bet."

"This isn't my normal vehicle, though, but I think I mentioned that to you last night while we were hanging out in the boat."

Upon mentioning the boat, both Reese and Niles simultaneously glanced in the mirrors outside their respective windows as if to make sure it was still tagging along behind them.

"You did," he clarified. Reese told him about how all of the other detectives were jealous that she was getting to drive the special-forces vehicle this week. "I'm sure that Riley would be equally impressed with your normal vehicle."

"The Charger has more power," she said, "and plenty of gadgets of its own."

"Which one is more fun to drive?" he asked.

"This one, but probably only because it's different than what I drive daily."

Reese and Niles talked about her police vehicles the rest of the way to the restaurant. When the door jingled as they walked in, the aroma of bacon and sausage invaded their nasal passages.

"Oh, my, it smells delicious in here," Reese announced.

They found a seat and thumbed through the menu. The options reminded Niles a lot of The Country Biscuit, which made him smirk because he instantly thought about Jenny. She wanted to tag along on the evacuation, but Mickey told her that it was a guy's trip. This was ironic because now he was shacked up with the blonde, and here Niles was sharing a meal with an attractive woman not named Eden for the very first time in his life. The latter seemed so odd for so many reasons, he couldn't help but think, as he tried to decide what he wanted to pick from the menu. Everything sounded tasty.

"Your face looks good," Reese randomly said to Niles as she peeked over the menu at him.

"Thanks," he uttered, but it must have been evident that a question mark was forming in his mind.

"I mean, you don't have any visible burns from the pepper spray," she explained.

Niles subconsciously reached his fingers to his cheeks and raked across them. "I think I'm good," he conveyed.

"Your eyes look a little bloodshot," she pointed out. "That's normal, though."

"My eyes aren't normally bloodshot," he teased. "Are you calling me an alcoholic?"

Reese stumbled into a laugh. "Funny guy," she said as the waitress set a steaming cup of coffee in front of her and an orange juice for Niles. "It's normal after being doused with pepper spray," she added after the waitress said she would give them a few more minutes to look over the menu.

"They still feel a little sore," he admitted.

"The feeling should go away within twenty-four hours," she relayed. "Is your body aching this morning?" she asked with an inquisitive frown.

"Not really," he said. "From the fight?" he asked.

"I guess that's why I feel kind of sore this morning," she concluded. "It's probably a mixture of fighting, running, and lying on the bottom of a boat."

Niles laughed. "It's a night we'll never forget."

Somehow, Reese had a feeling that those words would prove to be as accurate as any she'd ever heard. She didn't really know Niles North, but she knew he was a good man and a great dad. First impressions meant more than what most people realized, and she deciphered from their conversations that he was one of those guys whom a woman should latch onto and never let go of. She found herself wishing she could grab a hold of Eden, shake her, and beg her to flush all those pills down the drain. Explain to her that not many divorced men thumbed their ring finger every half an hour, wishing a wedding band was still wrapped around it.

"Fifty years from now, I'll probably be telling my grandkids about this ninja that I once knew," Reese said with a sideways grin as she carefully touched the rim of the hot mug to her lips.

Niles had to admit that he was having fun with Reese, but he knew that they could never be anything more than long-distance friends. "Make me sound like Bruce Lee," he requested.

"Are you going to do the same for me?"

"Of course," he said. "One day, when Riley's old enough to understand, I'll make sure to tell him about my sidekick superhero," he said with a wink. "Speaking of Riley, his mother messaged me and said that they were evacuating first thing this morning."

"Ooh, that reminds me, I heard that the dad of the missing boy turned himself over to authorities," she said.

"Eden told me the same thing, and I was so glad to hear it because I was afraid she was going to use that as an excuse to stay in New Bern. Of course, I'm glad that everything turned out okay with the little boy, too, but from what Eden said about his dad, he's actually a good guy."

"See, aren't you glad you're not in his shoes?"

"I guess so," Niles admitted.

For breakfast, Niles ate pancakes, and Reese tried the French toast. They both ordered bacon, she had a side of home fries, and he devoured a couple links of sausage. Both walked out with full bellies and struggled to climb into the Hummer. Reese wanted to check out Baker's Mountain, which was a little bit of a drive, but it also gave Niles a chance to show her Mickey's family's old tree farm, which was nestled at the edge of the mountain. Even though they probably weren't supposed to, they zigzagged through rows of perfectly aligned Christmas trees, and Reese reveled at how beautiful the hillside farm must look in the wintertime with snow on the ground and in the trees. They walked for more than an hour and took in the sights and sounds: squirrels dashing from one branch to another, birds flying and flocking, and they even spotted a family of deer climbing the rocky mountainside. The smell of the fresh mountain air was ever-present, and the sounds of nature reminded Niles of life at the treehouse. He found himself wishing that he could show it to Reese, and when he told her so, she seemed to love the idea. He thought she'd think like Eden, that a house in the trees was a silly place to live, but she seemed enamored by the lifestyle. As he talked about his home, he wondered if at this time tomorrow it would be floating down the Neuse River. He tried not to think much about the hurricane, especially now that he had the relief of knowing that Eden and Riley were on their way to Kentucky, but it kept coming up in conversation. At breakfast, people at tables around them were talking about the storm; the radio announcers were giving updates; and television stations from across the country had reporters on location in every town along the seaboard. Even though Niles wasn't there, he had a good idea of what it felt like to be in Eastern North Carolina right now. Unpredictable. Residents had no idea where the first tree would blow over, when the electricity would flicker and eventually go out, or how long it would take before floodwaters began to rise into the waterfront homes.

He tried to shove thoughts about the hurricane into the back of his mind as he and Reese hopped into the police vehicle and drove to Lake Hickory. They found a public access point and walked along the waterfront, fed the geese, and watched turtles dive under the murky water. When their stomachs began to growl, they talked about how lovely it would be to eat lunch at one of the picnic tables near the lake. Niles came up with the idea of having pizza delivered there, and both he and Reese were pleasantly surprised when one of the local pizzerias agreed to arrive there with an all-meat pizza in less than thirty minutes.

Reese retrieved the book, *Waiting at Hayden's*, from the vehicle and began reading beneath a blue sky and sunshine as Niles sat nearby, merely relaxing. She filled him in about all of the novels she snatched up at the local bookshop prior to leaving Chattanooga, specifically explaining how the one in her hand was tailored to where readers could shop the same clothes that the characters wore. She told him how she started reading it in the bookstore and had been looking forward to picking it up again. She was somewhat surprised when he seemed completely okay with her reading while they waited on pizza.

After sitting near Reese for a little while, Niles got up and went through a stretch routine that he often did back at home on a daily basis. Eventually, the pizza showed up; they ate lunch together at the picnic table and decided to stay at the park a little while longer since neither of them had anywhere to be.

Then, something completely unexpected happened. Something that would change the course of their lives. Niles uttered the words, "I'm so happy to know that Riley will not be anywhere near New Bern when the rivers rise." A moment later, his phone began to ring. It was Grandyma. He knew he had to answer, and by the time the call ended, the only words that he could remember hearing were, "Sweetie, Eden and Riley are not evacuating."

THE END . . . IS YET TO COME

A Note from the Author

Thank you for reading *When the Rivers Rise*! I am honored that you chose to invest your time in this book. If you haven't yet read my other novels, *A Bridge Apart*, *Losing London*, *A Field of Fireflies*, and *The Date Night Jar*, I hope you will very soon. If you enjoyed the story you just experienced, please consider helping me spread the novel to others, in the following ways:

- REVIEW the novel online at Amazon.com, goodreads.com, bn.com, bamm.com, etc.
- RECOMMEND this book to friends (social groups, workplace, book club, church, school, etc.).
- VISIT my website: www.Joey-Jones.com
- SUBSCRIBE to my Email Newsletter for insider information on upcoming novels, behind-the-scenes

looks, promotions, charities, and other exciting news.

- CONNECT with me on Social Media: "Like" Facebook.com/JoeyJonesWriter (post a comment about the novel). "Follow" me at Instagram.com/JoeyJonesWriter and Twitter.com/JoeyJonesWriter (#WhenTheRiversRise). "Pin" on Pinterest. Write a blog post about the novel.
- GIVE a copy of the novel to someone you know who you think would enjoy the story. Books make great presents (Birthday, Christmas, Teacher's Gifts, etc.).

Sincerely,
Joey Jones

About the Author

Joey Jones' writing style has been described as a mixture of Nicholas Sparks, Richard Paul Evans, and James Patterson. The ratings and reviews of his novels A BRIDGE APART (2015), LOSING LONDON (2016), A FIELD OF FIREFLIES (2018), and THE DATE NIGHT JAR (2019), reflect the comparison to *New York Times* bestselling authors. Prior to becoming a full-time novelist, Joey worked in the marketing field. He holds a Bachelor of Arts in Business Communications from the University of Maryland University College, where he earned a 3.8 GPA.

Jones lives in North Carolina with his family. Fun facts: He is a quarter of an inch from being six-foot tall. In his prime, Joey could dunk a ten-foot basketball goal. After his YMCA men's basketball team won the championship this past season, he says retirement from the sport—one of his favorite—isn't far away.

Joey Jones is currently writing his sixth novel and working on various projects pertaining to his published novels.

Book Club/Group Discussion Questions

1. Were you immediately engaged in the novel?

2. What emotions did you experience as you read the book?

3. Which character is your favorite? Why?

4. What do you like most about the story as a whole?

5. What is your favorite part/scene in the novel?

6. Are there any particular passages from the book that stand out to you?

7. As you read, what are some of the things that you thought might happen, but didn't?

8. Is there anything you would have liked to see turn out differently?

9. Is the ending satisfying? If so, why? If not, why not, and how would you change it?

10. Why might the author have chosen to tell the story the way he did?

11. If you could ask the author a question, what would you ask?

12. Have you ever read or heard a story anything like this one?

13. In what ways does this novel relate to your own life?

14. Would you reread this novel?

15. Are you looking forward to the sequel?

Also by Joey Jones

A BRIDGE APART

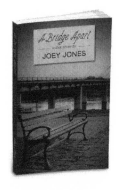

A Bridge Apart, the debut novel by Joey Jones, is a remarkable love story that tests the limits of trust and forgiveness . . .

In the quaint river town of New Bern, North Carolina, at 28 years of age, the pieces of Andrew Callaway's life are all falling into place. His real estate firm is flourishing, and he's engaged to be married in less than two weeks to a beautiful banker named Meredith Hastings. But, when Meredith heads to Tampa, Florida—the wedding location—with her mother, fate, or maybe some human intervention, has it that Andrew happens upon Cooper McKay, the only other woman he's ever loved.

A string of shocking emails lead Andrew to question whether he can trust his fiancée, and in the midst of trying to unravel the mystery, he finds himself spending time with Cooper. When Meredith catches wind of what's going on back at home, she's forced to consider calling off the wedding, which ultimately draws Andrew closer to Cooper. Andrew soon discovers he's making choices he might not be able, or even want, to untangle. As the story unfolds, the decisions that are made will drastically change the lives of everyone involved and bind them closer together than they could have ever imagined.

Also by Joey Jones

LOSING LONDON

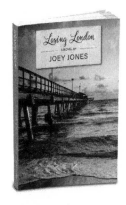

Losing London is an epic love story filled with nail-biting suspense, forbidden passion, and unexpected heartbreak.

When cancer took the life of Mitch Quinn's soulmate, London Adams, he never imagined that one year later her sister, Harper, whom he had never met before, would show up in Emerald Isle, NC. Until this point, his only reason to live, a five-year-old cancer survivor named Hannah, was his closest tie to London.

Harper, recently divorced, never imagined that work—a research project on recent shark attacks—and an unexpected package from London would take her back to the island town where her family had vacationed in her youth. Upon her arrival, she meets and is instantly swept off her feet by a local with a hidden connection that eventually causes her to question the boundaries of love.

As Mitch's and Harper's lives intertwine, they discover secrets that should have never happened. If either had known that losing London would have connected their lives in the way that it did, they might have chosen different paths.

A FIELD OF FIREFLIES

Growing up, Nolan Lynch's family was unconventional by society's standards, but it was filled with love, and his parents taught him everything he needed to know about life, equality, and family. A baseball player with a bright future, Nolan is on his way to the major leagues when tragedy occurs. Six years later, he's starting over as the newest instructor at the community college in Washington, North Carolina, where he meets Emma Pate, who seems to be everything he's ever dreamed of—beautiful, assertive, and a baseball fan to boot.

Emma Pate's dreams are put on hold after her father dies, leaving her struggling to keep her family's farm. When a chance encounter with a cute new guy in town turns into an impromptu date, Emma finds herself falling for him. But, she soon realizes Nolan Lynch isn't who she thinks he is.

Drawn together by a visceral connection that defies their common sense, Emma's and Nolan's blossoming love is as romantic as it is forbidden, until secrets—both past and present—threaten to tear them apart. Now, Nolan must confront his past and make peace with his demons or risk losing everything he loves . . . again.

Emotionally complex and charged with suspense, *A Field of Fireflies* is the unforgettable story of family, love, loss, and an old baseball field where magic occurs, including the grace of forgiveness and second chances.

Also by Joey Jones

THE DATE NIGHT JAR

An unlikely friendship. An unforgettable love story.

When workaholic physician Ansley Stone writes a letter to the estranged son of a patient asking him to send the family's heirloom date night jar, she only intended to bring a little happiness to a lonely old man during his final days. Before long, she finds herself increasingly drawn to Cleve Fields' bedside, eager to hear the stories of his courtship with his beloved late wife, Violet, that were inspired by the yellowed slivers of paper in the old jar. When Cleve asks her to return the jar to his son, Ansley spontaneously decides to deliver it in person, if only to find out why no one, including his own son, visits the patient she's grown inexplicably fond of.

Mason Fields is happily single, content to spend his days running the family strawberry farm and his evenings in the company of his best friend, a seventeen-year-old collie named Callie. Then Ansley shows up at his door with the date night jar and nowhere to stay. Suddenly, she's turning his carefully ordered world upside down, upsetting his routine, and forcing him to remember things best left in the past. When she suggests *they* pull a slip of paper from the jar, their own love story begins to develop. But before long, their newfound love will be tested in ways they never imagined, as the startling truth about Mason's past is revealed...and Ansley's future is threatened.

Made in the USA
Columbia, SC
08 November 2022